HAGAR

A NOVEL

HAGAR

A NOVEL

HAGAR
A NOVEL

LOIS T. HENDERSON

1817

HARPER & ROW, PUBLISHERS, San Francisco
Cambridge, Hagerstown, New York, Philadelphia
London, Mexico City, São Paulo, Sydney

Hagar was published in a hardcover edition by Christian Herald Books. Reprinted by agreement.

FIRST HARPER & ROW PAPERBACK EDITION

Library of Congress Cataloging in Publication Data

Henderson, Lois T.
  HAGAR.

  1. Hagar (Biblical character)—Fiction.   I. Title.
PS3558.E486H3   1983   813'.54   82-48398
ISBN 0-06-063861-3

---

86   10   9   8   7   6   5

Dedicated to
Al
With my love

PART ONE

And Abram went up out of Egypt,
he and his wife, and all that he
had, and Lot with him . . .
and Abram called on the name of
the Lord. . . .

GENESIS 13:1, 4b

1

The morning sun burned through the windows, blotting up the coolness which night had left in the corners of the room. The slave girl Hagar, who had been routed out of bed at dawn to minister to the young woman who had returned from the Pharaoh's rooms, was aware of the heat as though it were a threat. Even here in the women's quarters where the walls were thick and shadowed by tamarisk trees, the air was oppressive.

But the queer oppression was caused by something more than the morning heat, Hagar decided. She stood quietly in a corner, looking intently at the women who moved around her. There was fear and tension on the faces. Only the Hebrew woman, the sister of the nomad chief who had arrived during the flooding of the Nile, looked undisturbed. She moved past Hagar and when she saw the girl watching her, she smiled a warm, broad smile that lighted her dark eyes and smooth oval face.

Hagar touched her own thin, young face with tentative fingertips. Oh, to be as beautiful as the Hebrew woman, to have that burnished loveliness stamped on flesh that was round and tender. Oh, to be able to smile like that without fear, without anger. But the Hebrew woman was not a slave. Or an Egyptian. And she was no longer the bony, awkward child that Hagar was.

There was a sudden heightening of the tension in the
women who stood closest to the door that opened out onto
the porch. Something had happened, something terrifying,
and the news of it was moving across the grounds like a
wind. Hagar felt fear in the same way that she had felt it two
years ago when the battle that killed her parents and her
brothers and delivered her into the hands of the Pharaoh's
soldiers had occurred. She remembered very little of that
horrible day. Terror had washed her brain clean. She only
knew that she, who had been the daughter of a wealthy
man, who had been the pet of doting parents and generous
brothers, was suddenly a slave girl in the women's quarters
of the Pharaoh's palace.

A sharp, keen cry cut across the room, and one of the
women rushed out of the door. A jumble of words tangled in
the air, sorted itself into sentences, moved from woman to
woman.

"It could be the start of a plague," Hagar heard. "Her son
. . . the Pharaoh's son . . . has been stricken. He may die . . .
slaves have already died."

Into the babble of words, the voice of the Hebrew woman
fell with a strong, cool sound.

"It's a sign of our God's displeasure."

For a few seconds, there was silence in the room. The
woman had spoken with such a strange authority that the
other women seemed to wait for her to speak again.

"Our God is displeased because the Pharaoh has taken me
into his court," the woman said.

"Your god should be pleased," sneered one of the women.
"You and your brother are lucky you weren't taken into
slavery."

"He's not my brother," the woman said clearly. "He's my
husband."

There was silence again, this time laced with apprehension. Everyone *knew* that the Hebrew wanderer was the
woman's brother. They had both announced it when they
had arrived. And because the woman was beautiful, the

Pharaoh had taken her into his court.

"Of course he's your brother," one of the older women said sharply. "You, yourself, told us."

The Hebrew woman spoke defiantly. "No, I am Sarai, *wife* of Abram. I said I was his sister for—for reasons of our own."

"You lied! The words were spit out with venom. "If there *is* a plague, it's because you lied."

Some of the women began to push toward Sarai, to reach for her with clawed hands. Hagar saw a brief touch of fear on the smooth, golden face.

"If you touch me," Sarai warned, "if you touch me, you'll be punished by our God. Abram's God will strike you."

The Egyptian women wavered, hesitated, and Sarai walked past them through the door to stand quietly in the tamarisk shade.

Why am *I* afraid? Hagar thought. This is something between the woman, Sarai, and the women of the court. This has nothing to do with me. But her blood seemed to run jerkily through her body, so that she found it difficult to breathe.

"Here, girl!" One of the Egyptian women slapped Hagar's face. "Go for a jug of water. And try to find out what's happening. If possible, talk to slaves from the royal rooms and then bring news to us. Hurry."

Hagar ducked the hand which was raised to slap again and ran through the door. She stopped for one of the earthen jars that were piled along the edge of the columned porch, and then she turned to run across the open stretch of ground that led to the well.

But Sarai, who was standing on the porch, spoke unexpectedly. "You'll see it's as I said."

"It's nothing to me," Hagar said sullenly and saw the woman's eyes widen in surprise that a slave should risk such insolence. "I was born free," Hagar explained, shocked at her own boldness. "I haven't learned yet to be a good slave."

Sarai shrugged with apparent indifference. "Then you'll be slapped all the more by the women," she said.

Hagar began to move away, but Sarai's voice stopped her again. "Tell the slaves of the Pharaoh what I've said. Tell them that unless he lets me go with my lord, Abram, our God will bring tragedy to this house. Tell his slaves to tell him that."

Hagar glanced at her nervously and then sped toward the well. She didn't like all this talking about a god's power. Hadn't she learned that prayers were nothing more than smoke in still air? They went nowhere and achieved nothing. Young as she was, she knew that. Hadn't she cried out to all the gods of her family? Hadn't she begged for safety for her parents and her brothers? Hadn't she pled for her own freedom? And here she was, a slave girl whose face stung from only one of the many slaps she received for no reason at all.

So—let no one talk of gods who kept promises. Not even the beautiful woman who had such an air of authority about her.

The well area was crowded with slaves, and the talk was as excited and incoherent as it had been in the women's quarters. Hagar caught the word "plague" over and over. She could smell the fear around her, and she wished she didn't have to speak to anyone. But Sarai's instructions had been plain.

"The Hebrew wanderer from the east," she said breathlessly to a girl beside her. "They say it's his god who is causing the sickness."

The girl stared at her, and Hagar stumbled over the words. "The man, Abram—the one who came because there was a drought in his country—and the woman, Sarai—well, they're not sister and brother as they said. She's his wife."

Still the girl stared, her mouth slack and stupid. Such a one would never carry Sarai's message. Hagar turned to her right and found herself staring into Meryet's eyes.

"Meryet!" Hagar cried. "I was afraid you'd been sold."

"Little cousin!" Meryet's narrow eyes glinted with tears. "Are you all right? I've been worried but I've been sent to the royal kitchen to serve, and I was afraid to try to find you."

The girls' hands met and clung. Meryet was the only other person from Hagar's home who still lived in the palace. At first, they had shared a pallet on the floor and had wept and remembered together. But then Meryet had been taken from the women's quarters and Hagar had felt lonelier than ever before.

"What's this you're telling?" Meryet asked abruptly. "What do you know of the trouble?"

"The Hebrew nomads," Hagar said. "They came sometime ago—when the Nile was in flood—and the chief said that the woman, Sarai, was his sister. Our lord believed him and took her into his courts. She's very beautiful."

"But what's that got to do with the sickness?"

"She says it's because their god is angry and is punishing our lord," Hagar offered.

Meryet looked frightened. "Then our lord should be told so that he can appease their god."

"But who's to tell him?" Hagar asked. "Even if it's true—"

"I know some of the slaves who go into the royal presence," Meryet said swiftly. "I'll see that the story is told."

"You might be punished," Hagar cried apprehensively.

Meryet smiled. "I'll be very careful," she promised. "Tell the woman you've done her bidding. Maybe she'll be kind to you."

Hagar jerked her shoulders nervously. But before she could say more, Meryet was gone, flashing across the yard. They hadn't even had a chance to talk, and who knew when they could possibly have a chance to meet again?

Hagar lowered her jar into the well and lifted it carefully so that nothing would be spilled. Taking it on her shoulder, she moved through the hot, still morning toward the women's rooms. Sarai was still standing in the shade, the green leaves dappling her skin with moving shadows.

"Did you do what I told you to?" Sarai asked.

"Yes, my lady."

"Did you talk to someone who can carry the message?"

"Yes, my lady. To Meryet. She works in the royal kitchen and knows slaves who serve our lord."

A grave satisfaction smoothed across Sarai's face. "Good," she approved. "I won't forget this. And you say the girl's name is Meryet? Do you know her well?"

"She's my cousin, my lady. We were—we were captured on the same day."

"You were truly not born a slave then?" Sarai's voice held what seemed to be real interest.

"No, my lady. I was captured when Pharaoh's army over-ran my father's—"

A swift blow rocked her and only her deftness kept the water jar from crashing into fragments at her feet. "How dare you stand and gossip?" came the shrill voice of the woman who had sent her for the water. "You should be whipped for your insolence. Bring the water inside immediately."

Without even a glance at Sarai, Hagar hurried to obey. She had been whipped before, and there were scars on her back where the whip had laid the flesh open.

Sarai followed the girl. "It's my fault," she said. "I was asking her questions."

The Egyptian woman looked up with hatred glittering in her eyes. "It seems everything is your fault, doesn't it? The sickness, this slave's insolence. You're not making yourself very welcome here."

Sarai smiled and spoke softly. "I beg your forgiveness. I am, after all, a stranger here and not familiar with your customs."

Hagar tried to melt into the shadow cast by the door's edge, to become as invisible as possible. But the water jar was emptied into a basin and then thrust again into her hands. "Get more," she was told, "and this time, don't loiter."

Hagar clutched the jar against her flat chest and scurried toward the door. But Sarai moved as swiftly as she. "What's your name, little one?" she asked quietly.

Hagar looked up into the beautiful, dark eyes. "Hagar," she said. "They call me T'atet here, but my given name is Hagar."

"Then I'll call you Hagar, too," Sarai said and smiled again. "Now, go and do as you were told."

Hagar ran to the well and let down her jar. It was when she lifted it, cool and dripping, to her shoulder that she heard the sound of rage from the royal quarters. The sound swept through the morning air like thunder, and the jerk of terror in Hagar's heart daggered the blood across her eyes like lightning.

"Get me the Hebrew, Abram," Hagar heard in a loud, furious voice. "Get me Abram at once! *Hurry!*"

The last word, shrill as a scream, sent Hagar across the yard in a blind rush of panic. What it had to do with her, she did not know. She only flew, breathless, clutching her jar, toward the women's rooms, knowing that there was no real refuge for her there. There was no refuge for her anywhere.

Abram stood before the throne of the Pharaoh and bowed respectfully. "You sent for me, my lord?"

The Pharaoh, breathing hard, spoke in a tightly controlled voice, "Why did you lie to me?"

"I, my lord?" Abram looked mildly surprised.

"Yes. You. She was your sister, you said. I took her into my palace, thinking she was your sister. Now they say she is your wife. You could have caused me shame. I am told your god is angry, and my son suffers for it."

Abram looked at the floor.

"Have you nothing to say?" the Pharaoh demanded.

"No, my lord," Abram answered.

"*Is* she your wife?"

There was a long silence, and then Abram looked at the Egyptian ruler. "Yes, my lord," he said.

2

The Pharaoh himself was standing in the door of the women's quarters. This had never happened before in the time that Hagar had been there, and she shared the flutter of apprehension and amazement that swept the room.

The women prostrated themselves before their god-king, flattening themselves against the floor while their breathless voices whispered, "My lord—my lord—my lord—"

He stood in rigid silence, his eyes brushing over the prostrate women with a weary contempt. "The woman, Sarai," he said harshly. "I would speak to the woman, Sarai."

Hagar, lying on the cool floor, slid her eyes sideways to where Sarai crouched behind the partition. Now there was real fear on the oval face, and color bleached out of the lovely skin.

"My lord?" Sarai faltered and moved cautiously around the wall and into his view. "My lord?"

"You were part of the contemptible plan," he barked. "You and that man, Abram. To save his skin, you lied to me."

"Yes, my lord," Sarai whispered, but Hagar could see that the color was coming back into Sarai's lips. Even in this terrifying situation, there was some source of courage available to her.

"Leave my house!" the Pharaoh thundered. "Leave my city! Take what is necessary to appease your god. Take grain for your cattle, take cattle, take menservants and maidservants. You may have your pick of the lot of slaves. But choose soon—and go!"

"My husband, Abram, will decide on cattle and grain, my lord," Sarai spoke without hesitation as though she had planned what to say. "But I have chosen the slaves already—if my choice suits you, my lord. I want the girl, Hagar—and another—Meryet is her name. She serves in your kitchen.

"Which is Hagar?" demanded the Pharaoh. "Is she among this lot?"

"Hagar," Sarai said clearly. "Stand and come forward, so our lord can see you."

Her heart pounding wildly in her throat, Hagar got to her feet and moved toward the door where the Pharaoh stood. Even with her eyes downcast, she was aware of how his hard eyes raked over her thin body.

"She doesn't look like much," he said abruptly. "A captured slave. Take her and welcome. And the other, too. Only go. My son can't get well while you and your people crowd into our city."

"You are kind, my lord," Sarai murmured. "The God of Abram will bless you for your kindness."

The Pharaoh did not even answer. He turned on his heel and left the women's court as though the plague itself were chasing him.

Before the women could struggle to their feet, Sarai had grasped Hagar's arm. "Do you have any belongings?" she asked.

"A few souvenirs from home. Another skirt."

"Never mind the skirt. You won't wear these heathen dresses anyhow but something decent that comes up over your breast. Get your keepsakes. Hurry. We'll go at once."

Hagar scurried to the far corner of the room and groped beneath the pallet that had been hers. She felt the familiar knobbiness of a small bundle with a sense of comfort. Only a few trinkets—a bracelet of copper, a broken comb, and two small gods—tiny replicas of the goddess Hathor, the deity of love, happiness, music and dance; and of Sobek who had kept his worshipers safe in the river city of her birth. She had been decking the small idols with flowers when the soldiers had come, and somehow had been able to keep them clutched in her hands through all the terror that had followed. She had kept them—angry that they had never answered her prayers—but had been afraid to discard them, reluctant to throw away something which spoke so strongly of home.

"This is all," she said breathlessly to Sarai, aware that the women were standing, ringing them in with anger.

"We've been given permission to go," Sarai said to the women, her hand clutching Hagar's thin arm. The girl felt the clutching fingers tremble, but the trembling was not revealed in the calm voice. "You would be very wise if you did nothing to interfere with your king's commands."

A murmur of frustration came from the women, but Hagar watched them move, one by one, until the way to the door seemed to be clear. Sarai and Hagar had almost reached the porch when one of the women struck out swiftly. Hagar screamed as the whip came down across her shoulders.

Sarai's voice was loud enough to stop the hand that was raised for a second blow. "If you strike her again, I'll report it to the Pharaoh. She belongs to me."

The woman hesitated and then slowly lowered her hand. "Take her," she hissed with venom. "Take her and yourself away from us. But someday you'll be sorry." Her voice held the threat of dark prophecy. "Someday you'll ask your god to take this worthless wretch out of your house!"

Sarai smiled with superiority. "What can *you* know? Come on, Hagar. We'll look for Meryet and then find my lord, Abram, so we can start for home."

By the time the late afternoon sun was slanting redly across the sky, the group of nomadic Hebrews was moving with its animals a safe distance away from the Pharaoh's city. Hagar, walking beside Meryet, was too bewildered to really comprehend what was happening to her. She held on to Meryet's hand as though she were a small child, and felt pain in her shoulders where the whip had come down.

She had not realized that there were so many people in Abram's party. A few servants, she had thought, a few cattle and goats. Surely they must have been an impoverished group to have sought assistance in Egypt. But this crowd that jostled noisily along the dusty road was neither impoverished nor few in number. There must be hundreds of people, Hagar estimated dazedly, counting the women and children and the slaves who walked at the rear as she was doing. And the flocks were strong and healthy, moving patiently in the road's dust.

"Where are we going, Meryet? Do you know?"

The older girl smiled down at her cousin. "I don't know. Not really. These are nomads, you know. They're always traveling."

"But the woman, Sarai—she said we were going home."

Meryet shrugged. "Home could be anywhere—anywhere where there's water and grazing for the cattle. And a place to put up tents."

"Tents? You mean we'll live in tents?"

"What did you expect? A palace somewhere?"

"But—but—" Hagar stumbled over the words. "You seemed happy to go. You came running when Sarai called you."

Meryet shrugged again. "There are things you're too young to know. It wasn't happy for me there in the kitchen. You aren't the only one to feel the whip. And for different reasons. The woman, Sarai, looked kind."

"Oh, she is," Hagar cried. "She's—she's beautiful, isn't she?"

Meryet grinned. "Beauty can get you into trouble. If she hadn't been so beautiful, the Pharaoh wouldn't have taken her into his house. Was she one of his favorites? Was she called to his rooms often?"

Hagar tried to remember. It had been her duty to apply

green eye shadow and dark eye liner and to fasten the cone of greasy perfume to the hair of those who were called to the royal rooms. And it had been her duty to wash away the melted, waxy perfume that covered the shoulders of the women when they came back the following morning. But she had never ministered to Sarai. Perhaps one of the other girls had served her. Or perhaps, being Hebrew and not Egyptian, Sarai had put on her own cosmetics.

"I don't think she went often. Perhaps not at all. Maybe the Pharaoh was waiting until she was more accustomed to our ways."

Meryet leaned close to whisper, "Maybe her god protected her."

Hagar shook her head. "I haven't seen any statue—or amulet—or even a symbol. I think she only *talks* about a god."

"Well, no matter," Meryet said. "She's back with her husband tonight. And maybe life will be kinder to us here. It was worth trying, little Hagar. As if we had any choice," she added bitterly.

Sarai rode slowly on the back of a shaggy donkey. A thin cloth was pulled across her face to protect her from the dust that rose from the feet of the men and animals in front of her. She had not yet seen Abram face to face. There had been too much confusion, too much haste in their exit from the Pharaoh's city, but she had heard his voice raised in sharp command. He must have anticipated this exodus, or things could not have happened as swiftly as they had. Had Yahweh spoken to him again, had a warning come to Abram when he sat alone guarding his flocks? Sarai did not understand how the Voice came to Abram, but that it came, she had no doubt.

When she thought of seeing Abram, she felt a warmth in her cheeks and a trembling through her body. It had been a long time since she had been with him, and she had been lonely. She had been more than lonely; she had been frightened. She could acknowledge that now. She had been afraid that she would be called into the Pharaoh's room and would be forced to act the part of a concubine. She did not know, even now, if she would have gone obediently, or run screaming into the night, trying to find Abram.

So she had prayed, and Yahweh had heard her prayers! Even though she had been unable to offer sacrifice, even though she had been unable to cry aloud to Yahweh at dawn as Abram did, still she had whispered her desperate prayers in secrecy and they had not been in vain.

And tonight—tonight she and Abram would be together again, and she could tell him everything she had been thinking for all these days of separation. More than the touch of his hands, she longed for the closeness of his understanding.

Perhaps it had been her own loneliness that had attracted her to the girl Hagar, she thought. What an unattractive, thin, slant-eyed thing she was—bony and with a voice that was edged with insolence. But there was a terrible, lost quality in her eyes. And the thin, naked back had been scarred cruelly.

Of course, slaves must be whipped for disobedience, Sarai thought as she turned her head to see where Hagar was, but the child had been struck too many times for no reason. And she *is* only a child.

I need a child to fuss over, Sarai reflected honestly. Even if the child is a slave and homely. I'll get a decent dress on her and maybe some goat milk will put flesh on her bones.

"Are you comfortable, Sarai?"

Her head jerked up and she found herself looking in Abram's eyes. He looked merry and self-confident, and she saw the heat in his cheeks as his gaze ran over her face.

"Very comfortable, my husband."

"You're all right?"

She knew what he wanted to ask, what he could not even wait for the privacy of their tent to ask.

"I never left the women's quarters," she said and watched

relief and joy shine in his eyes. "I am, perhaps, not very desirable." But her modesty was false, and she knew that her eyes were shining, too.

"Desirable enough," he said mockingly but his hand touched hers before he rode away.

Maybe tonight, she thought, a child will be conceived. Oh, please, Yahweh, give me a son.

Meryet tugged Hagar's arm. "Look," she said. "That's Sarai's husband, I think. The chief of this tribe."

Hagar looked up, unable to see Abram clearly at first, but then a cloud of dust rolled by and she saw him plainly. He was a large man, wearing the loose, lightweight robe of the traveling nomad. His hair and beard were dark reddish brown, and his face was strong and kind.

He's much more handsome than the Pharaoh, Hagar thought. As handsome as my father was.

Abram drew up beside the two girls. "You're new with us." He spoke with certainty. "Where did you come from?"

"The Pharaoh gave us to your lady," Meryet said while Hagar only stared.

"His generosity astonishes me," Abram said with a wide grin. "Two children for me to feed and care for."

"I'm sixteen, my lord," Meryet said and added truthfully, "or nearly."

"And I, my lord, am twelve," Hagar said.

His eyes flicked to her shoulders. "And do they beat children in the Pharaoh's court?"

"The women are often angry," Hagar said, groping to understand something that she had seen but had never tried to describe. "They were angry because they—they were only women, not wives."

Abram nodded with satisfaction. "You see well, little one. If you're beaten here, it will be because you deserve it." He turned in his saddle and shouted to a dark-eyed boy who had ridden behind the herds all day, urging them forward. "Dothan," he shouted. "Come here."

The boy, dust covered and weary, came at Abram's bidding.

"Here are two new slaves," Abram said. "See to it that they're given a place to sleep tonight among the other slaves. I'll make you responsible for them for the time it will take to find a place for them and work for them to do."

"Yes, my lord," said the boy, but his attitude was in no way servile. He could almost have been Abram's son.

The impression was heightened suddenly when the man reached out a rough, affectionate hand and tousled the boy's hair. But Abram's next words denied the relationship.

"Get word to your father, my boy, that I wish to talk to him after we've stopped. As my steward, Eliezer must calculate my new possessions—these gifts I've received from the mighty Pharaoh."

Dothan laughed with his master and turned his donkey's head to ride away, but not before he had looked sharply at Meryet, skimming his eyes swiftly over the Egyptian dress that was caught under her breasts. Meryet did not meet his eyes, but Hagar felt sudden tension in the hand that held hers.

Abram spoke sharply to Dothan. "Go—as you were told." Then his eyes, suddenly stern, moved to Meryet's face. "You will find clothes such as the other women wear. And for the child, too. Our women walk before our God with modesty."

"Yes, my lord," Meryet said, her voice meek.

After Abram had ridden away, Hagar turned to her cousin.

"What does he mean?" she asked.

Meryet's shoulders moved in her characteristic shrug. "I'll have to find out. Each tribe has its own customs and its own god. We'll have to do what's proper for this tribe."

Hagar didn't answer. Her bare feet dragged in the dust, and she ached all over. She wished for one minute that she were back in the shade of the tamarisk tree at the women's court. Once every seven days they had been allowed to bathe in the river. Today would have been the day.

She moved her shoulders and felt pain. "I'm thirsty," she said.

"The people in the front have stopped walking," Meryet said. "There'll be a well, I'm sure. And our turn will come for a long drink of water." Then, after a silence, "Did you look at the boy, Dothan? The son of Abram's steward? Did you look at him?"

"Why should I look at him?" Hagar's voice was fretful. "And how do you know he's the son of Abram's steward? Who told you?"

"Abram himself, silly little donkey. Didn't you listen? But a man with many sons wouldn't be so affectionate with a steward's son. I don't understand all this."

"She doesn't have any sons," Hagar blurted out. She had almost forgotten the incident but now it surged vividly into her mind. "I heard her crying once, weeping because she was barren."

"Barren?" Meryet whispered in awe. "And her husband is still faithful to her?"

"I don't know," Hagar said. "I only know I'm thirsty."

Meryet was quiet and when she spoke, her voice was very matter of fact, but Hagar could see a tiny blaze of excitement behind her eyes.

"Be patient, little one," Meryet said. "You've stumbled—miraculously—into something that could be very good for us. A childless couple, a favorite slave who looks—looks—"

"Looks how?" Hagar said impatiently.

"Looks at me," Meryet said flatly, and Hagar saw the small smile of satisfaction that turned up the corners of her cousin's mouth.

3

Hagar and Meryet found some thin shade and watched wearily as Abram's tribe began what seemed almost to be a ritual. Fires were started, family groups came together, and wailing babies were silenced at their mothers' breasts. Tents appeared to sprout up in the sandy wash that was bordered by a stream bed where only a faint trickle of water remained of the spring torrent that had swept across the land. But there was still enough moisture to provide pasturage for the flocks and water for the people. Hagar was to learn that life would be spent searching for the treasure of water. If she had thought she loved the wide river in the city where she was born, she would learn to almost idolize spare streams, bubbling wells, or even the faint green that indicated water underground.

But on that first night, she knew nothing of how it would be to search for water, to long for it or to almost die for the lack of it. She only huddled, bewildered, watching the tents grow against the evening sky. They were made of goat skin but brightly colored. There was certainly nothing solid about them, nothing to make a person feel sheltered and secure, but they provided a protection from the wind and the sun and privacy for sleeping.

She had known only the rich home of her father and then the women's quarters of the Pharaoh's palace, where perhaps she was beaten but the surroundings had been elegant, and there had been adequate sanitation facilities even for the slaves. Here there was nothing.

And yet there was laughter. She heard it swelling up, soaring from group to group. Even the slaves, sweating as they tugged the tent ropes and pegged them into the soil, tossed laughter back and forth in the evening air.

The sound of laughter, the calling of small children playing, the bleating of the animals all began to fade into a haze and Hagar sprawled on the ground and slept. Meryet looked down at her and then shrugged and went to see what she ought to be doing. Let the little one sleep for a short while. Who knows what labor would be expected of them later on?

She found Dothan standing over a group of boys and men who were raising tents. His commands were insolent and merry, and one of the men threatened him with a ribald gesture, and Dothan moved away.

He saw Meryet looking at him. "They've been putting up tents since before I was born," he said lightly. "I irritate them."

"Then why do you give orders?" She asked the question meekly enough, but there was boldness in her heart.

Dothan spread his hands. "I was born to give orders."

"But—" She hesitated, not sure how to phrase the question. "But—you're not the chief's son, are you?"

"Near enough," Dothan said cockily. "My father, Eliezer, is Abram's steward—the natural inheritor if no son is born."

"But that is surely in the hands of the gods and a son may be conceived at any time?"

Dothan made a quick gesture to appease the gods. But his grin never wavered. "They have been married for many years—my master and his lady. There haven't been any children at all—not even girls."

"Well, then, he'll take another wife," Meryet argued.

"He loves her," Dothan said simply.

"Oh—love!" Meryet tossed the word away as though it were a dried seed in the wind.

"You don't believe in love?" Dothan said, still grinning.

"I believe in nothing," Meryet said flatly.

"Who are you?" he asked.

"I'm Meryet—daughter of Snefru. My father and Hagar's—the girl that you saw with me—were brothers. Our city was captured by the Pharaoh two years ago. Our parents, our brothers, all were killed. We were taken as slaves."

"Being a slave isn't so terrible," Dothan said in a consoling sort of voice. "I'm a slave and look at me! I'm sorry about your families, though."

"You may be a slave," Meryet said bitterly, "but you're a boy. Life is altogether different for boys."

"True," Dothan agreed cheerfully. "Come on, I'd better take you to my mother. She'll know where to put you. Where's the other girl?"

"I'll get her. Just a minute." Meryet ran to shake Hagar's shoulders, to drag her to a sitting position and whisper urgently in her ear. "Come on, we're going with Dothan. Hurry—wake up!"

Hagar stumbled after the other two, and she was sharply aware of the smell of food cooking, of the pungent odor of the smoke from cooking fires. Suddenly she was ravenous.

"I'm hungry," she said plaintively. "And thirsty, too."

"Well, here's water," Dothan said and stopped to hand her the water skin that had been hanging around his neck.

She lifted it to her lips and drank clumsily but instinctively, careful not to spill any of the precious liquid.

"Thank you," she said, handing the skin back. And for the first time she smiled.

Dothan looked surprised. "I thought she was born with a scowl on her face," he said wickedly to Meryet.

"Shame on you," Meryet said, but she grinned at him.

Hagar jerked away and walked stiffly alone as they approached a large group of women by the fire.

Dothan pulled a woman aside and began to speak to her, gesturing to the two girls, explaining something in a quick voice. In the midst of the words, Hagar caught her own name. And not spoken by the boy, spoken by the mother.

"Hagar," Dothan called. "Come here. This is my mother. You can call her Soshannah."

For a minute, Hagar hesitated, then she felt Meryet's hands pushing at her back, and she moved forward. The large dark woman who stood with Dothan looked at her curiously.

"You're Hagar?" The voice sounded disbelieving.

Hagar nodded her head.

"And our mistress has chosen you for her personal slave?" Still disbelief colored Soshannah's voice.

The words hardly made sense to Hagar either. In the harem, yes, she might have been chosen to be a slave to any one of the women. But in this tribe, Sarai was wife of the chief. She could have any slave she wanted. Surely Meryet was older and brighter and more able. Why had she chosen Hagar?

"Well—" Soshannah spread her hands in a gesture of resignation. "I'm not the one to question what our mistress does. You," she said to Meryet, "Dothan will show you where there's a pool. Wash the girl so she's clean. Here, wait, I'll get a decent dress for her to wear." She disappeared toward one of the tents and came back with some striped, rough material in her hands. "Here, put this on her, and we'll feed her and send her to the master's tent."

Dothan led them behind some straggling low trees and pointed out a small pool of water, dammed up for the animals. Hagar looked at it with distaste. How could she bathe where cattle and sheep had been drinking, where the ground was covered with their droppings, where anyone might come at any minute and see her?

"I'll stand guard," Dothan said, "But not for long. I've got too much work to do to play nursemaid to a girl."

Meryet stripped off the dirty Egyptian skirt, and Hagar's small bundle fell from the girdle. "What's this?" Meryet said. "Is it worth keeping?"

Hagar grabbed it fiercely. "It's mine," she muttered sullenly. "Sarai said I could bring it with me."

"All right," Meryet said indifferently. "Come on, hurry. He won't stand there forever."

Hagar shot one look at Dothan's slim back and then stepped into the tepid water. It felt slimy to her and she shut her eyes with a shudder as Meryet's hands rinsed off her thin body.

The rough garment that Meryet pulled over her head felt strange and uncomfortable. She had never worn anything before that came up over her shoulders, and the fresh whip cut stung fiercely. But she knew it was her duty to wear it so she tried to find some comfort in its vivid colors and the crude pattern woven into the material.

Dothan had disappeared by the time Meryet was satisfied with the condition of Hagar's hair.

"You're fixing me like I was one of the women being called to the Pharoah's room," Hagar said crossly, trying to move her head away from Meryet's hands.

"This is far more important," Meryet said. "If you please our lady, your life will be better than you can possibly imagine."

"In a tent?" asked Hagar in scorn. "Taking baths in a drinking hole for cattle?"

Meryet's voice was very tense. "But there will be some dignity in your life. In our lives—if you play it right. And I warn you now, little cousin, I'll be watching you. I'm not going to let your silly temper and foolish pride cheat me out of what I can have. Remember that."

There was such a threatening tone to Meryet's voice that Hagar felt even more desolate than she had been feeling before. She had thought that having Meryet with her would make life more pleasant. But Meryet seemed to have plans and ideas that Hagar couldn't even guess at. And she was too tired to try. She knew she ought to coax Meryet not to be cross, but she could only look at the ground and wish bleakly that her mother was not dead.

The food, though eaten in a rough, informal style that Hagar found distasteful, was good and satisfying. There were wheat cakes and stewed goat meat and fruit. Soshannah urged a cup of goat's milk on the girl, but Hagar, used to wine, turned her face away.

"You'll learn to drink it," Soshannah said grimly. "The mistress has ordered it for you to fatten you up."

Hagar was silent, because there was nothing for her to say.

When she had finished eating, it was full dark, and Dothan was waiting to lead her to Sarai's tent.

"Come on," he ordered, and Hagar got up to follow him.

"Your treasures," Meryet reminded her, and Hagar reached to pick up the knobby bundle. Meryet caught her hand. "Smile, little cousin," Meryet whispered. "Ask the goddess Hathor for the grace to smile."

Hagar looked at the older girl from under her lashes, and she was not sure whether the look in Meryet's eyes was a look of command or a plea.

Then, "I'll try," Hagar said, suddenly docile, and she was rewarded with a warm little pat from Meryet's hand.

She stumbled several times going across the unfamiliar ground, but Dothan never offered to help her. He seemed absorbed in his own thoughts. Finally he stopped and pointed to a tent which was set a little apart from the others.

"Here," he said. "Here's where our mistress waits."

He turned and left her, not even leading the way to the opened flap that served as a door.

With hesitant feet, Hagar moved toward the tent where soft light from an oil lamp spilled through the opening to make a wedge of gold on the ground.

"My lady?" Hagar called softly, almost fearfully.

There was a brief silence and then Sarai called, "Yes, child, in here. Come in."

Hagar entered the lighted interior and saw that it was grander than she had expected. There were colorful hangings, baskets and vases, and the rugs on the floor were soft to her naked feet.

Sarai was sitting on some cushions and, lying with his head on her lap, was the man, Abram. Hagar stopped in confusion. She was not ignorant of what went on between men and women, but in the courts of Pharoah, she had seen only lust. And her father had never sought out her mother for conversation as Abram had evidently sought out Sarai. Hagar stared with curiosity and she saw that Abram was relaxed and happy, and that Sarai's face was more beautiful than ever—glowing with a light more lovely than the lamp.

"Well, my lord," said Sarai, gesturing toward the child. "This is Hagar, gift of the Pharoah."

"I've seen her already," Abram said, grinning. "She looks a little better, I'll admit, but she's a skinny thing, my love. How can she serve you?"

Sarai reached out a hand and brought Hagar close to them. "Come here, little one," she said. "Would you like to serve me?"

Hagar looked at the dark, shining eyes. "I only know how to apply cosmetics," she said, unexpectedly modest. "And you don't need them, my lady. You're beautiful enough."

"An observant child," Abram said comfortably. "But I noticed that when I first spoke to her."

"You can learn to do other things," Sarai promised. "You can learn to spin thread and churn milk and weave. You can be here when I'm lonely—when my lord has taken the flocks away."

Hagar felt sudden warmth in her throat. "I'll do anything you require of me, my lady," she said in a solemn voice. "I'll serve you in any way I can."

Sarai smiled. "Are you tired?"

"Yes, my lady."

"There are rugs behind the curtain there in the back of the tent," Sarai said. "You can serve me best now by going to sleep. Tomorrow we'll talk."

It seemed to Hagar that Abram started to protest, but Sarai laid a gentle hand across his mouth. "She'll sleep in my tent every night," she said. "She can start tonight. She'll sleep like the dead. You'll see, my lord. She's exhausted."

Hagar hardly heard the words. She pulled the heavy

curtain aside, found the soft rugs and tumbled headlong into them to fall almost instantly asleep. She was only dimly aware how the heavy curtain shut out the light and muffled the voices of the man and woman so that their conversation was only a faint murmer, a ripple of sound like the river that had once flowed outside her window.

4

Hagar struggled out of the deep sleep that had held her all night. A sound had awakened her—the strong, vibrant ringing of a man's voice. He seemed almost to be singing, and for a few minutes she stayed snuggled in her rugs, listening to the rough music. And then she realized what it was. It was Abram praying to his God.

She had heard morning prayers all her life. Her father had been a righteous man, and her mother had chanted soft prayers to the goddess Hathor and the god Sobek each day as she put fresh flowers on the little altar in her room. It was probably because of her mother that Hagar had preferred Hathor and Sobek to all the other deities. Before tragedy had come into her life, Hagar had been a laughing child, and her mother had always said that the Hathor who was the soul of all merriment and music had blessed her at her birth. And Sobek, with his wide crocodile jaws, was security, it seemed, against all evil—until real evil came, and then Sobek had been as helpless as her father's soldiers.

But Abram's praying seemed different. There was such strong affirmation in it, such familiarity. Hagar crept forward to the curtain and pulled it aside to peek through the narrow opening. The door of Abram's tent faced east, and the sun was just coming over the edge of the horizon. Abram knelt at the tent door, and his strong voice seemed to herald the new day. Hagar listened to the prayer, puzzled over why it seemed different from other prayers she had heard.

The gods at home had been petulant, unstable, moved by small jealousies and angers, hungers and appetites. This Yahweh that Abram was addressing seemed to be someone only to be adored. It was a strange thing, and Hagar did not feel at all comfortable with it. It was odd, too, she thought, that Abram had only one god. It seemed to her that he ought to worship two or three in case one became angry or began to favor someone else.

Well, it's nothing to me, Hagar thought. The only thing that mattered to her was whether or not the woman would be good to her. If she weren't beaten, if she were given pleasant work to do and if the woman talked to her sometimes, she would be satisfied. The terrible loneliness that had tortured Hagar immediately after her capture by the Pharaoh's soldiers had gentled itself over the months into something that could be borne, and she had gradually built up a protective wall of indifference to everything around her. She hoped for no more than an absence of cruelty and pain.

At the end of Abram's prayer, a soft sound from Sarai turned Hagar's eyes away from the open flap of the tent. Although she had stayed inside the tent and had knelt in the shadows, nevertheless Sarai had joined Abram in his prayers. The sound that Hagar had heard had been Sarai's echoing amen. Men and women had not prayed together in Hagar's experience. But then, they had not talked as Sarai and Abram had talked the night before either. These people were different, Hagar realized, and she wasn't sure she liked their ways. It would take much getting used to.

Sarai started to get up and Hagar dropped the curtain, preparing to dive under the rugs and feign sleep. But just before the curtain shut out her view of the main tent, Hagar saw Abram lay his hand along Sarai's cheek and bend his lips to hers. The sight sent a shock running through Hagar's body. She had never seen that kind of gentleness before, and she was swept with a terrible desolation. Oh, that someone, *anyone* might love her like that, she thought.

The curtain was lifted, and Sarai looked in. Hagar had not even had time to close her eyes, and her heart gave a frightened jerk lest the woman think she had been spying.

"Hagar?" Sarai's voice was quiet but firm. "If you're awake, why are you lying here like a lazy little goat? Don't you know that the day has come?"

"Yes, my lady," Hagar stammered, scrambling free of the covers. "I heard him—my lord—at his prayers. I didn't want to disturb him."

"You should have joined us," Sarai said gravely.

"I, my lady?" Hagar stared at Sarai in amazement.

"Of course, child. Yahweh hears the prayers of all of Abram's people—even Abram's slaves."

A dozen questions stirred in Hagar's mind, but she suppressed them all. She would have all she could do just learning to live with these people whose life was so different from the one she had known. Her questions could be saved for a later time, when she felt secure and at home. If indeed she ever felt secure anywhere, ever again.

"Come," Sarai said briskly. "I'll show you how to find the slaves' tents. They'll show you where you can wash. Then find something to eat and come back here."

"Shouldn't I bring food for you first, my lady?"

Sarai smiled. "Not today. Abram has already brought me fresh milk and dates."

Hagar felt her mouth and eyes rounding with even greater astonishment. A man bringing food to a woman!

Sarai smiled but a warm flush moved up to her hair. "Oh, not every day, of course. No woman is ever treated like that. But he—my lord—is different from most men. And today— he's happy because we're no longer separated."

"Then why did he tell the Pharaoh that you were his sister?" Hagar blurted out before she could stop the words.

Sarai's eyes were suddenly angry. "You're insolent, my girl. You forget what you are."

'I'm sorry, my lady," Hagar mumbled. "I—you spoke to me so kindly I felt—felt as though I were talking to my mother."

Slowly the blaze left Sarai's eyes, but her mouth did not soften. "I want to be fond of you, child. But I won't tolerate any probing into what my lord does. Do you understand? His actions and his thoughts are no concern of yours." The words were sharp and decisive.

Hagar felt the ridiculous burning of tears in her eyes. She, who had reacted only with anger to the whipping she had received in the Pharaoh's court, now cringed before mere words.

Sarai saw the tears and put out her hand. "Don't cry. You're hungry and this is all new to you. I don't mean to be sharp, but you have to learn! My lord, Abram, answers to no one but Yahweh. If he should make a wrong decision—and neither you nor I dare wonder whether or not it was wrong—then that is his affair—his and Yahweh's. Do you understand?"

"Yes, my lady," Hagar whispered with trembling lips.

"Then go, as I told you," Sarai said kindly. "Look, do you see the gray tent there—the second one past the small shrub? That's one of the slaves' tents. They'll tell you what to do."

Her hand on Hagar's shoulder was gentle enough, and the girl moved obediently across the sandy wash. Although it was hardly full daylight yet, the camp was busy, women bawling orders to their children and slaves, men laughing together as they sent boys scurrying to round up any sheep or goats which had wandered too far. The sounds were cheerful, Hagar thought. It was as though these people were all one family. She saw Abram talking to a young man, but if he saw her, he gave no sign. Hagar didn't expect him to, and yet she knew that the woman, Sarai, was treating her more as a guest than as a slave. There was something here that Hagar couldn't understand.

The day was a strange one. Hagar found that she was allowed to move about the camp with no one watching or guarding her. It was only later that she learned that no one had to guard slaves in the desert; the stretching sands and the lack of water were unrelenting bars that kept every slave safely with his master. But after the time in the Pharaoh's court where her every move was observed by someone and where privacy was totally unknown, she found this comparative freedom a heady thing. Her duties were not light, but she discovered that all women worked—even Sarai. Much of the work, such as spinning and weaving and the dying of cloth, was saved for more permanent camp sites, Hagar learned. But even on the move as they were now, grain had to be ground for bread. Kneeling in front of a large rock which had been slightly hollowed, women rubbed the grain back and forth with a smaller rock, separating the kernels from the chaff. Hagar tried it at Meryet's suggestion, but found her back aching intolerably in only a few minutes.

"Baby!" Meryet scoffed lightly. "I had to do this for hours at a time in the Pharaoh's kitchen. These rocks are cruder, but the method is the same."

"I could learn to do it, too," Hagar said, "if I had to. If the lady tells me I must, I will." She had found an odd satisfaction in seeing the kernels of wheat roll from the chaff. "I liked it," she added defiantly.

"All women like it," Meryet said. "Even though it's backbreaking. There's something about it."

"The lady told me to just look around," Hagar confided. "It seems strange—just looking around."

Meryet nodded. "I know. Don't go past the tents. There might be scorpions. Or snakes. I don't know but there might be."

"I wish our lady had a baby," Hagar said abruptly. "I could take care of it."

Meryet laughed. "You're not much more than a baby yourself. You couldn't nurse it or clean it."

"I could!" Hagar insisted. "Not nurse it maybe. There'd be wet nurses for that. Or maybe the lady herself would nurse it."

Meryet glanced up scornfully. "A chief's lady?"

"She's different," Hagar said stubbornly. "I tell you, she's different."

"Oh, they're all different," Meryet conceded easily. "But whether for good or bad, I don't know. Anyhow, there's no baby—so take advantage of their childlessness and be—be very lovable."

"I don't think I could be like that—deliberately lovable. I wouldn't know how."

"You can learn," Meryet said almost grimly. "You can learn."

That evening, there was a sense of celebration after the evening meal had been eaten. The night before, there had been no gathering of the people for anything other than the work of erecting tents and providing for the animals. But tonight there was laughter and gossip, and the people began to meet together near the fire that burned outside of the tent of Abram. Abram himself sat with his back to the tent, and his voice was cheerful and confident.

Hagar, still uncertain about what was expected of her, slipped inside the tent and hid in the shadows. Sarai was with the other women and she had not given any directions to the girl.

"No, I don't agree with you. We were *wise* to go," Hagar heard Abram say strongly to the young man who sat beside him. "We couldn't have endured the famine without going to Egypt. Bethel-Ai had become almost a desert. The streams were drying up."

"But it was a dangerous risk, Uncle," the young man argued. "You might have lost Sarai, or we might have been taken into slavery."

Abram's warm laugh rang out. "Do you take me for a fool, Lot? Don't you think I know what I'm doing? Give me credit for sense, my boy. Didn't we come away richer than you ever dreamed?"

"In animals, yes," Lot said sourly. "But the slaves are a surly lot. The two girls are nothing, and the men aren't much better."

"The girls are Sarai's," Abram said easily. "The men will learn. Be patient, Lot. You always want everything to happen at once. Can't you wait?"

"If I have to, Uncle," Lot said humbly enough. "But my wife—she had hoped for a slave of her own. A girl with the sort of training that could be learned only in the house of the Pharaoh."

"Perhaps Sarai will give her one of the girls," Abram said, and Hagar felt her heart jump. "I'll speak to her about it. Just be patient, Lot."

Several boys had come up to the two men, and one of them spoke in a shrill voice. "Tell us a tale, Father Abram. Tell us a tale."

Abram laughed again and his hand went out with an easy gesture of kindness as he touched the boy's shoulder. "A tale, eh? A tale about what?"

"A tale about us," the boy cried, and the request was taken up by other voices. "Yes, a tale about us. Tell how we came from the land beyond the rising of the sun. Tell us, Father Abram."

Abram smiled at Lot, and Hagar felt a thrill of anticipation. There was nothing in all the world she loved more than a story.

The Egyptians were not good storytellers. There was no need for them to be, her father had often told her. Once a child had learned to read, there were tablets on which history and legend were written. But these wandering peoples would have no tablets with written words, she realized. They would have to depend on stories. It was much the better way, Hagar thought.

"Well," Abram began and his voice took on the subtly cadenced lilt of the storyteller. "Well, when I lived in the city of Ur—after my father Terah had been gathered to his fathers—the voice of Yahweh came to me. 'Abram,' he said, and my heart melted with fear."

As the sound of Abram's voice moved through the night, a

silence descended on the camp. Men and boys gathered quickly, eagerly, around their leader. Even the women and girls formed a circle beyond the light of the fire, and Hagar, inside the tent, crept closer to the door that she might not miss a word.

" 'Yes, my Lord,' I answered," Abram went on. " 'Have you called me?' "

" 'I have called you, Abram,' Yahweh said, 'to go forth from this city and to go to a land which I will show you.'

"But still my heart melted with fear. I knew only the land Between the Mountains. My father and mother were dead, my brother Haran had died, and I had only my wife, Sarai, and my nephew, Lot, and his family.

"Leaving a familiar land is a dangerous thing. How would I know where the watering places were? How could I pasture my sheep? So it came to me that I should say 'No' to my God."

There was a curious sucking in of breath which Hagar could hear plainly. How many times must they have heard this story and yet always there must be this fear that Abram would disobey his god. Hagar found that she was leaning forward in her desire to hear.

"But Yahweh spoke again," Abram went on. "Like thunder on the mountain, he spoke to his servant. 'Go out, Abram. Go out of your city, and I will make of you a great nation, and I will bless you and I will make your name great and you will be a blessing.' "

Abram paused and there was a fraction of silence and then a dozen voices joined his to chant the rest of Yahweh's promise. "And I will bless them that bless you, and curse them that curse you and in you shall all families of the earth be blessed."

Again the brief silence, but there was satisfaction and pride on every face. What a marvelous thing, Hagar thought with unaccustomed humility, to be able to believe the promise of a god!

"And so I did as Yahweh bade me," Abram said into the

silence. "I took Sarai, my wife, and Lot and his wife and all the souls who had come to Ur with my father, and I began the journey into Canaan."

There was a stir as the people settled more comfortably to listen to the familiar words.

"Sometimes it was difficult to know that Yahweh was leading us," Abram said simply. "The way was hard, and we traveled many days. But sometimes there was plenty of water and pasture for the flocks, and we began to prosper. We came to the plain of Moreh, and there was water and green grass there, but we were fearful because the Canaanites were in the land.

"Then Yahwah appeared to me again. On a dark night, when I stood looking over the vast plain, wondering what I was doing in this distant place, Yahweh spoke to me. 'Unto your seed I will give this land,' he said."

Abram coughed a little. "I had no son," he went on quietly, leaning forward to brush dust from his foot so that his face was hidden. "I had no son but I believed. So I built an altar there, an altar to Yahweh who is a mighty King and a mighty God."

"A mighty King and a mighty God," the voices chanted back at him.

"The Canaanites showed their teeth," Abram said, "but Yahweh kept them from biting us." There was a small ripple of laughter in the audience. "So we moved our tents and our people and our herds until we came to Bethel-Ai. And there I built another altar to the Lord."

He stopped as though he were finished, but one of the smaller boys spoke up.

"Tell us of Bethel-Ai, Father Abram. Tell us how it is."

"Bethel-Ai is a place of milk and honey," the voice of Abram chanted obediently. "Our tents were pitched on a small plain that was halfway up the mountainside. The sun did not scorch us by day nor the dews chill us at night. There was water enough for all and the grass was green for the flocks. There were dates and olives, and every man of us knew that Yahweh had led us to a land of promise."

"Then why did we leave?" The question was rhetorical.

"A famine came," Abram concluded. "Yahweh did not see fit to send the rain, and the water dried up and the grass withered in the noonday sun. So I led the people south and we came at last to the land of Egypt where the Nile gives water to a thirsty land." No voice prompted him then, no one brought up the shame of his lie about Sarai or the anger of the Pharaoh when they had been routed from the city. They may have been given gifts but there had been hatred in the faces of the givers.

"And now," Abram said clearly, "we are heading back to Bethel-Ai. We will see again the mountain and the plain, the water and grass. The Canaanite may bare his teeth at us, but we will pass unharmed into the land that Yahweh has promised us. For he has promised that he will make of us a great nation."

He lifted his face to the starry sky, and his voice boomed forth with the fervor of prophecy. " 'I will bless you,' says our God, 'and I will make your name great and you will be a blessing.' "

"Yahweh is a mighty God," Abram said to his people.

And they shouted back at him, "A mighty God and a mighty King."

Hagar felt dazed. The story had stirred her imagination and she had almost been able to feel Abram's fear over the command to leave Ur. She felt she could almost see the plain of Moreh and the mountain at Bethel-Ai where an altar had been built. But as for Yahweh, he was only another deity to be reverenced or to be ignored. She would ask Sarai, she decided, to show her a statue of their god. It would be easier if she had some idea what he looked like.

But when Sarai came into the tent, there was no time for questions. Sarai was impatient to have Hagar brush her hair and help her take off her dusty dress and bathe her feet in the shallow basin which had been filled earlier. It was obvious that she, too, had been caught up in the story, shaken by it somehow.

She dismissed the girl curtly, and Hagar crept behind the heavy curtain. She lay on the rugs, thinking about the story, remembering the way the words had woven a spell in the night.

Her mind puzzled over some of the difficulties. How could Abram believe the promises of Yahweh when Sarai was barren? How long would it take Abram to realize, as Hagar already realized, that a god had no more substance than the shadows that had fallen from the tamarisk tree?

5

The interior of Lot's tent was not as fine as Abram's, but it contained many items of beauty. The rugs, heaped for beds, had strong, lovely colors, and vivid hangings adorned the sides. Lot, who had finished dressing before he said his morning prayers, turned to look at his wife.

Even sleeping, with her hair rumpled about her face, Zahavith was beautiful, he thought. Life would undoubtedly be simpler if she were ugly enough that he could put her out of his mind and heart for days at a time. But she wasn't ugly. Her hair was a rich, warm auburn, and her mouth was wide and curved, with a dimple at the corner of her lips.

He hated to wake her. The children were already awake and playing outside the tent. They needed sterner discipline, Lot knew, but if he tried to exert it so early in the morning, Zahavith got irritated. She wanted to sleep as late as possible, and if the children cried or argued, their noise woke her up. Better to let the four of them, two boys and two girls, do as they pleased.

But the time had come when he must wake her. If he left his tent with his wife still sleeping, his uncle would ridicule him or worse, speak harshly. And there were others, besides Abram, who accused him of being entirely too lenient with Zahavith. But what could he do—when she was so enchanting if he were kind and so cold when he tried to be stern?

His hand on her shoulder was gentle and caressing. At first, she twisted herself away from its touch, but then suddenly, she lay still and not only permitted the touch but moved her shoulder to snuggle under his fingers.

"My lord?" she whispered, sleep slurring the words.

"Sunrise is long past," he said. "The children are outside—not fed yet—and it's time for me to go with my uncle."

She opened her eyes, and the dimple showed fleetingly. "And I'm being lazy again, my lord."

"If our life were different," he said passionately, letting his fingers move to her face, "if we were rich as the Pharaoh, you could sleep until noon."

She nestled her cheek against his hand. "Speaking of the Pharaoh, did you ask your uncle about the slave girl?"

If only once, Lot thought regretfully, she were warm and loving out of nothing more than a desire to be so. If only there were not always the request behind the touch. But that's the way she was, and there was no use wishing she were different.

"Yes, I spoke to him. He said Sarai might let you have one of the girls."

"Might?" She sat up and threw her hair back over her shoulder with an angry gesture.

But Lot was more aware of the way her auburn hair glowed against her creamy shoulder than he was of the anger.

"I'm almost sure you'll get one of the girls. Sarai is usually—obliging." He had almost said "generous," and that would have been a mistake.

"Obliging!" Zahavith spit out scornfully. "Why must I always be dependent on her—her generosity? Here I am—a mother of four children and another to be born—and she, who is barren, treats me like—like a servant."

A sense of justice made Lot want to object, but he had learned many bitter lessons in the years he had been married. And he was willing to say—or swallow—any amount of words to keep Zahavith happy. "No one has ever denied that your fertility makes you an excellent wife, my dear. I'm one of the most blessed of men," he murmured.

She yawned, a langorous sound, and pulled his head down beside hers. "Speak to your uncle again," she coaxed. "And make it clear that I don't want the little one—an awkward piece of skin and bone. I want the older one—she has an eye in her head and skill in her hands, I'm sure. She could teach me a lot about how the Egyptian women make themselves beautiful."

"You don't need lessons, my love," Lot said.

But she didn't want flattery. She wanted assurance that her request would be met. "Promise me," she said softly. "Promise me you'll ask for Meryet."

He didn't want to ask again. He had mentioned it when Zahavith had first suggested it, and he would have preferred that Abram make the next move, but he could not say "No" to the soft, fragrant creature who looked up at him from the rumpled rugs.

"All right," he agreed, and if he felt reluctant, he did not show it. "I'll ask him after the morning meal. But I'll need nourishment to face the ordeal." he added in a teasing tone.

She smiled, her dimple a flash of enchantment. "I'll hurry. I'll have your food ready before you can get your words gathered together for your uncle. Watch and see!"

And Lot watched to see, as he always did, that she was more beautiful than any other woman in his world. Let the others talk about Sarai; she was too cold and proud for him. Even with her greed and her temper, Zahavith was the one who made his bones melt like water even after all these years.

Hagar was sitting in the shade of Abram's tent, polishing a bronze vase. It was, she thought soberly, the most solid indication she had seen so far of Abram's wealth. This nomadic way of life lacked so many luxuries that she found it difficult to think of these people as wealthy, and yet she knew that only a rich man could own so costly an item.

The sound of running pulled her thoughts and her eyes from the vase in her hands. She saw Meryet coming toward her, racing along as though she were a child, and she seemed to blaze with excitement.

She dropped onto the sand beside Hagar and for a few seconds, she had no breath for speech. Hagar stared at her with fear.

"Is something wrong?" the younger girl asked, but Meryet only shook her head speechlessly.

"Well, then, why are you running as though seven devils were after you?" Hagar asked, turning back to her polishing.

"I've been talking to our lord Abram," Meryet gasped, and Hagar could see that her cheeks were scarlet.

"Well, what of it?" Hagar said impatiently. "If there's nothing wrong, then why are you so out of breath? What did he say?"

"He said I'm to be a lady's slave."

Hagar's heart jerked with the sudden memory of Abram's voice saying to Lot, "Maybe Sarai will give her one of the girls." Had he decided to let Meryet serve Sarai and was she, Hagar, to be given to Zahavith? She wasn't sure why such an arrangement would cause pain, but it would. She knew that.

Somehow she kept her voice cool. "Who are you to serve?"

Meryet's voice shook with excitement. "From today on, I'm to serve Zahavith."

Hagar felt relief wash through her.

"Meryet, how nice for you! What did our lord say?"

"Well, he said Zahavith wanted a girl to serve her. Not just any one of the slaves, but one who had been trained in Pharaoh's court. I told him—though it was hard to be honest—that I had not been in the women's courts as long as you had but had served for awhile in the kitchen. He just laughed and said well, then I'd know how to judge good food as well as good ways to make a lady beautiful. Oh, Hagar, this means that you and I will be better than ordinary slaves."

"I can't imagine why," Hagar said bluntly. "You, maybe, you're older. But—me—"

Meryet laughed, a soft, conspiratorial sound. "You'll find a dozen ways to make yourself useful. Sarai has needs that even she doesn't know about."

Hagar didn't answer. She only bent her head over the vase, rubbing it more briskly than before.

Meryet spoke dreamily. "It won't matter who inherits Abram's wealth—his nephew or his chief steward—I'll be there."

"You honestly think you'll profit from Abram's wealth?" Hagar's voice was sharp and angry. "You forget you're only a slave, Meryet."

Meryet's excitement was suddenly gone, and her voice was cold. "No, I haven't forgotten, little cousin. How could I possibly forget? But I won't always be a slave. There are ways, you know, to crawl up out of slavery."

Hagar glanced around swiftly. "Don't say that. Don't you remember what happened to the slaves that tried to escape from our father's house?"

Meryet laughed. "I'm not going to escape. Not by the way you mean. Not by running away. But there are ways."

A shrill whistle cut through the afternoon, and both girls saw Dothan swaggering along behind several other boys. He appeared totally unaware of their presence, but Hagar could see how his eyes slid around until he could not help but see them. She glanced at Meryet and was in time to see a look of pure satisfaction in the dark eyes. No word was spoken, but Hagar knew that the boy and girl had been sharply aware of each other even though only silence had stretched between them.

"Go ahead—aim for the moon," Hagar said bitterly, feeling young and inexperienced and angry. "Why be satisfied with being Zahavith's personal maid when you can be—whatever it is you want to be to Dothan."

Meryet's voice was suddenly wheedling. "Don't be angry with me. I wasn't born to be a slave, you know that. And there's no question about what I want to be to Dothan. I want to be his wife."

"His wife?" Hagar caught her breath in surprise. "I knew you were ambitious—but you're only—"

"Don't tell what I'm only," Meryet snapped. "If you'll listen to me and act the way I tell you, there's no stopping what we can be, you and I."

Hagar bent over the vase and didn't answer for a few minutes. She couldn't deny that there was something terribly exciting at the thought of growing—though marriage—or scheming—out of slavery and into the sort of position she once held in life. And what's more, Meryet was probably right. What was there to keep them from grasping at any opportunity to improve their situation?

Then she seemed to hear Sarai's voice, "Would you like to serve me?" and her own voice answering with a promise to do anything—anything—if her lady requested it.

"Well, maybe," Hagar muttered, hoping that Meryet would be satisfied with such an indefinite response.

Meryet got suddenly to her feet. "Work very hard, little cousin," she said clearly, as though she wanted to be overheard. "Remember I've been telling you that we must serve our mistresses with humility and faithfulness."

Hagar looked up in quick amazement and caught a warning look in Meryet's eyes. It was only then that she saw that Sarai was hurrying into the tent, her face hidden by a fold of cloth.

"Remember," Meryet said again.

"I'll remember," Hagar said, but her voice sounded sullen in her own ears.

Meryet slipped away between the tents, and Hagar sat motionless for a moment and then resumed her task of polishing.

When the vase seemed to glow with a satin sheen, Hagar slipped into the tent to place it on the small table near the tent opening. As she turned to leave, she heard the bitter, ugly sound of unrestrained sobbing. Her heart seemed to freeze. It was Sarai weeping, and Hagar had never heard such a sound of anguish before. Should she leave, pretending she had not heard?

She started to move toward the tent opening, but the heartbroken sobbing caught her and held her. Frightened and unsure, the girl stood uncertainly, balanced between a desire to run away and an odd feeling of compassion—totally foreign to her—which made her want to stay. For a long, agonizing minute, she teetered between the two feelings, and then she turned swiftly and moved toward the tumbled heap of rugs where the woman crouched weeping with despair.

"My lady," Hagar said, hardly recognizing her own voice. "My lady, don't cry so. I can't bear to hear you weep."

Sarai only wept harder, but her hand reached out to Hagar with a gesture that begged for help.

"What can I do, my lady?" Hagar whispered, daring to kneel beside her mistress. "How can I help you?"

"Oh Hagar." The words were muffled and blurred. "Oh, Hagar, I can't *bear* it."

"What, my lady? What can't you bear?"

"I've just discovered. . . . I've just learned. . . ." The voice wavered, stopped, and then went on in a broken, ragged whisper. "The way of women is upon me. I had hoped . . . I had prayed . . . that after the separation, I would . . . could bear my lord a son. But. . . ."

And here words failed her, and she wept again, more despairingly than ever.

"Oh, my lady," Hagar crooned, as though to a small, hurt child.

She never thought of Meryet's suggestion to be lovable. She only knew that Sarai was suffering, and that she wanted to help her.

"Please don't cry so hard. You'll make yourself ill. Here, lie down. Put this pillow under your head. I'll find some cool water and bathe your eyes. Please don't cry." She soothed with her hands as well as her words. In a few minutes, Sarai was lying with a soft, cool cloth over her eyes, and Hagar was sitting beside her, smoothing back her hair as though she were the mother and Sarai the child.

"Perhaps next month," Hagar ventured. "There's always a chance the gods will be kind."

"Yahweh has promised Abram a son," Sarai moaned. "And every month I fail him."

"If you . . . if Yahweh has promised a son, then Yahweh must see to it," Hagar said.

Sarai's swollen eyes opened and she smiled wanly at the girl.

"But I'm Yahweh's tool," she said, assuming the guilt with her words but revealing in her smile her pleasure at Hagar's putting the responsibility somewhere else.

"Then the god will use you," Hagar said, more to comfort Sarai than from any sense of conviction.

There was silence for a few minutes and Hagar wet the cloth and wrung it out again. Sarai glanced at her and then looked away.

"The whole tribe will know of my humiliation," she said thickly.

Hagar was indignant. "How? Who would tell them? They'll never learn it from me, my lady."

"They won't have to. Zahavith saw me . . . she knows why I began to cry. She'll enjoy the telling."

Her voice was bitter, and Hagar stared at the face that was still lovely, even with the marks of tears. "Does she hate you, my lady?"

Sarai's head moved restlessly. She didn't know why she was revealing her grief. It was not her habit to discuss these things, but there was a great sense of comfort in saying the words to the attentive child whose hands moved so gently on her hot forehead.

"She doesn't hate me. Not exactly. But a woman who has children despises one who is barren."

"Of course." It was the way women were.

"And she . . . she resents the fact that I have a larger tent and a richer husband."

"Is that why she asked for Meryet? So she'd have a better slave than you, my lady?"

"How did you know about that? Oh, of course, the girl probably told you."

"Yes, my lady."

Sarai reached up and caught one of the slender, brown hands that were smoothing the cool cloth across her eyes. "She asked for one of the Egyptian slaves," she explained gently. "I gave her the one I could most easily spare."

There was a long silence while Hagar clutched the strong, warm hand that held hers. Her voice was a husky little whisper when she spoke. "Thank you, my lady. I . . . I. . . ." But there was nothing to say, no way to explain her feeling of gratitude.

Sarai drew the small hand along her cheek and then released it. "I'm finished with my foolish mourning," she announced. "I mustn't lie here any longer. Here, help me brush my hair and then we'll get to work."

"No, listen," Hagar said. "Lie awhile. We can say you're sick. Then no one will know that you . . . that you came in to weep."

"But they'll know soon enough when there's no promise of a child," Sarai protested.

"But maybe next month," Hagar suggested. "Or the next. If Zahavith starts her gossip, there won't be any proof for what she says."

Sarai lay back, and a smile crossed her face. "All right," she conceded. "Maybe you're right."

Impulsively, Hagar lifted one of her mistress' hands and brushed it with her lips.

It was only later, spreading the story that Sarai was ill, that Hagar realized that she was doing exactly what Meryet had told her to do. And Meryet would never understand that what she did, she did out of pity and love . . . and not out of ambition or greed.

6

The tribe of Abram had stayed in the sandy wash long enough, and the time had come to start moving east. The confusion and chaos that had been an inevitable part of living in a foreign land was over now, and Abram's and Lot's slaves had begun preparations for leaving. The animals were sleek and healthy, ready for travel, and the people themselves were tired of living in a strange country and wanted to move toward Bethel-Ai. There would be many times of setting up and taking down the tents before Mt. Ebal loomed before their eyes, but at least they were going to leave the flat monotony of the Nile valley and head toward the land they loved.

The morning chosen for leaving was hot with a brassy sun in a brilliant sky, but the men moved with a strong sense of purpose and pleasure. These were hill people, and they had not been happy in the level land in spite of the fact that there had been water.

Lot and Abram stood together, giving orders, watching the preparations and the action.

"It seems as though every female sheep and cow we have has given birth," Abram mused. "Our herds have more than doubled in the past months. How many ewes, I wonder, dropped twins?"

"More than half, I think," Lot said with satisfaction. "It's a good feeling, isn't it?"

Abram nodded. "And I'm glad we divided the responsibility and the wealth of the animals between us, now that there are so many. Makes for more order, easier handling."

"Not every man would have been so generous," Lot murmured. "The animals were yours—you weren't obliged to share them as you did."

"Nonsense! I inherited my flock from my father, and my brother, Haran, would have had his share if he had lived. It was only right to give his portion to you—his son."

"But how many younger brothers get nearly half?" Lot argued, knowing that if Zahavith heard him, she would mock him for his dogged honesty.

Abram spread his hands in a careless gesture. "There are more than enough for all. Don't even think about it. Come on, help me with these boys of yours. They seem to be having trouble with that ram."

In the melee of bleating animals and pounding donkey hooves, the tribal chief and his nephew looked no different from the other men. They rode as hard, shouted as loudly and got as dirty as any.

Hagar, watching them from the edge of the camp site, grinned maliciously. Meryet's precious Lot certainly didn't look like a great man now, splashed with sheep dung and sweating in the heat. To hear Meryet talk, Hagar thought spitefully, Lot and Zahavith were some kind of royalty. She said they had finer table manners than anyone in the tribe and she insisted that their tent had some things more elegant than Abram's.

But Hagar was not impressed. She remembered too well that Meryet had tended to exaggerate when they had been children together, and her doll had always, according to Meryet, been finer than anything Hagar had ever owned.

If Abram was a little coarse at times, if Sarai mingled with the most common women in the tribe, they were still superior to everyone else, Hagar thought.

"Hagar!" Sarai's voice was sharp. "I've told you a dozen times to fold these rugs. Not roll them, *fold* them. Now come and do it right."

Sarai looked tense and preoccupied. Moving was always hard on her, she had confided to Hagar. New places were fine—even exciting—but the process of leaving the old place was difficult.

"Not that I care two beans about the *place*," Sarai had said, "It's the worry that the rugs will get dirty in the moving, or the hangings torn, or a vase scratched."

Knowing her mistress was more apt to lose her temper when she was upset, Hagar hurried to do her bidding.

She tried to fold the rugs more securely, but they were heavy and slid in her small hands.

"Here, like this," Sarai snapped. "Use your arms to fold them over. Look, watch me!"

Hagar, imitative as a monkey, soon had caught the knack, and the pile of folded rugs grew beside the tent.

"Tie them with that rope," Sarai instructed, "and then come and help me with these vases. And don't forget your own playthings."

"They're not playthings," Hagar retorted and then added quickly, "not exactly anyhow. They're gods from home."

"Gods?" Sarai stopped in the middle of what she was doing and stared at the girl. "Abram wouldn't want heathen gods kept in our tent. Yahweh is the only God in here."

"But where is he?" Hagar asked almost bluntly. She looked around and then asked the question that had been on the tip of her tongue often but had never been put into words. "I don't even know what he looks like. Don't you have a statue of him?"

Sarai looked shocked. "No one knows what he looks like."

"Not even my lord Abram?"

"No, not even Abram."

"But he must look like *something*." Hagar protested. "Look let me show you the little gods from home." She darted across the tent and picked up her bundle. The two small gods fell out as she unrolled the cloth. "See—this is Hathor, the goddess of music and love. Isn't she pretty? And this is

Sobek. See ... his body is human, but his head is like a crocodile. Wouldn't it be easier if you knew what Yahweh *looked* like?''

There was a fascinated disgust in Sarai's eyes as she stared at the small idols in Hagar's hands. "Don't bring them near me," she said, suddenly agitated. "I'm cursed enough—don't let them touch me. Yahweh will strike me.''

Hagar wanted to say, "I've slept with them under my pillow for months and nothing has happened to *me*," but of course she didn't say it. Instead, she wrapped the idols swiftly in the cloth again and pushed them out of sight.

"There," she said. "They can't do anything hidden in the cloth.''

Sarai was not comforted. "They shouldn't be in Abram's tent," she said. "They'll defile the place where Yahweh lives.''

"How can you say he lives here?" Hagar insisted. "I can't see him or hear him.''

Sarai didn't answer for a minute. "But sometimes I can *feel* him," she said at last. "And Abram can hear him—as plainly as he hears me.''

"Could *you* hear him?" Hagar asked.

"I'm only a woman. Only Abram's wife. Why should Yahweh speak to me?''

"Because you believe in him." Hagar felt a curious stubbornness stiffening the words. "What difference does it make who you are if you believe?''

"Oh, don't talk about things you don't understand," Sarai snapped. "You're only a child and a slave at that. Why do you try to understand things that only a man can understand?''

"Because," Hagar sounded sulky. "Just because.''

"You're insolent," Sarai said, but her voice was careless. She probably ought to punish the girl, but she hated to. The child's obvious adoration was such a soothing thing when life was difficult, Sarai thought.

"Well, never mind all that," Sarai said. "Come on and roll

these vases in the wall hangings. Careful now."

There was a sudden shout, and Hagar looked up to see Dothan racing past the tent, his voice raised in hot anger.

Sarai sighed. "I certainly hope the slaves aren't arguing again. They always get upset when we start to move the animals. Both sides claim the best ones."

"Both sides, my lady?" Hagar was suddenly a slave again. "I thought everything belonged to my lord Abram."

"And rightly should." Sarai spoke with asperity. "But Abram is generous sometimes beyond the bounds of good sense. He insisted some years ago on giving half of the herds to Lot. I've always believed myself that Lot asked for them."

"Is Lot so greedy, my lady?"

Sarai's smile was grim. "When a man has a greedy wife, he has to take care of her in whatever way shows itself. Run over there where the men are gathering. See if you can find out what's going on. It just wouldn't be seemly if I went."

"Yes, my lady," and Hagar was gone swiftly. This was better, she thought, than folding rugs and packing vases. She could hear shouts and cursing and the dull thud of blows. The wild cry of agitated ewes and the frantic bleating of lambs rose over the shouts of men.

The dust boiled in a cloud but Hagar slipped closer to the place where the trouble was. In only a few minutes she could hear some of the words and when a breeze dispersed some of the dust, she could see a little of what was going on. Some of Abram's and Lot's servants were arguing hotly over the animals, and the blows she had heard were those administered to some of the beasts as the men urged them to go in one direction or the other.

"These sheep are ours," one man shouted, his voice shrill. "Get your filthy hands off them."

"They're my lord Abram's," shouted another man, and his fist suddenly shot out and a streak of blood appeared on the first man's mouth.

"Why, you . . ." The two men were on the ground pounding at each other, their anger and pain blended in an ugly, furious mixture of sound.

Hagar saw Dothan dart in and try to land a blow on Lot's servant, but he was too light, and a thrust from another slave sent him headlong into the dirt.

A quick sound beside her jerked Hagar's head around. Meryet was watching the fight, her eyes blazing with excitement or anger, Hagar couldn't tell which.

"Hit him!" Meryet hissed between clenched teeth.

Hagar laughed. "Hit who?" she mocked. "Are you on the side of your lord—or your future husband? They're on opposite sides, can't you see?"

"Oh, shut up!" Meryet said and she slapped at Hagar, but the younger girl ducked.

The two girls stood glaring at each other, almost as angry as the men who rolled, panting and swearing, on the ground.

A decisive shout rang through the air, and it was loud enough and authoritative enough to stop the struggling men and to swing the two girls' heads around. Abram stood over the prostrate men, and his face was grim.

"What do you two think you're doing?"

The men scrambled to their feet, each trying to talk at once. Abram waved his hand at his own slave. "Zevi, what do you have to say?"

"He was trying to steal our sheep, my lord. See, I've marked your ewes with a notch in the ear, but he tried to take them anyhow."

"That's Lot's mark, my lord," the other man cried.

Zevi turned to his opponent furiously. "You lie," he yelled. "You're a dirty. . ."

"Quiet," Abram thundered. "Both of you—quiet!"

Lot was suddenly beside his uncle. "What's all the fuss?"

Abram's voice was controlled, but his face was suffused with anger. "The slaves are at it again. They seem to be claiming your animals for me and mine for you. Were you aware of any identifying marks?"

Lot slid his eyes away from his uncle. "They've been notching the ears, I think."

"Well, of course. We've always notched the ears. But do they use different marks?"

"Not that I know of, Uncle."

Zevi spoke with heat. "If you'll hear me, my lord. The notched ears are yours. Lot's slaves were supposed to take those with smooth ears. But when I checked them, I found your animals among theirs."

"He lies, my lord," Lot's slave began, but Lot quelled him with a look.

"The men get excited, Uncle," Lot soothed. "Tempers fray at moving time. You know it's so. Once we're on the way, once we've found grazing again, things will settle down. They always do."

"Must a man die to have peace?" Abram asked. "I won't put up with this. I warn you all. I will *not* allow it."

Zevi bowed his head. "Yes, my lord," he mumbled.

Lot bowed nearly as low as the slave, and seeing the obeisance, Hagar shot a triumphant look at Meryet and was rewarded with a glare.

"Then get to work and let me hear no more," Abram shouted. "Lot, oversee them. Check the ears yourself, if need be."

Lot nodded and rode away, and Abram glanced at Dothan who stood with his fists clenched as though he were ready to take on the first person to cross his path.

"Can you trust them, my lord?" Dothan asked, but his angry eyes were watching Lot, not the slaves.

"Dothan, you overstep yourself," Abram warned. "Lot is driven to many things, but he's an honest man. I'd stake my life on that."

Dothan spread his hands. "Yes, I guess he is. It would be easier if he weren't—if he actually *told* his slaves to steal you blind. But he doesn't. He's just conveniently away when things go on."

"Dothan!" Abram barked.

"Yes, my lord," Dothan was suddenly meek. "I have a hasty tongue. Forgive me, my lord."

The boy turned and followed the other men and Abram watched him go while his shoulders seemed to slump with weariness.

Hagar waited until Abram had moved away, and then she turned to Meryet. The older girl's face was a mixture of anger and arrogance.

"You're going to have to make up your mind," Hagar said. "It looks like you're going to have to be on Abram's side or Lot's side in this tribe. And Dothan belongs to Abram."

"And *I* belong to Meryet," Meryet snapped.

Hagar laughed. "You don't and you know it. You belong to Zahavith—and through her to Lot—and through him to Abram. And they'll all want your loyalty—so how are you going to do it?"

"I don't know yet," Meryet muttered. "I have to figure out a way."

"It's easier for me," Hagar said. "I belong to Sarai and I don't have any choice."

Meryet sneered. "And you're making good use of your position, aren't you? I've seen how you hang around Sarai, swallowing every thing she says as though her words were ripe figs. Oh, you're a smart one, you are . . . and to think I was the one who gave you the idea."

"That's not true," Hagar said swiftly. "I like her. I. . . ."

There were no words to explain the feeling she had for Sarai, no words that Meryet could possibly understand.

The two girls stood glaring at each other, as divided as the two fighting slaves had been.

"I thought cousins stuck up for each other," Hagar said a little bleakly.

For a minute Meryet stood stiffly, and then her face changed. Her eyes did not meet Hagar's fully, but a smile curved her lips.

"It's not really our fight, little cousin, is it?"

"No, it isn't. What do we have to do with cutting notches

in the silly animals' ears?"

Just then, Sarai's voice came faintly, and Hagar heard her name.

"I have to hurry," she said.

"I, too."

But neither of them moved for a few seconds. Then, "Let them fight," Meryet said. "You and I need each other. Don't we?"

Hagar nodded. "Yes," she said, "we do."

The smile they exchanged was a tentative one, but at least it was a smile, and then they were running to their mistresses. It wasn't a decisive peace, Hagar thought, but at least it wasn't open war. She wasn't sure she needed Meryet, but she was certain that she needed Meryet to need *her*.

7

Several months of traveling with Abram's tribe pushed the memories of her life in Pharaoh's court into the dim recesses of Hagar's mind. Her skin darkened in the constant sun, and her body became lithe and strong from the days of walking and from the duties that were hers when the tribe stopped. If she had not yet learned to laugh freely, she had at least cultivated the art of looking pleasant. And she had learned to drink the detested goat milk, so that her face was round and glowing.

"She really looks human, my love," Abram said one morning as Hagar served them fresh fruit and flour balls dipped in sour milk. "You've done a good job with her."

Slavery had taught Hagar many things, but she had not learned to act as though she could not hear the words spoken in her presence. So she made no effort to suppress a smile of pleasure at his words.

"You needn't look so self-satisfied," Sarai said, but a laugh took any sting out of the words. "The credit belongs entirely to me."

"Yes, my lady," Hagar said. "I know how good you've been to me."

"You'll discover I can change if you don't do as I say."

"Yes, my lady," Hagar said meekly enough, but she felt no apprehension. "Can I bring you anything else to eat?"

"No, not for me," Abram said.

It was improper enough that he took this morning meal in the privacy of their tent with Sarai beside him. It would have been unthinkable for Sarai to ask for more food if her husband refused it.

Hagar began to clear away the simple utensils, and the man and woman talked as though the girl were not even in the tent.

"I'm afraid we're going to have trouble with Lot's slaves and mine again," Abram said. "There are so many of them now and so many animals to be cared for that we simply can't have this quarreling. If they don't take turns with the watering places, and if they don't share what pasture we find, there's going to be serious trouble."

"Can't you command them, my lord?"

Abram glanced at the stout wooden staff that lay beside him. He was never seen without it, and it seemed to have as much power as Pharaoh's royal scepter, Hagar thought.

"I can command them," he said ruefully. "But that's not to say they'll obey the commands."

"My lord!" Sarai was shocked. "Who would dare disobey?"

"Not exactly disobey. If I say, Go, they go . . . but by a devious route. Do you know what I mean?"

Sarai shook her head. "Then punish them. Send them away. Whoever it is."

He laughed. "It's not as easy as that. Lot's my nephew."

Then she was really shocked. "You mean *he's* the one?"

"Of course not, but his slaves have strange ideas about what's his and what isn't."

"It's your own fault," Sarai said. "You shouldn't have given him half of the animals."

Hagar shot a swift glance at Abram. Surely he would reprimand such outspoken criticism from his wife, but he was only smiling tolerantly.

"Lot needed to have his own possessions," he said. "You don't understand his needs, Sarai."

"He lets that woman rule him," she said and tossed her head.

"And you think you don't rule me?"

Sarai was a strong woman, hot tempered and quick, contradictory in her moods, but now there was only tenderness and submission on her lovely face. "No, my lord, I don't rule you. You know I'm submissive to you . . . and to your God."

Abram took her in his arms. "I know," he said. "I know. I was only teasing. No man could have a better wife."

Suddenly tears rolled down Sarai's cheeks. "Not a good wife, my lord," she said in a strangled voice. "Not a good wife while I fail to bear a son."

But Abram only held her closer, and it never occurred to Hagar to move behind the curtain and out of their sight. They paid as little attention to her as they did to the hangings on the walls.

"Ah," he crooned against her hair. "I sometimes wish Yahweh had chosen someone else. If I didn't have Yahweh's promise to think about, having a son wouldn't matter."

"My lord!" Sarai's voice was nakedly incredulous, and Hagar felt shock burn through her body. Every man wanted sons.

"If I had to choose," he said solemnly, "without consideration for Yahweh's promises—I'd choose you, my love, over any other woman who could give me a son every year."

No other man in the world would say that, Hagar thought dazedly. She was totally incapable of even understanding the kind of love that moved Abram at that moment.

Sarai clung to her husband and said softly, "Yahweh will surely show us the way. Surely, my lord."

"Of course he will, but now let me go. I've got to deal with Lot. He's as embarrassed as I am over this whole thing."

"I'll wager Zahavith isn't embarrassed," Sarai said bitterly. "Somewhere you'll see her hand in all of this. I'm sure of it, my lord."

Abram looked at his wife in astonishment. "Do you really think so?"

"She'd sell Lot himself if he brought enough gold," Sarai said.

Abram grinned. "I'd say you were jealous, except that you've got nothing to be jealous of. No, don't point out that she has children. She neglects them. I caught the smallest one stealing a toy from one of Eliezer's little ones. A good mother would have taught them better. How can we expect Yahweh to lead us if our people don't do what's right?"

"My lord!" Hagar hardly knew that she was going to speak until the words were out. "My lord, does Yahweh *care* if you do right or wrong? Our gods cared only if we did things for *them*."

Abram looked up as if realizing for the first time that the girl was still there.

At first she thought he might be angry, but when he finally spoke, there was nothing in his voice to indicate anger. "Yahweh is a God of might and glory, but he's also a God of truth and honesty and duty. Didn't you know that?"

"How could I know, my lord?"

Abram looked at her for a long time. "You should have known it by observing us. We're Yahweh's people, and we should made it plain what kind of a God he is."

Hagar forgot that she was a slave and moved closer to the man and woman. "I never thought of that," she confessed. "I never thought of my father as being like Sobek, or my mother like Hathor."

"Sobek? The god with crocodile jaws? I saw statues of him while we were in Egypt. But Hathor? Who's she?" Abram could have been talking to Sarai or one of the men in the tribe.

"The goddess of music and love, my lord. Wait! I'll show you."

"No!" Sarai's voice rang out sharply. "I told you to leave those idols out of Abram's tent. Why didn't you throw them away?"

"Throw them away, my lady? But they're all I have from home."

"This is your home," Sarai announced. "You don't need any gods from Egypt. And certainly not in our tent."

Abram spoke abruptly. "Would you discard them if you believed that Yahweh was a greater God?"

"My lord," Sarai interrupted. "All you have to do is tell her to throw them away and she'll have to obey."

Abram glanced at his wife, and Sarai folded her lips together and looked guiltily at the ground. "I'm sorry, my lord," she said meekly. "I'm sorry."

Abram looked back at Hagar. "Would you? Throw them away willingly?"

"I don't know," Hagar said honestly. "How can I believe that Yahweh is greater? I don't even know what he looks like."

Abram sighed. How many, many times—first to his father Terah—and then to his brothers—and later to his tribesmen—had he tried to explain that you didn't need to *see* a god to know he existed. And why he even cared what this stubborn slip of a girl thought or believed, he had no idea. He only felt in his bones, in the way he felt so many things which later turned out to be right, that he must win her to Yahweh, not command her.

"Here, girl, sit here," he said and pointed to a pile of rugs near him, and she sat obediently.

"Who do you think made you. Hagar?"

The girl looked bewildered. "My father and mother?" she ventured.

"But who made them?"

"Their parents?" But even as she said it, she knew this was not the answer he was seeking. "I don't know who made the first person," she said quickly.

"*I* do," Abram said. "I know who the first man was and who made him."

"Truly, my lord?" There had probably been stories in Egypt of a creation, but there had been no real story tellers in her life. "Could you tell me, my lord?"

"A story just for us," Sarai murmured with pleasure. "The

men will wonder what you're doing in your tent so late."

"Let them wonder," Abram said. "It was Yahweh who made the earth, child. *He* was before the earth was. When there was only darkness over the face of the earth, Yahweh was. And he created everything—the dry land and the seas, the sun to shine by day and the moon to shine by night, the fish that swim in the sea and the fowl that fly in the air, the animals that walk on the earth, and finally man. Out of the dust he shaped a man and he breathed into him the breath of life and he called the man Adam. And Adam was made in Yahweh's image."

"In Yahweh's image?" breathed Hagar. "Then Yahweh looks like you, my lord?"

"I don't know. It's not important. Can't you see?"

"Did Adam have a wife?" Hagar asked, her mind skipping over the story she had been told.

Sarai laughed. "Of course! Yahweh knew how important a wife would be."

"He made a deep sleep to fall on Adam," Abram said, "and he opened his side and took out a rib and fashioned it into a woman. And when Adam woke, Eve was there to serve him and share his life."

Hagar's eyes were shining. "It's a lovely story."

But Abram was very stern. "It's not a 'lovely story.' It's a great truth. It's why we don't have a separate god for rain and drought, day time and night time, planting time and harvest. We have only Yahweh. We need only him. Because he made everything."

Hagar did not say, "How do you know?" She did not even think it. She knew, if she knew anything about gods, that knowledge came from what one had been told by people in authority.

"My lady Sarai told me that Yahweh speaks to you, my lord," she said instead. "How?"

It would have been easy for Abram to chide her for brazenness. But he only said, "I can't explain it, my child. Yahweh doesn't speak to me often, but when he does, the

Voice fills me until I can't hear anything else—not the voices
of people or the sound of the wind or the bleating of the
sheep. I am filled with the voice of Yahweh and that's all I can
hear."

Hagar looked up at Abram. "I'd *like* to believe, my lord. I'd
like to believe that Yahweh is a mighty god. But—I'm a
stranger in this land and a stranger to your god."

Surprisingly it was Sarai who answered. "I remember
how I felt in Egypt. I was a stranger and I felt as though I
might never belong anywhere again."

"In Ur, we belonged to the city," Abram said. "And in
Haran. But we're all strangers in *this* land. We don't have
houses or streets or a great palace and ziggurat to belong to.
I'm beginning to wonder if Yahweh sent us out so that we
had to belong to him. So he would be the only thing we could
depend on."

It was as though he were saying the words to himself,
making a discovery of great importance.

Hagar was quiet for a minute and then she asked, "Must I
throw the gods away, my lord?"

"No," Abram said. "I don't want them in my tent, but if
you'd keep them outside the walls, hidden, I don't care if
you keep them. Someday you'll throw them away—because
you want to."

"Thank you, my lord. It's just—just that my mother and
father gave the little gods to me." Unexpectedly there were
tears in her eyes, and it had been a long time since she had
wept for her parents.

"Yes, I know, I know," Abram said. "Now I must start
working." He got up to leave the tent and turned suddenly
to Hagar. "Your cousin, Meryet? Is she happy with Lot's
wife?"

"Oh, yes, my lord. She thinks Zahavith is—wonderful."

Sarai tossed her head but Abram went on with his questioning. "How old is she? I think she told me but I forget."

"Almost sixteen, my lord."

"Old enough for marriage soon." He turned to Sarai.

"Dothan is getting very tense and irritable these days. Wants to pick a fight with anyone who comes along. Maybe he needs a wife to settle him down. I've been reluctant to match him up with just any slave girl. He is, after all Eliezer's son and . . . if there is no heir. . . ."

"They're still young," Sarai said, averting her eyes. "Why don't we wait, my lord?"

"Well, think about it," Abram said and strode out of the tent.

"There's corn in that basket over there," Sarai said as though nothing unusual had taken place, as though they had just finished the morning meal. "Go and grind it."

"Yes, my lady." Hagar took the basket and moved behind the tent where the grinding stone was, grateful for the opportunity to be alone to think.

She had become fairly adept at grinding the grain, and she could work quite a long time before her back began to ache. This morning she moved with a gentle rhythm, smelling the warm smell of the grain as the chaff blew away.

It was only when she heard Meryet's voice that she looked up from her task. "Is your lady in her tent?" Meryet asked.

"I think so. She was a few minutes ago. Why?"

"My lady has need of some oil. Is there any in your tent?"

"Yes, a little. I hope you use it sparingly."

Meryet shrugged. "My lady Zahavith likes her cakes well coated with oil. Who am I to tell her to use it sparingly?"

"Especially if it should make her angry with you," Hagar said.

Meryet merely grinned. What would she say, Hagar thought, if she knew that Abram was actually thinking of her as a wife for Dothan? But I won't tell her, Hagar thought spitefully. I won't share what I hear in the privacy of our tent.

As though the thought of him caused him to appear, Dothan was suddenly in front of the two girls. But this time, he never even looked at Meryet. He was agitated and clearly angry.

"Where is my lord?" he asked Hagar.

"I don't know. He left the tent some little time ago."

"Don't you have any idea where he went? I have to find him," Dothan said, the words sputtering with anger.

"He said something about wanting to see Lot."

"He'd better see me first," Dothan said. "Because then he might have something to say to Lot."

"What's wrong?" Hagar asked.

"Someone has kicked away the stones that dammed up the water for Abram's cattle," Dothan said, evidently willing to tell even a humble slave girl just because the words were bursting to be said.

"Oh, *no*!" Hagar breathed. There was no crime greater than allowing the water for the animals to be drained away from the drinking hole.

"If I find out who did it," Dothan said, "I'll kill him. With my own hands. Oh, there's Abram over there. My lord, my lord, wait!" And he was gone.

Hagar looked at Meryet, and there was something about the older girl's face that hit Hagar with a jolt above her heart.

"You knew," Hagar whispered in disbelief. "You already knew."

Meryet spoke too quickly. "How could I know? Don't be silly."

"Someone told you."

"Who could possibly tell me? Do you think I know everything the slaves do?"

"Then you heard something," Hagar persisted. "I know how people talk in front of slaves, particularly women slaves. As though we were just part of the furnishings of the tent. You heard something, Meryet. Admit it."

"If I had heard anything, I wouldn't tell you," Meryet snapped.

Hagar glared at her cousin. "And I won't tell you what I know either."

"What do you know?" Meryet's voice was suddenly wheedling, but Hagar was thoroughly angry now as well as frightened.

If the trouble had gone far enough that the men were interfering with the water supply, then it was surely serious. By now Hagar knew enough about the scarcity of water and how Abram had to negotiate with other dwellers of the land for the right to use springs and wells to understand how precious water was.

"Surely Lot wouldn't. . . ," Hagar began.

Meryet interrupted sharply. "My lord Lot is an honest man. He wouldn't do anything so terrible. For all you know it was Abram's own slaves who did it . . . trying to make Lot look guilty." But there was no conviction in her voice.

"Maybe Lot didn't do anything." Hagar said, "but his slaves did. And you know who. Or you could guess."

Meryet turned away but not before Hagar had seen the confusion on her face. "Don't try to talk about things you're ignorant about," Meryet said. "If I knew anything, don't you think I'd tell my lord Lot?"

"Not if you thought Zahavith didn't want him to know," Hagar hazarded and was rewarded with a hot flush on Meryet's cheeks. "You better tell what you know," Hagar advised. "I don't know how to tell you to do it, but if you don't want real trouble in this camp—and *you* might be in more trouble than anyone else—you'd better see that someone knows what's going on."

Meryet didn't even answer, but Hagar saw that she headed back toward Lot's tent instead of completing the errand that had brought her to Sarai's tent.

Hagar could see Dothan talking excitedly to Abram and then she saw them walk rapidly away together. Ought she to run after them and tell them what she suspected about Meryet? No, after all, she didn't know anything for sure, and surely Abram would be able to solve the problem. But her heart was troubled as she turned back to the grinding of the corn.

8

Meryet slipped into Lot's tent and looked for Zahavith. She had no idea what she was going to say or do, but she was badly shaken. It was disturbing enough that Dothan hadn't even looked at her, but it was even worse that Hagar had suspected something. Hagar simply couldn't be depended on anymore, Meryet reflected. She was so smitten with Sarai that she probably repeated everything she heard to her mistress.

Not, Meryet comforted herself, that she had said anything to Hagar that could be repeated. True, yesterday she had heard Zahavith say lazily that she could almost wish Abram would have bad luck with his flocks if Lot could benefit from it. And the comment had been made—deliberately?—in front of Dolel, that stupid slave who worshipped the ground Zahavith walked on and would do anything in his power to please her.

But I didn't make any accusations, Meryet's thinking continued. So Zahavith can't hear anything that will make her angry with me. If only I thought Dothan would ask Eliezer or even Abram for me, then I wouldn't have to worry about Zahavith. But how can I be sure? I've tried every way I know to hear something or learn something that would reveal how Dothan or his father feel, but I'm as unsure now as I was the first day we came and Dothan looked at me.

Zahavith spoke from the inner recesses of the tent. "Meryet, is that you?"

"Yes, my lady."

"Did you get the oil?" Zahavith came out and looked expectantly at Meryet's hands.

"Sarai wasn't there, my lady," Meryet lied. "Everyone was all upset—something about someone tampering with the water hole for Abram's cattle."

Zahavith's eyes widened. "What happened?"

Meryet shrugged. "I don't really know, my lady."

Zahavith turned away but not before Meryet saw a flicker of excitement in the dark eyes. "No matter. I'll find out when my lord comes back."

There was a scraping noise at the opening of the tent, and Dolel stood there, grinning cheekily at his mistress. "My lady, there's a merchant caravan stopping at the water hole. I'm told there are cosmetics to be sold. Kohl to darken your eyes and small ivory boxes to hold it."

"I need kohl badly," Zahavith said. "Mine is nearly gone. Where's my lord Lot? Find him, and ask him to buy some for me. Is the caravan selling or trading?"

"Selling, my lady. They're on their way to the next market city, and they're stopping only a short while to water the animals. But I heard them say they would sell cosmetics to any lady in the tribe who wanted it."

"Then find Lot. He has a few small chunks of copper somewhere. The caravan owner may take them for the kohl. Go and see."

But still Dolel hesitated. "My lady," he said. "Abram and Lot are talking. I don't think they want to be interrupted. It's something about the watering hole for Abram's animals."

It was obvious that Zahavith was torn between her desire for the kohl and her reluctance to irritate Lot.

Then her face brightened. "Here," she said, "take these," and she pulled two silver bracelets from her slender arm. "See if they'll be sufficient."

"Yes, my lady." A grin nearly split his face. "Perhaps my

lord Abram will give Lot more silver for the right to use our watering hole—which is full to overflowing."

"You fool!" Zahavith snapped. "Why should Abram pay for what is rightly his?"

"Oh, no, my lady. Our watering hole is Lot's alone. That's why. . . ."

But Zahavith would not let him finish. "Be quiet!" she said, flashing a quick look at Meryet. "Be quiet and go see about the kohl."

"Yes, my lady." A clawed hand secreted the bracelets in some recess of his robe, and he was gone.

"They were such lovely bracelets, my lady," Meryet mourned. "I wish you hadn't used them to buy the kohl."

"When else—and how else—could I get it?" Zahavith asked. "Besides, I'll get other bracelets. We're getting close to some of the cities where there are many caravans—cities like Sodom and Gomorrah. My lord Abram will *have* to go down into the plain if his slaves can't protect his watering places in the mountains. And then we can live near cities and marketplaces and great palaces."

Meryet didn't answer. So that was what Zahavith had in mind—something to force Abram down out of the hills, down into the watered valley. Meryet turned away with her habitual shrug. It was nothing to her where the tribe went.

Her duties done for the present and certain that Sarai had no need for her, Hagar left Abram's tent and began to walk through the shadows of the late afternoon. The tribe had moved from the valley up into the foothills, and this was Hagar's first experience with land that thrust itself in curves and folds against the sky. She found an outcropping of stone, warm from the sun, and sat down on it, cupping her chin in her hands and staring out over the valley from which they had come.

The distant hills were a dark, clear blue against the evening sky, and the nearer hills were tawny and rosy gray. The foliage was scarcer than in the fertile valley of the Nile, and the trees were different from any she had ever seen. The sturdy dark trees with needles instead of leaves were cypress, Sarai had told her, and the tree with golden fruit just now ripening among the glossy leaves was the apricot. The fruit was much to be desired, Sarai had said, and there was a grove of the trees near where Hagar sat. Because the apricots were nearly ripe, the tribe would stay where they were for several weeks in spite of the fact that they were getting closer and closer to Bethel-Ai. Reluctance to leave the ripening apricots made the water trouble even more serious than it would have been under normal circumstances. If, indeed, that were possible, Hagar reflected.

She looked longingly at the hanging fruit, wishing she could pick one and bite into the succulent flesh, but she knew the danger of trying to eat fruit that was still green, so she turned her eyes from the trees and gazed again at the surrounding land. They were north of the Negeb now—the desert area with its threat of death and thirst—and Hagar had heard the songs of thanksgiving around the camp fire, songs that celebrated the fact that the Negeb was behind them.

This, then, was the start of the land of Canaan—this land of hills and mountain streams and strange trees. There would be greener hills further north, Sarai had said, but Hagar was fascinated by this golden, stony land where they were.

The swift sound of sliding pebbles jerked her head around, and she found herself face to face with a tall, thin boy who was a total stranger to her. Her heart jerked with fear because she had heard of nomads who attacked those who traveled through the land. She looked quickly beyond the boy to see if there were any others with him, but evidently he was alone.

"What are you doing here?" The words came simultaneously from both of them, and without meaning to, they both smiled.

The boy answered first. "I'm getting away from my master

for a few minutes. The head of the caravan. For just a little while, I'd like not to be yelled at or beaten."

Hagar nodded sympathetically. "I know. It was once like that with me."

"You're not a slave any longer then?"

"Oh, yes, but my mistress is kind. In the Pharoah's court, things were ... different."

The boy nodded. "We've just come from Egypt," he said. "We're on our way to Damascus. My master bought me from my parents when I was small, and I travel with the caravan. I hate him," he added as calmly as he would say the sun was shining.

"Your parents sold you?" Hagar gasped.

The boy spread his hands. "We were very poor. A man must eat."

"But his own son?"

"One of seven," the boy said.

"My name is Hagar," she said, wondering why he stayed to talk to her.

"And mine is Simeon." He turned his back to her and looked out at the hills, drawing in a deep breath as he did so. "It's so beautiful," he said. "After the stink of the cities, it's so good to be here. This is my country."

Hagar was silent, and the boy turned to look at her. "If you're a slave, why don't you run away?" he asked. "There's no one watching you."

"Why don't you?" she countered.

They both looked out across the wild, rough country.

"It would be hard to live on apricots that aren't ripe yet," Simeon said and grinned.

A shout came toward them. "Simeon! Simeon, get over here!"

"Simeon, get over here!" the boy mocked. "Someday, I swear I *will* run away—when I'm near a friendly tribe—or when I'm older. And I'll have my own caravan route—and no one will beat me any more. No one!"

"This is a friendly tribe," Hagar ventured, not even sure

why it would be pleasant to have this boy be a part of it.

He laughed. "Friendly? The slaves were screaming at each other over by the water hole, and it looked as if the chief had his hands full. They were shouting about water and flocks, and it sounded as though blood would be shed any minute. No, thanks, I'm not interested in asking for refuge from a man who looks like he'd bash in the head of the first person who spoke to him."

The shout was louder and more insistent. "Simeon!"

"You'd better go," Hagar said nervously. "He'll beat you."

"Probably," Simeon said carelessly. He turned to clamber over the rocks toward the sound of his master's voice. But suddenly, he looked back over his shoulder. "Maybe someday I'll see you again. Caravans and tribes have a habit of meeting. I'll look for you."

And with only the sketchiest gesture, he was gone. Hagar felt an odd little rush of pleasure. Of course, she would never see him again—it was ridiculous to think so—but he had been friendly and warm. And he had called the land beautiful. Not many boys, she thought, used their eyes to see the beauty of the sky and land. Simeon, she thought. It was a name she had never heard before. She wondered what it meant.

By the time the camp fires had been built and the evening meal was finished, a sort of peace had come to the tribe. But word had gone out that Abram wanted all of the men— slaves and kinsmen—to gather around his tent. They came, some eagerly, some dragging their feet, but all of them sure that this was not a night for story telling. Zahavith, her eyes darkened with the new kohl, had sat in front of her own tent until Lot had made her go inside. It wasn't proper, he told her, for women to be seen when men wanted to talk.

Sarai and Hagar were behind the hanging curtain, discretely hidden, but they made no attempt at conversation. Sarai obviously wanted to listen to what was going to be said, and Hagar was busy with her thoughts that skittered like sand fleas from the water trouble to the boy who had talked to her as though she were another boy and an equal.

Abram's voice was harsh. "You know why I've called you here," he said. "You all know that the stones were pushed from the watering hole which had been made for my cattle and flocks. None of you are fools. You know that the culprit will be found and punished. But it will go easier for the guilty one—or ones—if a confession is made."

Silence lay heavy in the night, broken only by the crackle of the fire and the uneven sound of men breathing.

"Yahweh has said we must not do evil things to one another," Abram said. "But this is evil. It will take days before the water level can be built up again, and in the meantime, all of the animal's must share Lot's drinking hole."

Lot spoke without hesitation. "And you're welcome, of course, Uncle. I wouldn't have anything if it weren't for you." He turned to his slaves. "See that his cattle and flocks are watered first."

"First, my lord?" It was Dolel who spoke, and his voice was shrill with indignation. "But I thought. . . ." The words stumbled to an awkward stop.

"You thought what?" Lot's voice snapped.

"N-nothing, my lord," faltered Dolel.

"Dolel, come here," Lot commanded, and Abram sat in silence, letting events move without him. "Are you the one who kicked away the stones?"

"I thought . . . thought . . . you wanted it," the man blubbered.

Lot leaped to his feet, his face red in the light of the fire. "*I? I?* I wanted evil done to the man who has cared for me like a son? You stupid fool!" He knocked Dolel to the ground with a furious gesture and then without raising his voice, spoke to two of his slaves. "Tie him up. Give him twenty lashes. No, thirty."

Then he turned to Abram and dropped to his knees in front of his uncle. "My lord," he said brokenly, touching his forehead to the ground, "My lord, I confess for my slave. The slave is mine—my responsibility—and so the fault is mine."

Abram reached out to touch Lot's shoulder, then he spoke. "Let everyone leave. I want to be alone with my nephew."

When the last man was gone, Abram spoke gently. "Dolel is not really your slave, Lot. He belongs, heart and soul, to Zahavith. He'll do the most menial tasks for her—I saw him bartering for women's cosmetics from the caravan today. Perhaps he would do evil things for her, too. Come now, get up."

"She's not really evil, Uncle. She's only foolish and greedy."

"Foolishness and greed that threaten our water supply can't be tolerated, Lot. You know that."

The sound of the whip came from the other side of the camp, and Dolel's screams spilled into the night air.

"Yes, my lord," Lot said humbly. "But what am I to do? I love her."

And Abram, who loved his barren wife more than most men loved, could only nod in sympathy. "We'll talk about it tomorrow," he said. "I'll ask Yahweh for guidance. It may be . . . it just may be that we'll have to . . . well, I won't talk about it now. We'll discuss it in the morning."

"Yes, my lord," Lot mumbled and walked away, his shoulders bowed, his hands clenched in knots of frustration. As Dolel's last scream rang through the night, Lot knew that the beating had been given to the wrong person—but there was nothing he could do about it. His love for Zahavith rendered him powerless.

9

Long before daylight, Abram was kneeling at his tent door, wrestling with the problem that seemed almost overwhelming. If he had learned nothing else in the years of wandering, he had learned that a man must have peace within his own tribe or he was lost. Survival was difficult for the wisest, strongest tribes, but for one split by dissension and jealousy, it was almost impossible.

It wasn't only the water rights, although that was of critical importance. It was also the need for solidarity among the members of a tribe in case of attack. Vicious, merciless bands of marauders roamed the deserts, and a tribe which could not form a solid wall of unified strength would be slaughtered.

Abram lifted his knotted fists to his mouth. In silence, his anguish flowed out of him to Yahweh. Show me what to do, he begged. Speak to me as you have before, O Lord.

But there was no Voice, only the tortured thoughts twisting in his mind. Lot was basically a good man, a righteous man, and Abram loved him. Yahweh must surely know how much he loved his nephew, how he looked on him almost as a son. It would seem that his inheritance should go to Lot instead of Eliezer and so to Dothan. Lot was, after all, blood of his blood, bone of his bone. But when he thought this way, there was no peace in him at all. This, for some reason, was not what Yahweh wanted.

Then what do you want, Lord? Abram moaned in his heart. And what shall I do with Lot? What can I do to bring peace into my tribe?

Let him go!

The words came with such startling clarity that Abram jerked his head around to see if Sarai had spoken them. They were, after all, the same words she had said yesterday when they had discussed the disobedience of the tribesmen. But Sarai was sound asleep and there was no sound at all from Hagar's part of the tent.

The words came again, filling Abram with a great sensation of sound even though the air was silent. *Let him go!*

"Go, Lord? Go where?"

Wherever he chooses to go!

Abram sat back on his heels and looked, puzzled, to where the first hint of dawn was lighting the edges of the sky. "You mean, let *him* choose any part of the land he wants?" Abram felt a smile tugging at his mouth and dared ask his irreverent question. "Should I give him time to talk it over with Zahavith?"

Did Yahweh laugh? Oh, no, of course not. Yahweh was a great and a mighty God who would never demean himself so. It was only dawn trembling beyond the hills; it was only laughter moving in his own heart, thought Abram. But if the Voice did not answer the question directly, Abram felt that Yahweh was approving the ridiculous suggestion. Yes, Lot should be allowed to discuss it with Zahavith. Her wants and needs must be met if Lot were ever to be happy, and Abram desperately wanted his nephew to be happy. If I never have a son, Abram thought, then may my brother's son live long and be prosperous.

Satisfied now that Yahweh had pointed out the way he ought to go, Abram began his morning prayer of adoration and devotion—keeping his voice low and hushed at first, but then crying out with a great abandon as the sun crept higher in the sky, and bands of rose and pearl formed over the eastern hills. He heard a stirring behind him in the tent and knew that Sarai had joined him in prayer. Probably Hagar, too, was kneeling but whether out of belief or duty to her mistress, he did not know.

Hagar, herself, hardly knew. She had wakened out of a deep sleep with a sense that something had disturbed her, some strange and distant sound. But when she strained her ears to hear, there was only silence broken gently by the soft sound of Sarai's snoring. She turned over to sleep again and heard the first quiet words of Abram's song of praise.

That's the sound that woke me, she thought—but she knew she had heard something *before* Abram started to pray. Thoroughly awake now, she listened to Abram's words of adoration. If Abram is made in Yahweh's image, she thought as simply as a child, then surely Yahweh must be a great God. When she knelt to pray, she didn't know whether she was praying to Yahweh or to the man who stretched out his hands to the growing light of day.

"Hagar," Abram commanded when the morning meal was finished. "Run to Lot's tent. Tell him I want to see him at once."

"Yes, my lord," Hagar said.

"Are you going to send him away?" Sarai asked. To send a slave into the inhospitable desert would be Sarai's idea of justifiable action, but Lot was Abram's nephew.

Hagar didn't hear Abram's answer because she was already running toward Lot's tent. Her heart was pounding with more than the exertion of running. What if Lot were really sent away? That would mean that Meryet would go, too. And Hagar didn't really know how she felt about that. Meryet was her cousin and the only person in all the world who shared her childhood memories, whose blood was truly her blood. And yet—Meryet had become an ambitious, scheming girl who upset and frightened Hagar.

Is it only that she frightens me, Hagar thought with a burst of insight, or am I jealous of her? Am I jealous of the fact that Abram is thinking of her as a wife for Dothan? Do I want that position myself?

As the wife of Dothan, she would still be able to serve Sarai. She would belong to the tribe of Abram in a very real way—Sarai's favorite slave and also wife of the boy who might someday inherit Abram's wealth. It wasn't fair, Hagar thought, that Meryet should be put in that position when Meryet was loyal to no one but herself. It wasn't fair. So . . . of course I'm jealous, she acknowledged to herself. But I have a right to be.

Meryet met her at the tent opening. "What's wrong?" she said, worry already in her face.

"My lord Abram wants to see Lot at once," Hagar said.

"Why?"

"What do you mean—why?" Hagar's voice was hot with anger. "It's none of your business why—just do as you're told."

Meryet stared at her cousin and then turned, without speaking, and went inside.

Hagar did not wait for Lot to join her but ran back the way she had come. She was shaken by her self-discovery. It wasn't pleasant to think that she was jealous of her only living relative. It wasn't a happy thing to know that she and Meryet both coveted the position of Dothan's wife. Oh, not that she liked Dothan at all, Hagar admitted to herself. He was a braggart and treated her with a sort of mild contempt. It was Meryet he looked at. But people didn't marry for love. They married for convenience and for expedience. Sarai and Abram were different. And no doubt even their marriage had been arranged like everyone else's and the love that had grown between them was a sort of miracle.

When Hagar got to Abram's tent, Sarai told her to go out back to grind corn, and Sarai herself joined her there to make small cakes, mixing the ground meal with water and oil. They worked in silence, and so when Abram and Lot began to talk, the conversation could be heard plainly.

"You asked for me, my lord?" Lot asked.

"Yes, I did. Sit here beside me."

There was a silence and Hagar dared not even look at Sarai.

"Yahweh has told me what to do," Abram said. "It's a sad thing for me—a bitter thing—but it's something that I have to do."

"What is it, Uncle?" Lot's voice was taut with apprehension.

"We have to go our separate ways," Abram said. "I can't have this quarreling in the tribe. You know that."

"If I punish the slaves enough, maybe there won't be any more quarreling."

"No, my men are as guilty as yours. Perhaps not as guilty of wrongdoing but just as guilty of anger and hatred. And I want peace between us, Lot; you and I are almost brothers."

"But, Uncle, where would I go?" Lot sounded frightened, as though he were certain that his uncle would banish him toward the Negeb.

"That's for you to say," Abram announced. "You're the one to make the decision."

"What?" Lot's astonishment sharpened his voice.

"I mean it, Lot. I want you to go to your tent and discuss it with Zahavith—no, don't interrupt—I've thought this out carefully and Yahweh has moved my heart to the certainty that this is what has to be done. I want you to talk to Zahavith and the two of you decide which part of this land appeals to you."

Hagar felt Sarai stiffen and saw how still her hands had become on the little cakes.

"Look," Abram said. "Isn't there enough land for all? If you choose the right, then I'll go left, but if you choose the left, then I'll go right. The choice is yours, Lot."

"But that's not fair to you, Uncle," Lot said.

"Nevertheless, do as I say. When you've talked with Zahavith, when you're sure she's satisfied with your decision, come back and we'll discuss it further."

"But, Uncle. . . ."

"Don't make this harder for me, Lot," Abram almost shouted. "Yahweh has commanded me, and I command you."

"Yes, my lord," Lot said and there was the sound of his sandals moving out of the tent and away.

Sarai was up and around the tent in one swift flash of movement. "My lord," she said, her voice high and breathless. "Are you mad?"

"Mad, Sarai?" Abram's voice was cool.

"Yes, mad. You know what she'll do. She'll urge him to take the best land, the watered areas, and we'll be stuck with the hills and the rough places."

"I feel closer to Yahweh in the hills," Abram said. "And as for water, Yahweh won't let us die for lack of it. You've got to trust me, Sarai."

"You're already sure that he'll take the Jordan Valley, aren't you?" she asked more quietly.

"I imagine so. But I'm not worried."

Hagar straightened her back and sat on her heels, listening frankly. What would it all mean to her? True, there was water in the valley—Sarai had pointed out the silver thread that was the distant Jordan River. But there were cities there, too, and people and confusion, quarreling and bickering. In only a few weeks, she had learned to love this silent, rocky land. If Abram was sure that they could survive on it, then she rather hoped that Lot *would* take the valley.

"What about the girl, Meryet?" Sarai was saying. "Will you keep her as a possible wife for Dothan? Or have you given up on that idea?"

"I talked to Eliezer," Abram said. "He thinks it's early yet to talk of marriage. We'll let the girl go with Zahavith. If it becomes advisable to send for her, we can send a messenger. They're not going to the very ends of the earth, you know."

Sarai's voice trembled as though she had felt a sudden chill. "But they're going far, my lord. Farther than we realize, I think. Zahavith will insist that they go to the cities, I'm sure.

To Sodom, perhaps. She was made for cities, my lord."

"So were you once," Abram said. "You weren't born to this wilderness."

"I've learned to love it," Sarai said. "Look, my lord, Lot's returning already. It didn't take them long to decide, did it?"

"Maybe we misjudged her," Abram said. "Go now and let me talk to Lot."

The younger man's voice was breathless. "I've talked to my wife," he announced. "It seems she has very strong feelings on the subject."

"I'm not surprised," Abram said dryly. "And what's your decision?"

"Well, if you're really serious, Uncle, if you really meant what you said. . . ."

"Am I in the habit of lying?"

"Oh, no, no! It just seems so . . . unreal to me. But, Zahavith says she would like the valley of the Jordan. She longs to be near the cities, Uncle. Please believe me. It's not that she's greedy for the water."

"It's all right, Lot. When Yahweh told me to give you a choice, I suspected that Zahavith would want to be near the cities. This wandering life is hard for women who are soft."

His voice was not insulting, but Hagar felt a thrill of the same pride that brought Sarai's chin arrogantly into the air. Abram didn't think them soft. Or weak.

"Shall we go today, Uncle?"

"The sooner, the better for all," Abram said heavily. "Prolonged farewells only cause sorrow, and the sooner the slaves are separated, the less quarreling we'll have. And with you gone, the water hole will be more than adequate for my flocks."

"Will . . . will I see you again, Uncle?"

Abram spoke slowly. "I certainly hope so. Our paths may cross. Lot . . . listen to me. I'll take you to the feet of Yahweh every day in prayer. I'll ask him to cherish you and protect you and keep you pure. And if anything happens to you—if you're ever in danger or in trouble, try to get a message to me. I promise you that I'll do everything in my power for you. Everything."

Lot's voice shook with emotion. "I'll be grateful to you all my life, my lord. You've been kinder than a father. No father would understand how I feel about Zahavith, but you've always understood."

"I love my wife, too," Abram said. "Now, go and start your preparations."

In a matter of hours, Lot and his followers were ready to travel. Hagar stood with the others of Abram's group and watched as Lot's family and slaves and cattle and flocks were gathered together. Everything was done quietly; the shock of this decision to divide the tribe seemed to have rendered everyone speechless. But finally Lot stood before his people, his sturdy donkey beside him.

"Are you ready then?" he asked, and the call went down the line.

Lot turned to Abram who stood alone. For long moments the eyes of the two men locked, and then Lot came over and embraced his uncle. He made no effort to hide the tears that wet his face.

"Goodbye, Uncle," he said brokenly, kissing Abram's cheeks. "I leave part of my heart with you."

"Leave your heart if you will," Abram said, "but take the knowledge of Yahweh with you. Be righteous and honest and decent as Yahweh would have you be. Go in peace, my son, and may the peace of our God go with you."

Sarai walked over to Zahavith, and the women hugged each other. In the actual moment of parting, they both seemed reluctant to separate even though they had never been fond of each other.

"Go in peace," Sarai whispered.

"May Yahweh bless you," Zahavith said, "and may your . . . your prayers be answered."

The people began to move, and for a few seconds Hagar couldn't even see Meryet. Were they to be separated like this, probably forever, without even a goodbye?

Then Meryet ran from the column of people, and threw her arms around Hagar.

"I've lost everything," she wept against Hagar's shoulder. "Dothan's father didn't ask for me, and now Lot has been sent away. I've got nothing . . . nothing."

Let her think so, the jealous part of Hagar said. Let her go without hope and without joy. She thinks she's so much better than I am. Let her grieve.

But something happened. Some echo of the unknown sound that had wakened her seemed to ring through her head. And in that instant, the jealously was pushed aside by something Hagar didn't even understand.

"No, listen," Hagar whispered. "Abram—my lord Abram is already thinking of you as a wife for Dothan. I didn't tell you before, but it's true."

"But I'm going away," Meryet wailed.

"Abram said it's not to the ends of the world," Hagar said. "If he needs you, he'll send a messenger for you."

"Are you telling the truth?" Meryet stared at her cousin.

"*I* never lie," Hagar said and Meryet dropped her eyes.

"I know." Meryet had never sounded so humble before. "Oh, Hagar, I hope we see each other again. I hope. . . ."

But Zahavith was calling. "Meryet, come quickly before you're left behind. Hurry!"

There was time for only one quick kiss, but Meryet's face was glowing when she pulled away from Hagar.

"Pray to Sobek and Hathor for me," she whispered to Hagar. "Put flowers on them every day. Oh, Hagar, please!"

"I'm not even allowed to have them in the tent," Hagar said. "But . . . but I'll ask . . . Yahweh to bless you."

"Oh, Hagar. . . ." And Meryet was gone, darting to her place in the long column of people and animals.

Hagar watched them go, then turned with a peculiar sense of desolation. Her last connection with her childhood was gone. She was, for this instant, as alone as she had been in all her life.

But then she heard Sarai's voice. "Hagar, come on now, we have too much to do to stand around."

"Yes, my lady," Hagar said and went gladly to her mistress who represented everything that was now safe and secure in Hagar's world.

PART TWO

These kings made war...
And they took Lot...
and there came one that
escaped, and told Abram
...and he smote them....

GENESIS 14:2a, 12a, 13a, 15a

10

From her favorite place high in the rocky hills of Hebron, Hagar sat looking at the vastness of the plains. The day was so clear that it seemed to her the very edges of the world were visible, and she imagined that she could see all the way to the valley near Sodom and Gomorrah. She wondered, as she had wondered before, if the passing years had been as kind to Meryet as they had been to her. Had Meryet, too, grown softer, rounder, more gentle in the secure, familiar warmth of tribal life?

Or was it true that Lot's tribe really had been absorbed into the city of Sodom? Passing caravans had occasionally left messages indicating that Lot now lived within the city walls of Sodom instead of in the neighboring plains. But of course no one knew anything for sure.

And did Meryet still dream of being called back to marry Dothan, Hagar mused, or had she stopped waiting long ago for Abram's messenger?

Not that Dothan had married anyone. He had grown up to be as carefree and arrogant a man as he had been an arrogant and carefree boy. He was evidently unwilling to tie himself down to the responsibilities of marriage, and neither Eliezer nor Abram pushed him. Hagar often wondered if Dothan still remembered Meryet, still dreamed of her.

But that was foolish with a dozen pretty girls still unspoken for in the tribe—a few of whom were actually qualified to marry Abram's probable heir.

There's me, Hagar's thoughts always concluded. Not that I want him, but I'm going to have to marry someday, and better Dothan than some.

The familiar thoughts slowed and ended as Hagar became aware of a small disturbance at the foot of the hills. There was the kind of dust that was raised by donkey's feet, but she knew of no one who was absent from their tribe, no one who was expected. Abram needed to be told of this.

She ran, fleet footed, back to where the tents clustered on a stony plateau. There was only a slow stir of activity in the heat of midday. The young men and boys were off in the pasturing areas with the flocks and herds, and probably Abram was resting in the shade of the tent as he customarily did.

Hagar came close to the tent opening.

"My lord," she called. "My lord, I must speak to you."

Sarai answered, her voice irritable with sleep. "What is it, Hagar? Must you disturb our lord now? He's been sleeping."

"I think someone's coming," Hagar said. "Down in the valley but heading for here."

"I'm coming," Abram growled. "Wait a minute."

He appeared in the tent opening, rubbing the sleep from his eyes. He always seemed older, Hagar thought, when first waking. But when he was fully awake, he looked robust and vigorous and she found it impossible to think of him as being any age at all.

"What are you jabbering about, girl?" He looked crossly at her. "Sometimes I think you fancy yourself as a sentry ... always sitting up on that hill."

Hagar allowed herself to smile. "Not a sentry, my lord. I like to be alone, that's all. But there *is* someone coming. I thought you ought to know."

"Well, of course I ought to know. Where? Show me where."

She led him up the steep, rocky path, and his feet were as

sure on the stones as hers. When they reached the corrie that served as her shelter when life was difficult, she pointed down toward the plain.

"There," she said. "See ... there's dust. As though a donkey were coming. Or even two of them. Not a caravan though, my lord. Perhaps a messenger."

"From Lot," Abram said quickly, his words echoing her thoughts. "Whoever it is seems to be coming from the direction of Sodom. I ought to go to meet him—or them."

"But, my lord, what if it's not someone from Lot? What if it's some wanderer who would harm you?"

"Am I a weakling?" Abram demanded, his voice suddenly angry.

"Of course not, my lord, But even soldiers have other soldiers at their side."

He peered at her from under his eyebrows. "You're developing a pretty tongue in your head, aren't you?"

"It's true, my lord."

He turned away from her to look down in the valley and then swung around to face her.

"You've grown up," he announced as though he had only discovered it. "I keep thinking of you as a child—but you're not a child. And haven't been. Do you long for marriage? Do we wrong you in keeping you so close to our tent?"

"My life is yours, my lord," Hagar said meekly.

He stared at her and then said almost idly, "Perhaps you're the one we ought to marry to Dothan. Maybe I should insist. . . ." His voice trailed off and he gave her a long, speculative look. "You've turned out to be a good-looking girl," he said. "I never thought you would when we got you."

"Thank you, my lord."

"Don't thank me. Thank Sarai. She's the one who's shaped you into something suitable for a man. Rounded you out and smoothed down the rough corners of your temper. And as for your looks, you were born with those."

"Yes, my lord," she murmured, but she felt warm from

his approval. "Look, they're coming closer. There are two. I can see them now."

"We'll let them come up to the camp," Abram said. "If they're friendly, they'll come openly. If they're not friendly, at least we'll not be taken by surprise. Let's get down to the tents."

By the time the distant dust specks had materialized into two weary people astride two equally weary donkeys, everyone in the tribe had gathered in the open place in front of Abram's tent. The crowd was made up almost entirely of older men, women and children, but it would have been a formidable enough gathering, had the travelers been enemies. Evidently they were not, for they continued to come toward the crowd waiting for them.

The travelers slipped from the backs of their donkeys and came toward Abram. Odd, Hagar reflected, that they should know so surely who was the chief of the tribe.

The man—young and travel-stained and apparently weary to the point of dropping—looked vaguely familiar to Hagar. Perhaps he *was* one of Lot's slaves, after all.

Then her eyes met the eyes of the second traveler and she saw it was a woman. For long silent seconds, the two stood staring at each other, amazement on Hagar's face and relief on the other's.

"Meryet!" Hagar cried, insensible to the fact that it was not her place to run in welcome toward the travelers. She threw her arms around her cousin. "Meryet, where did you come from?"

Meryet only hugged her speechlessly, but Hagar felt the tears that fell and her arms were aware of the terrible weariness and weakness of the body she held.

"Shh!" Meryet whispered at last. "Let him talk—Simeon."

Simeon! The name cut through Hagar's memory with the sharpness of a blade. Of course. It was the boy who had stood beside her near the appricot grove, looking at the land with appreciation. What in the world was he doing here . . . and with Meryet?

"My lord!" Simeon was bowing before Abram, but he
swayed with fatigue, so that Abram brought him erect with a
quick hand.

"Come," Abram said, "Sit in the shade of my tent. Hagar,
bring dates, bread and fresh water. Can this truly be
Meryet? Tell us about Lot, my child." He bridled his
curiosity and spoke hospitably. "Here, both of you, sit here.
Hagar, food... water." Hagar ran to carry out her orders, but
there was a trembling in her whole body. It was wonderful to
see Meryet again—wonderful. And yet... only a short while
ago, Abram had actually spoken of arranging a marriage
between Dothan and Hagar. Would Meryet's coming spoil
that? Oh surely not. Meryet must be married to Simeon or
they would not have come together across the plains and
foothills. Hagar's hands shook, almost spilling the precious
water, but eventually she had a tray of dates, some small
wheat cakes, water and wine.

Nothing of importance had been said while she was gone,
she realized as soon as she came into the tent. Abram, with
warm hospitality was only bidding the travelers welcome,
asking after their comfort, offering water to wash their
hands and feet.

But when the food had been served, the questioning
began.

"You've come from Lot?" Abram said.

"From Sodom," Simeon replied.

"Lot's not dead?" Abram asked in sudden fear.

"I hope not, my lord," Simeon said and exchanged a look
with Meryet.

"What do you mean?" Abram's voice was rough.

"If you'll let me tell you, my lord," Simeon suggested. "It's
a long and a sad story. May I say it in my own words?"

Abram sat back, hiding his impatience with courtesy. "Of
course. Please tell me everything—but when you're ready."

Simeon drank deeply of the fresh water and quickly ate
several dates. Then he looked up and met Abram's waiting
gaze.

"I'm Simeon," the young man said. "I've run away from my master—a caravan leader. I was through here once before, some years ago, and I remember your tribe."

His eyes flicked swiftly to Hagar's face and then back to Abram, but she felt the look as though it had been a touch. Would he look at her like that, married to Meryet?

Abram inclined his head in acknowledgement. Simeon's admission of running away from his master put him at Abram's mercy.

"I was heading for this place—it was my own country once—when I found this girl—Meryet—alone and terrified and nearly dead. I questioned her—but I did not touch her, my lord—and I found that she had escaped from Sodom."

"Escaped?" The word came out in spite of Abram's attempt to wait patiently.

"Not from her master, my lord. From the town. There had been war there—killing and rape and capture. Somehow she had escaped. Unharmed."

Hagar was suddenly and breathlessly aware of her perfunctory prayers to Yahweh that Meryet would be safe. Was it possible. . . ?

"But her master, my lord, and his family," Simeon went on. "They were captured by King Amraphel and King Tydal and others. There were four kings from places north of here, one of them near Damascus. I don't know all the names. Neither does she," he added, jerking his head toward Meryet. "But most of the people of the city were captured. "She"—again the jerk of his head toward Meryet, "she got away. When I found her, she was unable to go further alone. But she said if we could get to Hebron, we would find shelter. I believed her and we came," he ended simply, apparently too tired to elaborate any further.

"But only captured," Abram persisted. "You didn't hear of Lot's death?"

This time, his question was directed to Meryet and she lifted her face to his.

"Captured for slaves, I believe, my lord. My lady,

Zahavith, was screaming with rage and fear, and they laughed when they tied her up. But there was no talk of killing."

"And how did you know we were in Hebron?"

"My lord Lot spoke of it often. He hoped to see you sometime again. He talked to someone from every caravan that came into Sodom so that he might know where you were."

Abram was silent, thinking furiously. "Four kings, you say?" he suddenly barked to Simeon.

"Yes, my lord."

"How many followers?"

"I don't know, my lord."

"Many," Meryet spoke up. "Thousands, my lord."

"But *I* have Yahweh," Abram mused. Then he turned to Hagar. "See that these two are given a place to rest. Feed them, and give them something clean to wear. Tonight, after the evening meal, we'll talk again. You are welcome here," he added courteously to Simeon and Meryet and then turned abruptly and went into the inner recesses of his tent.

Eliezer took Simeon with him, the rest of the crowd dispersed, and Hagar and Meryet found themselves alone at last. Meryet devoured the food that Hagar brought her the way an animal would, stuffing it into her mouth with shaking fingers. For a while they were silent and then Meryet looked at Hagar.

"Dothan?" she asked simply. "Is he married?"

Hagar shook her head. She should have known that Meryet wouldn't risk her life to try to find her cousin. It was Dothan who had drawn her, Dothan and the wealth of Abram.

A look of surprise and gratification spread across Meryet's face. "Am I to be so lucky?" she murmured.

"It isn't luck," Hagar snapped, stung into defending something she had hardly recognized before. "It's more than that. I *told* you I'd pray for you."

Meryet reached over and put her hand on Hagar's. "You must have," she said soberly. "The life there—in Sodom—it's evil. Oh, not in Lot's house. Not yet. Zahavith is foolish and greedy and sometimes cruel." There was a sudden bleakness in Meryet's eyes that twisted Hagar's heart with unexpected pity. "But they aren't as evil as the others. The men of Sodom—they're worse than animals. I was afraid to ever step out of our door—oh, not that I'd be raped. That would have been too normal for them."

"Meryet. . . ," Hagar breathed in horror.

Meryet was grim. "I was stupid to have ever wanted to serve Zahavith. She's so greedy she even allowed marriage between several of her daughters and the men of that place." Meryet shuddered. "It's good to be here," she said, looking around the peaceful compound. "I'd forgotten what quiet and decency were like. Oh, Lot tries to be good—he does truly—but. . . ." And her old familiar shrug finished the words.

"What of Simeon?" Hagar asked at last.

"What of him?" Meryet echoed. "He served as a guide. He brought me here. But he possesses nothing—nothing. I wouldn't care if I never saw him again."

"But he was good to you."

"And I was good to him. I brought him to Abram."

"I don't understand why you're not married yet," Hagar said after a brief silence. "You're more than old enough. Why didn't they marry you to someone before now?"

Meryet looked grim. "Lot wanted to. I had to be . . . very clever to persuade Zahavith she couldn't spare me to any man. It was one time her greed came in handy to me."

Hagar was silent. There was nothing more for her to say.

"Hagar," Meryet said, "help me get cleaned up. Is there water for washing? I want to oil and smooth my hair. Have you a comb? And something to darken my eyes? Just a little. It's getting late and the men will be coming back with the animals."

"And you want to be beautiful for Dothan?" Hagar could

not help the bitterness which filled the words.

"As beautiful as possible," Meryet replied simply.

Simeon, refreshed by the rest and the food which had been given to him, sat around the fire with the men of Abram's tribe that evening.

"We're going to war!" Abram announced and there was a gasp of complete surprise and then a flurry of questions but Abram silenced them all with a glare. "My nephew Lot and his family are in danger. If we start now, we can catch up to the kings who captured them. We'll attack from the rear —we've done it before—and we'll harass them until we have Lot securely in our hands. Then we'll retreat."

A murmur of protest surged through the crowd, but Abram ignored it. "I have Yahweh's promise," he announced in ringing tones, in the voice of prophecy. "Just as I've had his promise before. Didn't he say we would possess this land—possess it in peace and prosperity? And hasn't his promise come true?"

"You also said Yahweh promised you a son." The words were mumbled by someone deep in the crowd.

Abram's eyes blazed. "Who said that?"

There was only silence as the impassive, sullen faces stared at him.

"I heard the slave girl say there were thousands in the army that captured Lot," one of the men argued. "Can we defeat thousands, my lord?"

"Of course not!" Abram's voice was sharp. "I never suggested defeating them. I spoke of harassment—sly attacks at vulnerable points. Yahweh will show us the way. As he has before. You know yourselves that he protects us."

There was silence as each man thought of the prosperity and peace they had known for years. Few tribes could claim such blessings. Perhaps what Abram said was true.

"I'm with you, my lord!" a young man shouted, and other voices began to join his, until the whole camp was crying out with approval, their protests and fears forgotten.

"Eliezer and I have taken a count," Abram went on. "There are 317 of us—318 if Simeon joins us."

"Gladly, my lord," Simeon called out, his face blazing, his fatigue forgotten.

"We'll leave at dawn," Abram said. "Eliezer will call out the names of the men who are to go. The rest of you will stay here and make a sacrifice to our God. You will live in virtue until we come home with Lot safety beside us." His voice rang out with confident authority. "Our God is a mighty God."

"A mighty God," the men shouted back at him like a great amen.

Hidden by shadows, Meryet and Hagar had heard everything.

"How can he be so sure?" Meryet asked.

"I don't know," Hagar said morosely. "Yahweh hasn't given him a child, but he seems to go on believing."

"Well," Meryet confided, "if he comes home safely, I have an idea that will change our lives—your life and mine. Maybe even Abram's."

But Hagar only heard the words, "*If* he comes home safely," and a terrible fear ran coldly through her. Abram *must* return safely. There would be no point in living if he were killed.

"Oh, please, Yahweh," Hagar found herself praying silently but with a greater passion than her prayers had ever held before, "Please, Yahweh, bring him home. Bring my lord safely home."

11

The days crawled by. Everyone knew that if Abram were to be successful in his raid against the marauding kings from the north, it would have to be done swiftly, so each morning that dawned seemed less promising than the one before.

Sarai, Hagar and Meryet sought comfort in being together. Sarai's eyes were red and swollen from weeping, and Hagar was quiet and withdrawn, suffering with the mute endurance of a small animal. Only Meryet made a determined effort to be cheerful.

"If Yahweh spared me—along with Simeon—to come and tell Abram of Lot's capture, there must have been a reason. Surely Yahweh will protect his own," she said.

Whether Meryet spoke from any sort of conviction or whether she was merely saying what she knew Sarai wanted to hear, Hagar could not even guess. Hagar only knew that she, like Sarai, clung to the words, repeating them in her own mind at night as a sort of talisman against despair.

On the fifth morning, Hagar went up to her private spot on the hill. It was more than a refuge in this difficult time. It was a perfect place to watch for messengers, and she stared out over the plains for hours at a time.

She picked some scarlet poppies and exotic-looking but coarsely-named "dove's dung." Even in her grief, she could not ignore the brave, sturdy desert flowers that grew with such brilliance in the rocky crevices. When she reached her place of sanctuary, her hands were filled with color.

"I'll sacrifice them to Yahweh," she thought suddenly, aware of the fact that Abram's people gave only grain or birds or animals as sacrifice, that the offering of flowers was a spillover from her childhood.

"They're all I have, Lord of my lord," she whispered, placing the blossoms on a flat rock that could serve as an altar. "I don't own any animals—I don't grow grain. Will my flowers suffice as an offering?"

She knelt and felt the sunlight beating against her bowed head. And in that minute, she thought of something.

"Wait," she cried softly as though Yahweh would stand in that place until she returned. But that was foolish because surely Yahweh was with Abram, not here. "Wait," she begged anyway, "I'll be back."

She raced to where she had hidden her old childhood treasures. Spread on her hand, they seemed small and humble to offer to Abram's god. But they were the only things that were truly her own, the only things that Abram's generosity had not given her.

The bracelet was discolored, and the comb lacked most of its teeth. But the two little statues were unblemished.

"I'll give the statue of Sobek to Yahweh," she whispered breathlessly to herself, and knew that she was relinquishing at least part of the faith of her childhood. She was acknowledging—or hoping—that Yahweh was a greater deity than the Egyptian god. In giving Sobek away, she was doing what Abram had suggested years ago when he said that someday she would give up the idols of her own volition.

But she couldn't give them both up, she realized. The dainty, delicate little statue of Hathor reminded her too much of her mother, and to give it up would be almost like losing her mother all over again. She remembered the day her mother had given her the idol—a day of sunshine and laughter and gifts—long before death or fear or slavery had come into her life.

With a strange mixture of guilt and relief, Hagar re-wrapped the tiny statue of the goddess and pushed the small bundle back into its hiding place.

She heard Sarai's and Meryet's voices in the tent as she turned to run back up on the hill, and she wondered briefly what they found to talk about. Well, nothing that concerned her, she was sure.

Back in her rocky solitude, she laid the small articles on the altar with the flowers. But just placing them there wasn't enough. With fingers that trembled, she picked up a smaller rock and brought it crashing down. The splintering sound went through her like pain. For long minutes, she gazed at the broken fragments. There! the little god was demolished, destroyed, offered up to Yahweh. Before she could weaken, she smashed the comb and bracelet, making them totally unfit for human use. Then with a greater humility than she had ever known, she sank onto her knees before the stone which served as her altar.

"Oh, Yahweh, I've given this all to you. And all I ask is that my lord come home safely. Please hear me, Lord."

The silence seemed to beat around her like a pulse, and she wondered if she would ever know, as Abram did, that Yahweh heard her prayer.

Then suddenly the silence was not so complete. There was a scrabbling sound and Hagar leaped to her feet, her heart pounding thickly.

"Who is it?" she said, the words choking with fear.

"Shh!—it's me—Simeon."

She stared at him in disbelief. It was as though she were reliving that day so long ago, when they had met near the apricot grove, except that now Simeon was no longer a boy and his face was gray with dust and fatigue.

"What are you doing here?" she gasped. "Where is my lord?"

The fatigue disappeared in the brilliance of his sudden smile.

"I've come with a message," Simeon announced. "I volunteered because I know this land so well. The news is good, little one. Your lord has done everything he said he would."

"You mean he's safe?"

"Safe *and* victorious!"

"He has Lot?" Her voice was disbelieving. After all, Meryet had said the conquering kings had thousands to follow them.

"He has Lot indeed. And Lot's family. Safe."

"But where?"

"Down on the plains. They'll be in sight by late afternoon. He wants everyone to go down to meet them—to celebrate the victory before Lot and his family head for Sodom."

Hagar stood and stared at Simeon while waves of joy ran through her. Could any of Abram's success be due to the sacrifice just made—if it could be called sacrifice—or to the prayers that accompanied it? But no, that was ridiculous. Abram had been safe long before her sacrifice had been made.

"Oh, Simeon," she gasped at last. "Oh, thank you."

His hands reached out and caught at her shoulders. "There are other ways to thank a man who has been to war," he said roughly and pulled her into his arms. His mouth on hers was hard and hungry, and held her fiercely.

For a second she was too surprised to move, but then she began to struggle. When he finally released her, he was laughing and she was trembling with anger and something more.

"A reward to the victor," Simeon said. "I'd like even more, of course, but I have a message to deliver."

"You won't get any more rewards from me," she said icily. "What kind of girl do you think I am?"

"I'm just thinking of tonight—when the wine is flowing—and everyone is under the spell of victory."

"We're not pagans who carouse and get drunk . . . we're decent people who. . . ."

But Simeon only laughed at her. "Men are men and

women are women," he said, "and Abram will want to repay me for the risks I've taken."

"You're insolent!" Hagar raged.

"You're insolent yourself, girl," he retorted. "You're only a slave, after all."

She glared at him, more angry at the way his kiss had stirred her than she was at his taunting remarks.

"I may be a slave," she said, "but I'm not something to be handed over to the first man who talks to Abram of payment. Other men have served him, you know."

"Dothan?" Simeon guessed shrewdly. "But Dothan has no taste for you, my pretty. Dothan has other desires, and I'll wager *he* won't be thwarted when the time comes."

"That's Dothan's affair," she snapped, but cold anger iced her veins. Even a stranger knew that Dothan didn't want her. Some honesty in her, however, made her recognize that if it had been Dothan who had kissed her, her heart would not be pounding in the erratic way it had been beating ever since Simeon had pulled her into his rough embrace.

"You'd better stop this stupid talk and take your message to the tribe," Hagar managed to say at last after a taut silence had fallen between them.

"I hope they're kinder than you," he muttered. "A man dreams for years . . . and then discovers the girl is made of stone. Or are you?" He wheeled on her and his teeth glinted in a savage smile. He was close to her, not really touching her, but overwhelming her with his intensity. "Are you?" he repeated in a milder tone, and this time his embrace was gentle, and his lips against hers were soft and sensuous.

When the kiss ended, they were both breathless. "No, not of stone," Simeon said with satisfaction. "I didn't think my memories would play me false. Don't stiffen against me, girl. I won't take you here . . . with the dirt of battle on me and men's blood on my hands. But someday—if not to-night—someday you'll come to me. Willingly. I swear it."

She stared at him, her eyes going involuntarily to his hands, and then she whirled away from him. "Hurry!" she begged. "Come and tell them that my lord is safe."

He followed her without speaking again until they came together to the tents.

Down on the lower plain, the night was filled with merriment and joy and reunion. Even Sarai and Zahavith seemed glad to see each other, and their excited talk made a counterpoint to the rougher talk of men.

"Of course you'll give Meryet back to us," Zahavith said to Sarai. "Abram gave her to me years ago."

"But there was always an understanding that if Dothan wanted to marry someday, we would ask for Meryet." Sarai's voice was cordial, but the words were firm.

"Dothan? Eliezer's son? Abram's ... heir?" Zahavith's voice climbed with each questioning word, then dropped to the sound of conspiracy. "Although I've always thought it strange that Abram's nephew wasn't the legal heir."

"That's not the way Yahweh wants it," Sarai said.

Zahavith's spread hands dismissed Yahweh and his wishes. "Who can know what a god wants?" she asked.

"Abram knows," Sarai insisted.

"Oh, then you've had the child Yahweh promised," Zahavith said silkily, "and I just hadn't heard?"

Sarai hesitated, and Hagar, who had overheard the conversation, interrupted. "Do you know where Meryet is, my lady?"

Sarai turned to Hagar with relief, glad to be spared from answering Zahavith's question. "Why, no. I thought she'd be with you."

"She should have stayed with me," Zahavith cried. "I'm the one who grieved, thinking she was dead until I saw her only a short time ago. Why didn't she stay here with me?"

"I'll look for her, my lady," Hagar said to Sarai and slipped away before Zahavith could say anything else.

The light and shadow cast by the huge fires both concealed and revealed. A sudden wave of warm light brushed away a deep shadow, and Hagar saw Meryet at the distant edges of the crowd. But she was not alone. Just before the shadow covered her again, Hagar caught a glimpse of Dothan. He and Meryet stood looking at each other.

Almost reluctantly, Hagar made her way to them. "My lady is looking for you," Hagar said, and Meryet glanced at her as though she had never seen her before. "We're supposed to be serving the wine."

"Is Zahavith with your mistress?" Dothan asked, his eyes never leaving Meryet's face.

"Yes."

"Then stay here," Dothan instructed Meryet, and turning to Hagar, he said, "Go and tell them that you can't find her. Tell them you'll keep looking. Only look in the opposite direction. You understand?"

"Why should I?" Hagar snapped.

"Because I said so," Dothan returned, and there was such sudden authority in his voice that Hagar ran to obey. All his casual indifference was gone, and there was strength in him that Hagar acknowledged with respect.

Abram looked up to see Dothan leaning over his shoulder with an urgency foreign to that casual young man.

"My lord," Dothan said, "my lord, I must speak to you."

"Not now, boy, can't you see that I'm talking to Lot—and to kings?" Abram's voice was only a low whisper, but Dothan stopped before its intensity. "Here, sit here, my boy. You've all met my steward's son, Dothan." His glance and gesture took in the strangers who sat around the fire. "King Bera of Sodom, Dothan, and King Birsha of Gomorrah."

The boy bowed his head with courtesy, but Abram felt the impatience quivering in him. "It will wait," Abram murmured in Dothan's ear. "It will keep a minute or two. Right now we have grave matters to settle." Once more his voice came up to its usual pitch. "These gracious kings want to share their bounty with us."

"Well, why not?" Dothan asked reasonably. "Without us,

they would have been poorer by far. You're the one, my lord, who rescued Lot and other inhabitants of the towns. You're the one who brought back their treasures."

"I only rescued Lot," Abram said stubbornly. "I only did what Yahweh told me to do. I don't want my hands soiled with greed."

"My lord," Eliezer said smoothly, "perhaps my son is right. Perhaps a normal gift in gratitude for your efforts is only fair."

For several minutes Abram was silent, and then he spoke with decisiveness. "Ordinary soldiers deserve rewards, it's true. Men who fight out of loyalty to a human leader need to be paid. For example," he turned to the kings beside him, "I will gladly take payment for the food my men consumed, for the weapons that were broken or lost. That's only right. Just as I plan to pay the young man, Simeon, who brought me news of Lot's capture and who went to battle with us. Enough to start a small caravan of your own," he said suddenly to Simeon as though there were only the two of them there, and Simeon's gratitude shone in his eyes and smile.

"And as I plan to reward Dothan," Abram continued, "with whatever it is that he wants."

Dothan sat back with a long audible sigh.

"But as for me," Abram said, "I want no part of your money because I don't want to be in your debt. I want to owe nothing—except to Yahweh."

"But, my lord," several men began.

"No!" Abram shouted, suddenly angry. "Why don't you listen to me? Why don't you feel Yahweh's plans as I do? Isn't there anyone—anywhere—who can tell me I'm right? Must I always be alone, standing against all of you with only Yahweh at my back?"

The next words came out in a whisper frayed with self-doubt and loneliness. "And am I even sure that Yahweh is with me? Or. . . ."

A startled cry from one of the men acting as sentry cut through the silence that had followed Abram's outburst.

"Who comes?" the sentry called in loud tones.

"We come in peace," a voice said. "Put up your knife. We come seeking Abram, servant of the Most High God."

Abram's breath hissed out in amazement. Then, with a sudden radiance on his face, he scrambled to his feet to hurry and give obeisance to the old man who was walking into the circle of firelight.

12

"My lord," Abram said warmly. "Welcome! Welcome! I don't know your name, but if you come in the name of Yahweh, you're welcome at my fireside."

"My name is Melchizedek," the old man said, "I'm the king of Salem, but I serve the Most High God, and he sent me to find you."

With gentle, urgent hands, Abram led the old king to the place of honor by the fire and then knelt reverently beside him.

"No, sit," Melchizedek said. "I have much to say to you."

"But first, wine and food for you and your followers," Abram said. "We're making a celebration, my lord. That's why you find us here instead of at my tents."

At a gesture from Abram, Dothan ran to give orders that food and wine be brought to the strangers, and after Melchizedek had taken some refreshment, Abram began to ask some questions. "How did you know my name, my lord? How did you know where to find me?"

"The Most High God told me," the old king said simply.

"You mean," Abram's voice trembled. "You mean that you, too, hear the voice of our God, hear it plain enough to shape words in your mind?"

Melchizedek stared at Abram. "How well you say it, my son. I've never met anyone else, you know, who listens to our God. But he knows you're his servant—just as I am his priest. He has sent me to tell you this, to bless you."

"When I most needed it," Abram muttered. "It's not easy, my lord, being the only one who hears."

A wry smile twisted the corner of the old king's mouth. "I know. I know. I've caught myself wishing he spoke more loudly at times—or in a more universal language."

The look that passed between the two men was one of shared amusement, affection and understanding.

"I know more than your name," Melchizedek went on. "I know that the battle you have just fought was a miracle—that 318 men defeated the plans of several thousands. I know that the Most High God delivered your enemy into your hands."

There was no way for King Melchizedek to know this, Abram thought dazedly, no way except through Yahweh. Their number had been known only to them, because their frantic yells and skilled harassment had led the enemy to believe they had ten times as many men as they actually had.

Abram bowed his head again and spoke in humility. "You *must* have been sent by Yahweh. Now, perhaps my followers will truly believe."

"We do believe, Father Abram," a voice cried out, and then another voice and another. "We believe that you *are* the servant of Yahweh and that he speaks to you."

In the shouting and acclamation, Melchizedek looked at Abram with the fondness a man might feel for his son.

"This night is a blessing for me, too. Could we go apart, do you think, and talk alone?"

"Of course. Dothan, see that King Melchizedek's followers are cared for . . . and those who are with the kings from Sodom and Gomorrah. May Lot come with us, my lord?" he asked Melchizedek, and the old king nodded his head.

"Dothan, you will see to everything?"

"Everything, my lord." Dothan spoke with his new authority.

"Then we'll go," Abram said, and he and Melchizedek

and Lot moved away from the shouting crowd and into the shadows of the night.

Hagar, carrying a flask of wine, felt her elbow suddenly caught by a strong hand.

"Did you hear what he said?" Simeon's voice was excited. "Did you hear what Abram said?"

"Yes, I heard." She tried to keep her voice level but his touch made her heart jerk.

"A caravan of my own," Simeon gloated. "It's what I've always dreamed of."

"I know," she said. "You talked about it the first time I saw you."

"You see." His tone was almost accusing. "You remember, too."

"I never said I didn't remember."

Simeon looked at her in the flickering light of the fire, and it was as though he held her in his arms again.

"I'll ask Abram to keep you for me," he said hoarsely. "I can't take you with me now. My life will be dangerous and difficult until I'm established with a safe route. But I'll come back and marry you."

"It's not my place to make any promises," Hagar said breathlessly. "I belong to Sarai."

"You belong to me," he said recklessly, "and if I could get you away from this place, where we could be alone, I'd *make* you mine."

"And then leave me?" Her voice was almost taunting. "Possibly with your child in me?"

He stared at her. "I wasn't brought up to think of those things," he muttered.

"So, have you scattered your sons across the desert, wherever the caravan stopped to water its animals?" Her voice was high, but there was pain in it as well as mockery.

"I had a girl or two," he said, stung into an honesty that was new to him. "But some tribes do not cherish their women."

"The cherishing must begin with men," she said.

"Then someday I'll learn to cherish you," he murmured, reaching out to touch her. But she drew away. His confession had hurt her more than she would have believed possible.

"Why do you want *me*," she asked, "if other girls are so willing?"

He stared at her intently and when he answered, his voice was very serious. "Because you're different," he said. "Because you have a mind as well as a body. Because you're the only girl I ever wanted to *talk* to . . . as well as kiss. I don't even understand it, but I know you were made for me. I'll always feel that way, no matter what happens."

It was what she had always wanted, she thought . . . to be part of someone else so that she would never have to be lonely again. His words stirred her even more than his kisses had.

"We'll have to wait and see," she whispered breathlessly, and when he touched her cheek, she shyly kissed his hand and watched his eyes catch fire. Then she turned and ran to the security of her work.

Abram, Melchizedek and Lot walked back toward the dying fire after hours of conversation. All of the things Abram had known dimly, all the dreams he had dared to dream were sharpened, brought into hard focus by the words which he and Melchizedek had shared. It was as though Yahweh had spoken with a human voice, and Abram felt lifted out of himself by the glory of it all.

But he was troubled about Lot. Even though Melchizedek had confirmed Abram's suspicions that the cities of Sodom and Gomorrah were evil and corrupt, Lot was stubbornly determined to return.

"Zahavith loves it there," Lot argued.

"But the things that are done there are an abomination to Yahweh," Abram cried.

"But not in *my* house, Uncle," Lot said. "I don't permit anything that is evil to be done in my house."

"And how long do you think you can hold out against

them?" Melchizedek asked.

"As long as my uncle speaks to Yahweh for me," Lot said simply.

Abram sighed. "As long as I have breath in my body," he said, "I'll ask Yahweh to bless and spare you."

"I'll add my prayers to his," Melchizedek said, "but I still think you're wrong to go back."

"I have to," was all that Lot would say.

"I can't let Meryet go with you," Abram said suddenly. "Dothan wants to marry her. He hasn't asked me yet, but I know he does."

"Zahavith will be angry," Lot said.

"Then she'll have to be angry," Abram declared, "and eventually get over it."

"Tell her, my boy," Melchidezek suggested, "that you had a choice between going to Sodom without Meryet—or staying here with Meryet. Her anger, then, won't be directed at you."

Lot looked at the old king with gratitude. "I'll do it," he said.

Melchizedek touched Abram's arm lightly. "Even we who talk with God must deal with the problems of men."

The camp was silent when the three men got back to the fire. Sprawled in fatigue from the journey or huddled together to keep warm, the people of Abram slept.

Only Dothan sat by the fire, awake and waiting.

"The kings of Sodom and Gomorrah are gone, my lord," he announced. "Part of their men went with them, and part stayed to take Lot and his family safely to the city."

"And everything else is well, my boy?"

"Everything, my lord."

Abram looked quizzically at Melchidezek. "Will you linger with us for some weeks, my lord? You could share our celebration when Dothan, my present heir, takes Meryet as his wife."

"I haven't even asked you," Dothan gasped.

"Am I a fool?" Abram asked. "Haven't I watched you

since she has come back? Will you stay, my lord?"

"Only until sunrise," Melchizedek answered. "My errand—but for one thing—is complete."

"And that one thing, my lord?"

"When dawn comes, I want all of your tribe gathered here together. There is a ceremony that the Most High God would have me perform. But now, we have a few hours to rest. I'm an old man and weary."

In only a few minutes, Melchizedek, Lot and Dothan were wrapped in their robes and asleep. But Abram knelt, unconscious of his fatigue, yearning toward Yahweh, his God who had not forsaken him.

In the morning, the men of the tribe gathered around the place where Melchizedek and Abram stood together. The eastern sky glowed with the color of apricots and a fresh breeze sweetened the air.

"Men of Abram," Melchizedek said when the silence was complete, "you've heard why I've come, and you know that the Most High God sent me. Until he spoke to me, I had never heard of Abram or of his people.

"But now I know you, and I know that you sing the praises of the Most High God and you tell your children about him. For this, you and your descendents will be blessed.

"But it is Abram's faith which is as sweet as incense in the nostrils of his God. The Most High God has chosen Abram to lead you, and it is to Abram that he will speak."

The people were nodding, their faces burning with the color of the rising sun and with the fervor of Melchizedek's words.

The old king turned and the people watched as Abram dropped to his knees.

"Blessed are you, Abram," Melchizedek intoned, "for you are the servant of the Most High God."

"Blessed is Abram," the men murmured, "for he is the servant of the Most High God."

"Blessed is the Most High God who has delivered your enemies into your hand," Melchizedek cried.

The voices of the men rose from a murmur to an exultant shout. "Blessed is the Most High God who has delivered our enemy into our hand!"

When the shout died away, Melchizedek took wine and bread from his own leather pouch.

"In reverence to the Most High God," he said, "eat and drink with me."

Abram broke a piece of the bread and put it in his mouth, then tipped the wine skin to his lips and drank briefly.

"So I am fed," he said simply, and Melchizedek leaned over and kissed his forehead.

"So you are fed," he said and took some of the bread and wine for himself.

"Yahweh's name be praised," Abram said and knew that, from this hour on, his faith would never falter again.

It was several days before normal tribal life could be resumed. Lot and his family left for Sodom as soon as Melchizedek and his followers, carrying the tithe that Abram had given him, had ridden away. This time, there was less sadness at Lot's going, because this time it was Lot's own desire to leave. Zahavith's anger over leaving Meryet behind had been vehement, but by the time they rode away she was no longer shouting, and her fury was reduced to a sullen refusal to speak to anyone. It was, Hagar reflected, a relief to have everything behind them—the war, the victory, the presence of Lot and Zahavith, the miraculous coming of Yahweh's priest, even the pain and resulting loneliness of Simeon's departure. All of these events had hurt or changed her. It was good to know that there was only work to be done and little to trouble her heart.

Of course, there was Meryet to think about. Meryet was sleeping in Abram and Sarai's tent, sharing Hagar's corner with her. But Meryet had a way of taking over, and in a few days it seemed as though it were Meryet's corner, Meryet's privilege to serve Sarai, Meryet who hurried to do Abram's bidding. Hagar felt a peculiar sense of loneliness—as though she were no longer who or what she had always been.

As she had become accustomed to doing, she went one afternoon to her small sanctuary up on the hill. She had not been there since the day she had made a sacrifice to Yahweh. She stood looking at the dusty jumble of dead flowers and the broken bits of treasures.

"It was a foolish thing to do," she said aloud, "a childish thing to do." And with a sweep of her hand, she sent the contents of the make-believe altar onto the ground.

"What are you doing?"

Hagar whirled around to see Abram standing and staring at her.

"My lord," she gasped.

"I was coming down from the hill and heard you talking to yourself and throwing things around. What's going on?"

He looked so comfortable, so kind standing there, the sunlight bright behind him, that she found herself pouring out everything. She told him how she had desired to make a sacrifice and had only a few trinkets to offer, only a childhood idol to break.

Abram listened in silence and then went over to stir the broken fragments with his foot.

"And you think Yahweh despises such sacrifice?" he asked gently.

His gentleness broke down her last reserve. "I don't know what to think," she cried. "I'm so mixed up, my lord. I *do* believe in Yahweh now. If I needed any proof, I had it when you were victorious over thousands and when King Melchizedek proclaimed you as the servant of Yahweh. But I can't feel Yahweh would listen to *me*."

"Why not to you?" He sat on a rocky ledge, as though he had all day to talk to her.

She sat across from him. "Because I'm only a woman, because I don't seem to be able to . . . to matter to anyone."

"You matter to Simeon," he said.

Her head jerked up. "He spoke to you?"

"Of course. Didn't you know he would?"

She only shook her head. She was not sure she had really believed anything Simeon had said.

"If he becomes successful enough to take a wife, I've told him you might be . . . available."

He was laughing at her, she thought, but the laughter was kind.

"Does my lady know?" Hagar asked.

"She knows."

"And?"

He shrugged. "She was just happy that you wouldn't be leaving now."

"But she almost acts as though she liked Meryet better than she likes me." The words were out before Hagar knew she was even going to say them. Was that her problem? Was she only jealous again?

Abram looked thoughtful. "Meryet is a strong person. She can exert influence, I think. But Sarai loves you; of course she does. And in only a few days Meryet will be going to Dothan's tent. Then life will be just as it was."

She smiled. "I'm sorry, my lord. I acted like a child."

He was very serious. "But not when you worshipped Yahweh—even though you did it in your own way. To break the idol—to give up something precious for our God—*that* isn't childish. It may very well have been your prayers, my child, which helped us win the victory."

"Truly, my lord?"

"Yes, truly. You're not like most of the slaves—you have a mind and a heart. It won't make life easy for you, you know."

"I know."

He stood up as though to leave, then turned toward her again. "What of this thing with Simeon? If he comes and asks for you, would you be willing to marry him?"

"If I cannot serve *you*, my lord, then I would be willing."

He looked startled. "Serve me? But you've always served me—or served Sarai which is the same thing. Still. . . ." He paused and then spoke abruptly, "Well, it's in Yahweh's hands."

"Yes, my lord."

"And in the meantime, be happy for Meryet," he said. "She's your cousin and it's your duty to share her joy as well as her trouble. Do you understand?"

"Yes, my lord," she said slowly. "I'll be happy for her. I will.

"I know I spoke of Dothan and you. . . ." he began but she hurried to interrupt.

"No, no, my lord. It's all right. Dothan has always wanted Meryet—and she him. What you said to me has been forgotten."

He searched her face. "Well, we'll see. Simeon is a brave young man . . . and a smart one. The only thing is . . . we'd hate to give you up."

He smiled at her and then left her alone in the hot, bright stillness of her private spot.

We'd hate to give you up, he had said. And could she endure going away? Could all of Simeon's kisses make up for the loss of Abram and Sarai? Well, there was no use worrying about it now. Now was the time to think of Meryet's marriage to Dothan. After all, she didn't know whether or not Simeon would ever come back.

13

Sarai looked up from her spinning to see Abram standing beside her. She smiled her welcome, but inquiry filled her eyes. It was not usual for him to come to the tent in mid morning.

"Do you want something, my lord?" she asked.

"I want to talk to you." He sat beside her, grinned with affection and touched her cheek. "Must you spin while we talk?"

"No, my lord, but it seems strange to sit with idle hands."

"Well, your brain won't be idle, so let your hands rest."

Abram glanced over to where Meryet and Hagar were grinding corn and indicated with a gesture that he wanted them sent away.

"You girls find something to do somewhere else," Sarai said, feeling a sense of surprise. What did it matter what one said in front of slaves?

Hagar left quickly, not even glancing over her shoulder, but Meryet made such a long business of gathering up dishes and utensils that Sarai felt she was lingering deliberately.

"Meryet!" she called.

"Yes, my lady. I'm going. I'm going." But the sidelong look she gave Sarai was one of conspiracy, a sort of prompting with her eyes.

"What's that all about?" Abram asked. "She acts as though she wanted to tell you what to say to me."

"It's nothing," Sarai said. "Meryet has been speaking about . . . something. But I have to think about it a great deal before I talk to you about it, my lord."

"You're sure you can't tell me now?"

"Yes." The answer was abrupt, and when Abram looked at his wife, he saw that her head was bent and her lips were quivering.

"Is something the matter?" he asked.

She shook her head. "You didn't come to talk about me," she said. "You came to talk about something else, I'm sure. What, my lord?"

"About the marriage of Dothan and Meryet," he said. "It's an unusual situation, and I'm not sure how to handle it. Do I make the contract with Eliezer, or should I have had Lot make it? Someone has to represent the bride."

Sarai pursed her lips thoughtfully. "I know. I've been thinking about it, too. She belonged to us, my lord, before we let her serve Lot and Zahavith. I don't think they even enter into it. The thing to determine is whether or not any gifts should be made. It seems silly, doesn't it, for Eliezer to give you a gift, when everything he has has been given to him by you?"

"But once I've given it to him, it's his, and if he wants to return it, he has a right to do so."

"Do you *want* a gift?" She could not keep the surprise out of her voice. "You wouldn't take anything from the kings of Sodom and Gomorrah."

"That was different," Abram said. "They would have bribed me with their gifts. Oh, subtly, of course, but they would have tried to use me. If Eliezer gives me a gift, it will preserve his pride in himself. He won't be in my debt then, but I in his. In his own mind, I mean."

She smiled at him. "I wouldn't have thought of that. No wonder men respect you, my lord."

He was silent, but her approval brought a smile to his lips.

"So, what shall it be?" she asked.

"I could ask for their firstborn," he said soberly, and she jerked toward him.

"Oh, no, my lord. What good would that do?"

"If we raised the child from birth, it might seem more like ours."

"But it wouldn't be *your* child. Yahweh has said it must be *your* child. A child of theirs wouldn't be any more a natural heir than Dothan is. You're not really serious, my lord?" In her agitation, she clutched at his robe, worrying the sleeve in her hands.

"No, I guess I'm not really serious," he soothed. "It's just that sometimes I wonder if Yahweh wants me to just keep waiting patiently or if he wants me to *do* something about a child."

Her voice was so low that he had to lean close to her to hear. "I'm too old to bear a child my lord. The way of women no longer comes to me."

"You couldn't be with child?" The sudden hope in his voice made her wince with pain.

"No, my lord. There are other ways to tell if you carry a child. I'm as barren as I ever was," she said bitterly.

"And as lovely," he interposed gently. "You look as young to me as you did when you were a bride."

"My lord," she whispered, her lips trembling.

Indifferent to the fact that it was daylight, that anyone might see them, he drew her into his arms and kissed her deeply. "If love alone could make a child," he said, "we would have a thousand heirs."

For long minutes she nestled in his arms, then drew away.

"But what about Dothan and Meryet?" she asked, trying to put her own emotion aside. "Shall we celebrate as though she were a daughter of the tribe? What gift would you really want?"

"The gift of Dothan's service," Abram said. "I have it already, but if it's sworn to and if the contract is legal, then Eliezer has done something for me, and I won't have to worry that Dothan will ever be lured away."

Because you need an heir, Sarai thought, but she did not say the words.

"And as for celebration," Abram went on, "six days of celebration, certainly, as we would do for a son. Dothan deserves it. But I hope the people will understand that it's Dothan's celebration . . . not Meryet's. It would be different if it were Hagar getting married."

"Why?" The single word came out harshly.

He stared at her with amazement. "Because we've had Hagar since she was a child. She's like a daughter to us. Why would you even ask why?"

"I'm sorry, my lord. I've been thinking about . . . about things which Meryet has brought to my mind. It has me a little confused."

"Well, you must be confused if you think that Meryet and Hagar are equal in our affection and responsibility."

"Do you . . . do you love Hagar?" she asked hesitantly.

He stared at her as though she had lost her mind. "What do you mean, do I love her? She belongs to us, and she's a good and faithful girl. She thinks too much sometimes, but she's like our own child. Don't you feel that?"

"Yes, of course, my lord. You must forgive me. My mind seems to be wooly today."

He laughed. "Then you'd better clean it out somehow. You have a lot to do to get ready for this celebration. It's only a few days away."

"I know," she agreed. "I just wish we had more honey. Some of the date honey has spoiled."

He laughed again. "That's a woman's worry," he announced. "Not mine, fortunately. I don't know any way to sweeten spoiled honey. How many goats and sheep are you going to want killed for eating?"

"It'll be better to just kill a few from day to day. There's no time to cook things elaborately. We'll just roast them. You might set several boys and men to making a trench for roasting."

"Yes, my lady," he said mocking her gently. He kissed her again before he stood to leave. "A wedding's a joyful thing," he added. "I only hope that Dothan will be half as happy as I've been. But he won't be. No one could."

She flushed like a girl. "Go on about your work," she said and he went as meekly as one of her slaves.

He waited until he was safely out of her sight before he even allowed the question to come to the surface of his thoughts. If she *were* too old to bear a child, was there any hope now for a miracle? Any hope at all? Yahweh had promised a son, and Abram believed in the promise. But what of Sarai? Why had Yahweh permitted him to love her so much when he had made her barren?

For five days Abram's tribe celebrated in honor of Dothan and his bride. There was laughter and feasting, story telling and singing. All work, except caring for the animals and preparing food for the people, was put aside. It was a time of joy and merrymaking.

On the last night before Meryet would be led by a group of girls to Dothan's tent to become his wife in fact instead of just in promise, the celebration went on for hours. But finally, at Abram's suggestion, the people went to their own tents to sleep.

Meryet and Hagar, sharing Hagar's pallet for the last time, talked briefly and then a silence fell between them.

"Do you really want to marry Simeon?" Meryet asked in a sudden, soft whisper.

Hagar jumped. She and Meryet had never even discussed Simeon. "How did you know there was any talk of my marrying him?"

"Sarai told me."

Hagar spoke with anger. "Why should she tell you? What are you to Sarai?"

Meryet gave a whispered laugh. "You get excited so easily, Hagar. Listen, I'm not trying to take *your* place with her. But I need my own place."

"Why?"

"Because Dothan isn't really a true heir. You know that and so do I. If Sarai . . . if she were to die, and Abram married again, Dothan could be disinherited in nine months. But if Dothan were a sort of partner, if he were to share with Abram as Lot did, and if I were wiser than Zahavith, then nothing could change our status. Can't you see? I only want to become . . . let's say. . . *necessary* to Sarai. A sort of confidante. But you, Hagar, she thinks of you as her child."

"Does she? Does she really?"

"Of course. Only you're *not* their child—no, don't get angry. There's something I want to say to you before I leave to live with Dothan."

"What?" Hagar asked, her curiosity overcoming her irritation.

"You realize, don't you, that Sarai can't even hope to have a child any more?"

"Of course I realize that," Hagar answered with heat. "I've been in her confidence for years, you know, not days."

"I know," Meryet soothed. "Anyhow, if childbearing is impossible for her now—if she can't even hope from month to month any longer—than how is Abram to get his promised heir?"

"I don't know," Hagar admitted. "I do believe in Yahweh, but I don't know if he can perform *that* kind of miracle."

"There are ways of helping Yahweh," Meryet said smoothly. "The promise has never been that Sarai would bear a child. It's just Abram's stubborn love for her that has kept him married only to her all these years."

"What are you saying?" Hagar was truly shocked. If Yahweh had promised Abram a son, then that surely meant the son would be born of Sarai.

"I'm saying," Meryet went on in her soft whisper, "that, according to everything I've heard, Yahweh promised that it would be Abram's seed that would grow and multiply. Nothing has ever been said about who would bear the seed."

"Meryet!"

"Don't be stupid, Hagar. Dothan and I have just been told what's involved in a marriage contract. If a wife is barren, it's her duty to give her own slave to her husband to bear his child."

The silence stretched between them for so long that Meryet began to wonder if Hagar had heard what she said.

"Surely you know that," Meryet finally said impatiently.

"I've known it was done." Hagar's whisper was faint.

"Well?"

"But not Abram. He and Sarai are different."

"Nonsense!" Meryet said. "Abram is just like any other man."

"No, he isn't. He's . . . he's been chosen by Yahweh to lead his people."

"*And* to have sons," Meryet said shrewdly. "Sarai should have given you to him several years ago. If she'd been smart enough to know there aren't really any miracles, she would have done it."

"Me?"

"Oh, Hagar! Who else?"

"I don't want to talk about it," Hagar said and turned onto her side, away from Meryet. "Go to sleep."

But Meryet raised herself onto her elbow and shook Hagar's shoulder. "Don't be altogether foolish. It's not for you to say, anyhow. If Sarai decides to do it, you'll have to obey, but it will be better if you're prepared, so you can help her."

Hagar turned back. "You mean you've talked to *her* about it?"

"Of course. And she's thinking about it. She loves Abram that much," Meryet said.

Hagar didn't answer, but this time Meryet let the silence go on. She had said all that needed to be said.

There was no wedding ceremony in Abram's tribe. There was only the procession of laughing teasing girls who led Meryet formally from Abram's tent to Dothan's. Meryet, flushed, happy, proud, pretended to pull against their hands, pretended to resist their urgings, acted as though she wanted to escape and run back to the tent of Abram. But while Hagar remembered girls who had truly pulled against their escorts, who had wept at leaving the tents of their parents for a marriage they had not really wanted, she knew that Meryet's actions were all pretense. Few girls had gone to their husbands' tents with more willingness.

When Meryet had finally been pushed into Dothan's tent, when the flaps had been rolled or pulled down, when the last lamp had been blown out, then the girls all made their way back to their own tents, all of them feeling a little lightheaded from the amount of wine consumed and the merriment that had filled the past six days.

Hagar crept into the darkened corner of Abram's tent without even a glance to where Abram and Sarai were already settled for the night.

"Did she go to his tent willingly?" Sarai asked suddenly, raising her voice so it would carry beyond the curtain.

"Oh, she acted as though she didn't want to," Hagar said, coming back into the central part of the tent, "but it was all pretending with Meryet. She's wanted this for a long time."

"Dothan, too," Abram said. "I hadn't realized how much until the girl came back. Maybe he hadn't either. Well, they're together now, so . . . may they know joy!"

"May they know joy," Sarai and Hagar repeated as though a toast had been made.

Hagar went back to her pallet but she couldn't sleep. She felt certain that Sarai was as wakeful as she was. I wonder if she's weeping, Hagar thought. She's probably thinking of Meryet, young and happy, and maybe able to conceive Dothan's child almost immediately. She must be suffering, Hagar thought, and I can't do anything to help her.

Or if she thinks I can help her by having Abram's child, what will it mean to *me*, Hagar wondered. What about Simeon? And what would it be like to lie with Abram, to bear his son?

He's like a father to me, she mused. He's more than a father, she admitted to herself; he's more of a god than Yahweh is!

It's all so easy for Meryet, Hagar's tortured thoughts went on. She schemes and plots and plans, and then she goes safely to Dothan's tent and takes her place as wife of the steward's son. But Sarai and I—we lie awake, torn between Meryet's ideas and Yahweh's promise, not sure which of them will give Abram a son.

14

Hagar was so tortured by conflicting emotions for the next few weeks that she hardly spoke to anyone. She did her work and then fled to her sanctuary and sat looking out over the rocky land. She could not think coherently, and she found it impossibly to pray.

One day Sarai, who rarely left the camp compound, came slowly up the path to Hagar's hideaway. The location of the place was no secret, and it was only Abram's and Sarai's generosity and tolerance which had allowed Hagar to think of the spot as her own. Out of breath from her climbing, Sarai stood in the patch and looked at Hagar who was so absorbed in her own thoughts that she hadn't even heard Sarai's approach. Seeing the girl in this sun bright, silent place, Sarai was suddenly aware of her in a new way. She was really almost beautiful, Sarai thought. I've been seeing her as the scrawny little child she was when she came. I hadn't realized how she has changed.

"Hagar!" Sarai said, and the girl jumped.

"Oh, my lady," Hagar gasped. "I didn't hear you."

"What do you find to do up here?" Sarai asked, almost crossly. "There's no one to talk to and nothing new to see."

"Oh, no, my lady," Hagar cried, eager to defend the place she loved. "It's new every day. The sky changes with the seasons, and there are flowers after even the smallest rain, and even these tiny lizards which live under the stones are interesting. As for no one to talk to, I like being alone. I can think better."

"Think about what?"

Hagar spread her hands. "Oh, everything. And nothing."

Sarai moved over to sit on the rocky ledge where Abram had once sat. "You're an odd one," she said. "Do you ever think about Yahweh?"

"Oh, yes, my lady," Hagar said eagerly. "I once made a sacrifice to Yahweh here. It wasn't a true sacrifice, but my lord Abram said that Yahweh would never despise it."

Sarai nodded. "That was the time you smashed the little god."

"Did he tell you about it?" Hagar asked in surprise.

"Yes. He was pleased."

Hagar was sure that Sarai had not come to talk about the hideaway and what Hagar did in it, but perhaps it was difficult for her to approach the true purpose of her coming.

"I'm sorry I can't offer you water, my lady," Hagar said. "I know it's a hot climb up here. Is there anything I can do for you?"

Sarai looked steadily at the girl. "Do you remember a promise you made to me a long, long time ago when I asked you if you would like to serve me?"

Hagar's heart began to pound. "Yes, my lady. I said I would do anything for you. Anything."

"Is it still true?"

"Oh, my lady, you know it's true," Hagar cried. "Anything. I'd do anything."

"Even bear my lord a son?" The words came out abruptly, harshly.

Hagar knew a sudden gratitude to Meryet. If she had been totally unprepared for this moment, her own astonishment would have made her insensitive to Sarai's pain.

"If you and my lord believe it to be Yahweh's will," Hagar said.

Sarai turned her head away and bit her lip. "It wouldn't be

easy for me," she confessed.

"Oh, my lady," Hagar ran to where Sarai sat and knelt beside her, pressing her face into Sarai's lap. "Oh, my lady, I know how hard this must be. Yahweh himself must stand amazed before your courage."

"Hush, girl, that's irreverent," Sarai said, but her hand came out to touch the dark head in her lap.

"Does my lord agree?" Hagar asked, her voice muffled.

"I don't know. I haven't even talked to him about it," Sarai admitted.

Hagar's head jerked up. "Then why speak to me? It's not for me to refuse or consent."

"That's true," Sarai said, "but I had to know how you felt about it. I mean I had to know...," and her voice trailed away.

Hagar searched for words to help Sarai, but there were no words available.

"I wanted to bear my lord a son," Sarai cried. "I never once thought the promise couldn't mean me."

"I didn't either," Hagar said. "I think of you and my lord as being ... well, almost one person."

Sarai looked at her gratefully. "But Yahweh has spoken only of Abram's seed," she said. "Meryet is right about that. And I'm too old to hope any longer. I'm going to speak to him, Hagar. I'm going to tell him that you're willing to serve as the ... the vessel to bear the seed."

For a second, Hagar felt a surge of resentment. She was more than a clay pot, more than a jar used to carry corn. But in Sarai's mind of course she would be no more than that.

"My lady," she murmured and bent her head submissively.

"My lord," Sarai said several days later when Abram woke from his midday nap, "would you walk with me beyond the tents? I want to speak to you ... alone. Where no one can hear."

Abram stared at her with sleepy astonishment. She had

never made such a suggestion before, and if the people were to see them walking together in the middle of the day, they would wonder and perhaps even gossip.

"It's very important, my lord," Sarai insisted. "But I can't talk to you here . . . where Hagar comes and goes . . . where Meryet might stop in."

"Come then," he said.

She did not speak until they had reached a place far away from the camp.

"Stop here," Abram commanded. "It's not safe for you to go further."

"Shall we sit on this rock, my lord?" Sarai asked, and they sat together.

"Well?" he said after the silence had stretched tautly between them.

"My lord, Yahweh has promised you a son. No—don't speak. Listen to me. Yahweh has promised *you* a son, but he has never said that the child must be mine."

"This is ridiculous," Abram began, but she silenced him with her hand across his lips.

"If you had loved me less," Sarai said, "you would have taken another wife long ago. You know you would."

"Are you telling me to take a second wife?" Abram demanded. "Because if you are, I won't even discuss it with you."

"Not a second wife, my lord. I'm not brave enough for that."

He took her hand, lifted it to his lips and pressed a kiss into the palm.

"But my slave, my lord." Sarai went on, saying the words quickly before her courage failed. "My slave to bear a son."

"Your slave? Hagar?"

"Yes, my lord."

Abram stared at Sarai with a baffled expression on his face. "But I've practically promised her to Simeon."

"You've given Simeon more than enough, my lord. Certainly Yahweh's promise is more important than a promise to a stranger."

"She's . . . she's almost like a daughter," Abram argued.

"I'm not suggesting that you love her, my lord. Only that you give her a child to bear."

Abram looked at Sarai, and in that moment they were both remembering the lie to the Pharaoh, the risk they took to save Abram's life.

"I don't know," Abram said. "I don't know if it's Yahweh's will."

"Does Yahweh expect you to wait forever for the promised child? Will Yahweh give me a child when I'm old?"

Abram sighed and turned away. He *did* believe that, he knew. He believed that Yahweh could do anything. But Sarai was right, too. There had never been anything specifically said about Sarai in Yahweh's promise. Only that Abram himself would have sons.

"I don't know, my love," he said at last. "I don't know."

"Perhaps Yahweh would speak to you again," she suggested.

"I don't call him, you know. I'm not the one who can summon his voice."

"But if you tried," she persisted. "If Yahweh cares, and if he knows what we're thinking, surely he'll speak to you."

"I'll try," Abram said at last. "If he definitely says no, then you'll simply have to have faith."

"But if he says yes?"

"He may not give a definite answer."

"Stop avoiding my question," she cried hotly. "If Yahweh says yes—or if he leaves the decision to you—will you take Hagar?"

"Do you really want me to?"

She lifted her chin, and he saw again, as he saw every day, that the years had only faintly dimmed her beauty. She was still the loveliest thing he had ever known. "I want you to have a son," she said.

"Then . . . if Yahweh doesn't forbid it," he said but did not complete the statement.

"Thank you, my lord." She stood as if to walk away. Then she hesitated and flung herself into his arms, clinging to him as though they had been separated for months. "And you'll always love me, won't you?" she cried.

"Always," he said, swept away by the intensity of her need. "Always, always."

The hot day moved silently on, but they were aware of nothing but each other and their love.

15

Abram had been praying all night, and he felt the air begin to freshen with the coming of day, but still Yahweh had not spoken. Despair started to build up in him, and Abram's tears fell as he called on God.

"Hear me, O Lord. I'm alone and frightened. I don't know what to do. I don't know what to do."

Don't be afraid.

The Voice was always totally unexpected even when Abram had been pleading for its coming.

"My Lord and my God," Abram gasped, wiping his tears away with his hands.

Don't be afraid, Abram. I am your shield, and your reward will be great.

"But what can you give me since I am still childless?" Abram dared to ask. "You haven't given me any seed. There's only Dothan, the son of Eliezer of Damascus, who was born in my tents. Is he to be my heir, Lord?"

The son of Eliezer will not be your heir.

"But, Lord...."

Abram's protests were pushed aside.

Your own son shall be your heir.

My own son, Abram thought, and felt hope swell in his heart.

The Voice spoke again.

Look toward heaven and number the stars if you are able to
number them. So shall your descendents be.

Obediently Abram looked up. The western sky was still
dark and the stars shone against the satin blackness. Like a
child, Abram began to count, and in only a minute his eyes
were dazzled and blinded by the multitude of jeweled
sparks above him.

"I can't possibly count them," he protested.

The Voice repeated the promise.

So shall your descendents be.

Abram fell on his face in sudden awe. There was no
question in him of how or when; he simply believed.

After a few minutes of silence, he lifted his head, planning
to ask who would bear the promised child. Would a miracle
happen to Sarai, or was it his duty to take Hagar and begin
the lineage that Yahweh had promised?

But the Voice cut into his thought before the question
could be shaped.

I am the Lord who brought you from Ur of the Chaldeans, to give
you this land to possess.

The problem of Sarai and Hagar fled from Abram's mind.
He heard only the words of promise, and he ached for a
confirmation, a sign.

"How am I to know that I possess the land?" Abram
asked.

Bring me a heifer three years old, a she-goat three years old, a
ram three years old, a turtledove and a young pigeon.

The Voice stopped.

Abram gaped at the heavens where the eastern sky was
slowly paling.

"Am I to sacrifice them?" Abram asked, but although the
Voice did not speak, he knew this was not Yahweh's inten-
tion.

Then I'll bring them, Abram thought, and Yahweh will tell
me what to do. Ordinary sacrifices had been made with little
or no ritual. As long as the burning flesh sent its smoke up
toward the heavens, Abram had felt his duty had been

performed. But there was something more expected from him now. He was sure of it.

But first, Abram's thoughts went on, I must cleanse myself to get ready for whatever it is Yahweh wants me to do. He went to the watering hole and stripped himself and bathed, washing even his hair and beard. Then he walked, with only his shawl wrapped around his hips, to his tent where he found clean robes to cover his nakedness. He covered his head but he put nothing on his feet. So will I stand in humility before my God, he reflected.

Then, until the sky was bright with day, he knelt by his tent in speechless adoration. He was not even aware that Sarai and Hagar had come to kneel beside him, then had crept back into the tent, awed and frightened by the radiance which shone in his face.

At full daylight, Abram stood.

"Will you eat, my lord?" Sarai faltered.

He didn't even hear her. He moved as a man in a dream over to the animals and chose a heifer, a she-goat and a ram, all without blemish and all three years old. He tied ropes around their necks and then put a glossy turtledove and a fine young pigeon into a bag. The birds lay quiescent in his hands, and none of the animals cried out or struggled against him.

Still unspeaking, Abram led the animals to the place where Yahweh had spoken to him.

As though each motion were being dictated to him, Abram slit the throat of each animal and laid it on the ground to bleed and then he wrung the necks of the two birds. There was no outcry or struggle, and Abram was selfishly glad. He had been a shepherd so long that even killing for food was unpleasant for him. He did it because a man must eat, but he had never learned to enjoy it.

When the animals had stopped bleeding, Abram cut the carcasses in two, splitting them in equal parts. The task was long and laborious, and the heat of the day made the work even more difficult. But Abram persevered until he had finished, and it was then that he began to dimly understand what he was doing.

With the deliberate motions of a ritual, he laid the pieces of the carcasses in two rows. On one side he placed half of the heifer and the she-goat and the ram and then several feet away, but parallel to the first row, he placed the second half of each animal. The bodies of the birds were left whole and placed at one end.

Abram was covered with blood and sweat when the task was finished, but there was a look about him which kept other men from offering to help. Many came to see what he was doing, but each one went back to his own task after only a minute or two. It was so evident that what was occurring was something between Abram and his God that no one even dreamed of interfering.

"Now what, Lord?" Abram asked, weary and out of breath.

He heard no voice, but it seemed to him that he was supposed to wait without sleeping until Yahweh would speak again. After the long night of prayer, his eyes were heavy, but he forced himself to stay awake and alert.

That these actions were to lead to a covenant, he now had no doubt. The killing and dividing of a carcass was a traditional covenant ritual, and it was usual for those who entered into a covenant to walk between the pieces of flesh. But how Yahweh would carry out his part of the ritual was something Abram's tired mind could not even grapple with.

The sudden approach of several vultures was a shock. Of course, they came when a carcass lay even a few minutes in this heat, but Abram was not prepared for the scavengers. His heart leaped in apprehension as the first bird began its long dive toward the split body of the ram. Abram grabbed his staff and ran wildly toward the diving birds, brandishing the stick and shouting.

The vultures continued to wheel soundlessly in the sky, coming lower from time to time until Abram drove them away.

His arms grew heavier and heavier. The hours of fasting and prayer and work were taking their toll. His shouting at the vultures was reduced to a hoarse croak, and he knew a real terror that the slaughtered animals would be desecrated or consumed by the scavengers.

Suddenly he was aware of long strips of cloth being flapped in the air, and he saw the vultures wheel away, screeching in fear.

He turned his head, wondering who had come to his aid, and he saw Sarai. Could that mean that she was the one to be involved in the covenant? But beyond Sarai, also waving furiously, was Hagar.

Abram dropped wearily onto the sand, content for a few minutes to let the women help him. He had not realized until he looked up at the wildly waving scarves and the frightened birds that the day was drawing to a close and the sun was going down. Absorbed in his work and the effort of keeping the scavengers away, he had been completely unaware of the passing hours. But now he was suddenly overcome with a fatigue so deep he could not force himself to his feet again. Sarai and Hagar would keep the birds away, he thought, and felt his eyes close and darkness flow into him.

Sarai and Hagar did not speak. The fluttering scarves were all that were necessary to keep the vultures away, and so they concentrated on the effort that was needed to keep the scarves moving. Then, suddenly, the birds were gone, disappearing into the evening sky.

Sarai took a deep breath and dropped onto the sand. She wasn't sure what she had been doing or why; she only knew that it was important to Abram that the carcasses be kept untouched, and Hagar had seemed to understand, too. They smiled wearily at each other and then turned to look at Abram.

He lay in a sort of stupor, but his eyes were open, and even as they stared at him, he began to speak. It was not his own voice that they heard, but a hoarse cry which spoke of things that neither woman understood.

"The Lord has spoken," Abram said in his voice of terrible prophecy, "that my descendents will be sojourners in a land that is not theirs, and will be slaves there. They will be oppressed for four hundred years!"

Abram's eyes held a darkness.

"But Yahweh has promised that judgment will be brought on that nation," Abram went on, "and afterward my people shall come out with great possessions.

"But as for me," Abram said more normally, his voice softening, "I will go to my fathers in peace, I shall be buried in a good old age. And my people shall come back here in the fourth generation, for the iniquity of the Amorites is not yet complete."

His voice ceased and his eyes closed. Sarai and Hagar looked at him but made no move to touch or wake him. Without even glancing at each other, they left Abram and went back to the tent. They had heard a mystery and perhaps it was not for their eyes to see what came after.

Abram woke when it was full dark and he felt as refreshed and rested as though he had slept for hours. And he knew exactly what he had to do.

He touched the young pigeon with his finger, identifying himself with it, and then walked slowly between the rows of carcasses. With this action, he bound himself to Yahweh; he was, from this hour on, committed to obedience to his God.

But he did not know whether there could be a matching sign from Yahweh, for Yahweh no longer walked on earth as he had once done in the Garden of Eden.

But when Abram seated himself and looked toward the animals, he felt astonishment run through him. A light, like a flaming torch or a smoking fire pot, moved between the rows of carcasses. Surely it hesitated briefly by the turtle-dove, and just as surely it moved along the same path that Abram had walked.

"My Lord!" Abram whispered, his mouth dry.

And the Voice surged through the night with promise.

*To your descendents I give this land, from the river of Egypt to
the great Euphrates.*

The Voice went on, defining the boundaries of the land
that would belong to Abram's sons and their sons after them.
And Abram listened, knowing that by this act of covenant
Yahweh had committed himself to his people.

It was several days before Sarai dared approach Abram
with the question that had been eating at her. Abram had
gathered the tribe together to tell them of the promises of
Yahweh, repeating the words over and over until even the
smallest child knew them by heart. But he had said nothing
about her suggestion that Hagar bear his child, and at first
she was afraid to question him.

When the dazed look finally left his eyes, however; when
he began to move and speak normally, even to grumbling if
there were no dates for him to eat before he slept, she felt her
time had come.

"My lord," she murmured one night, "My lord, what did
Yahweh tell you?"

"I've repeated a score of times what he told me." Abram's
voice was sleepy and irritated.

"But not about . . . about Hagar. You haven't mentioned
that."

"He didn't tell me," Abram answered shortly.

"Did you ask?"

"Not exactly."

"Why didn't you? You know how important it is!" she
wailed.

"Shh! She'll hear you," he whispered.

"Well, why didn't you?" she persisted.

"It didn't seem right. Not the right time, perhaps. Or not
the right question."

"Then the decision has to be yours," she said firmly. "The
promise of a child can't be ignored, can it?"

"Sarai—I'm tired. We'll talk about it again."

"We'll talk about it *now.*"

The insistence of her voice fretted at his nerves. Why couldn't she go to sleep?

"All right. Talk."

"Will you take Hagar and give her a child?" Sarai asked patiently.

"What would Hagar think about it?" he hedged.

"What does that matter?" she countered. "And besides, she's willing."

"You mean you've discussed it with her already? Without getting my permission?"

She moved away a little, stung by the anger in his voice.

"I needed to know how she felt," she said sullenly.

Abram moved his shoulders restlessly. When he spoke, his voice was irritated. "Well, since you and Meryet and Hagar all think it's such a wonderful idea, it would seem that what I want is totally unimportant. So . . . all right. I'll do it."

Sarai was silent for a long time, and then she spoke in a voice which was resolute and calm. "She'll give you a son, my lord. I'm sure of it. We'll talk to her in the morning."

"*You'll* talk to her in the morning," Abram snapped.

"All right. *I'll* talk to her," Sarai agreed. "We'll give her her own tent, and . . . ."

Abram groaned and pulled Sarai against him so that her words were muffled against his chest. "Don't talk," he begged. "Whatever you and Hagar do—and Meryet, too, I suspect—will be all right with me. And if the girl conceives, then I'll have to accept the fact that it's probably Yahweh's will. But for tonight, my love, let it be."

"Yes, my lord," she whispered.

For a long time after he slept, Sarai lay awake. But she did not weep. To have wept would have been to admit that what she was planning was wrong, and she was sure that this was the only way Abram could father a child. Yahweh had said

Abram would have a son, but nothing had come of the promise. Well, if Yahweh would not give Abram a son, then she and Hagar would.

PART THREE

Now Sarai Abram's wife
bare him no children; and
she had an handmaid, an
Egyptian, whose name was
Hagar... and gave her
to her husband Abram....

GENESIS 16:1, 3b

16

There was no troop of laughing girls to lead Hagar to the new tent that would be hers. There were only Meryet and Sarai, carrying pillows and rugs that they could spare, sharing a few hangings and baskets. Hagar helped them, but she found no pleasure in the new goat-hair tent that several of the men had pitched far enough from Abram's large tent to be private but close enough to seem to belong to it. She was empty of feeling, except for a kind of apprehension that gnawed at her stomach. If she had married Simeon, she thought, she would have been a wife, the head of a household. If she had even married one of the common slaves, she would have understood her position. But to be given to Abram was an uncertain thing at best. She was neither wife nor concubine, nor, if she conceived, a slave in the ordinary sense.

"There!" Meryet said at last, "Does it please you?"

Hagar looked at the small tent without actually seeing it. "It's fine."

"There's no cooking place," Sarai said briskly, "but you'll eat in our tent as usual."

"Oh, no," Hagar cried involuntarily, stung out of her seeming indifference. "That would be too hard for you, my lady. My lord will eat with you, but to have to look at me and know. . . and know. . . no, I'll go and eat with the slaves."

"Hagar, listen to me," Sarai said sharply. "My heart has already broken over this thing—over the fact that I can't bear my lord a son. What I'm doing, I'm doing for him. He doesn't come to you with love—or even desire. It may be," she added, "that he won't be able to lie with you after all. But I suppose that's up to you." The last words came bitterly.

Hagar felt pain dart through her. She had obediently, even willingly, given up any hope for a life of her own to do what Sarai wanted. Now to be taunted was more cruel than she could bear without retaliation. "I'm not experienced where men are concerned, my lady," she said. "Perhaps you could teach me what to do."

Sarai's eyes blazed and her hand raised as though she would strike the girl who faced her, but then she forced herself to be calm.

"Let Meryet teach you," she said and turned and left the girls standing alone in the new tent.

"She's upset," Meryet soothed.

"I *know* she's upset. She loves him. I'm not a fool, Meryet. But I deserve some kindness, too." Hagar said.

"She'll be kinder, once the thing is accomplished," Meryet predicted. "Once you're pregnant, she'll think of you as a sort of cradle for the baby until it's delivered into her arms. Then the child will be hers, and she won't resent you any more. It's the idea of Abram coming into this tent tonight that is simply tearing her apart."

"It's tearing me apart, too," Hagar muttered.

"Oh, now, listen. It's not so terrible. All you have to do is. . . ."

Hagar thrust up her hands as if to push the words away. "Don't instruct me as though—as though you were teaching me to weave."

She flung herself away from Meryet's astonishment and ran swiftly up into the hills. She raced along the familiar path, her breath sobbing in her throat, hardly able to see the stones under her feet for the tears which blinded her.

Nobody cares about *me*, she cried silently. I'm not even

sure that Simeon cares, and now he can't have me. I won't know how to please my lord, and I may not even be able to bear a child. I may be as barren as Sarai is.

She reached the little corrie she loved and flung herself down on the sunbaked ground. Not since she had first huddled weeping in the Pharaoh's court had she cried like this, letting the sobs tear out of her throat, making no effort to stop the tears.

"Help me, oh, help me," she cried in her anguish. "Yahweh, I need someone to help me."

Gradually, the terrible weeping began to diminish, and then she heard the sound of feet on the path. It was probably Meryet with her plans and advice.

"Go away," Hagar said, her face still hidden against her arms. "Just go away."

"Not until I've talked to you."

"My lord!" Hagar gasped and struggled to get up from the ground.

Abram made no effort to help her but only stood patiently until she had wiped her wet face with the hem of her robe and had smoothed her hair with her shaking hands. When she felt that she could bear to face him, she made a gesture to the rocky ledge that served as a place to sit.

"Will you sit, my lord?"

He nodded gravely and moved over to the ledge. "You, too," he said. "Sit down here."

Obediently she sat beside him, but there was no way she could stop the sobs that caught in her throat with a childish sound.

"My lord?" she asked at last.

"Why are you crying?" he said. "Are you so frightened?"

"Oh, no, not frightened, my lord. Or . . . at least not frightened of *you*."

"Sarai said that Meryet insists you won't even let anyone instruct you in . . . being a wife."

"But I'm not to be a wife, my lord," she said steadily.

"A sort of wife," he insisted. "If you bear my child, you'll be cared for in this tribe as a second wife."

She only bent her head. She might be cared for as a second wife, but that changed nothing.

"Hagar, listen to me. You know I love Sarai," Abram began.

"Oh, my lord, of course I know. Haven't I seen you together for years? Don't I know how you look at her ... and she at you? You don't have to tell *me*," she cried.

"Perhaps not. But I want to talk to you about it. And don't interrupt ... just listen. I love Sarai and I had hoped she would bear the son Yahweh promised. It hasn't worked out that way. So she ... we've decided that *you* would bear the promised child. Can you possibly think of it as an honor?"

"Oh, yes, my lord. I. . . ."

"No, wait. I'm not finished. I've got to be honest with you, child. I've been honest with you far too long to change now. Because I love Sarai, I can't love you ... that way."

She opened her mouth to speak but he waved her to silence.

"But ... as a man wants a woman, I can want you. And if a child is born, the child will be the result of ... sharing. Not rape."

The intensity of his voice told her how important this was to him.

"It never occurred to me that you would ... rape me, my lord. I was afraid that I would be so undesirable you wouldn't be able ... able to do what Sarai wants," she admitted.

He laughed. "You don't have much regard for yourself. You're very pretty, you're young—and I'm a man. It will be all right; believe me, it will."

She had thought her weeping was finished, but his gentleness flooded her heart and spilled over in tears.

"Don't cry," he said. Almost clumsily, he reached for her and pulled her against his chest. His hand patted her back and she felt the strong, sturdy beating of his heart under her cheek.

They were silent for a long time, and gradually her tears diminished and then stopped. But still he held her, and she began to relax against him, feeling a sense of comfort in his arms. It wasn't going to be so bad, she thought.

His hand moved tentatively along her shoulder and down her arm. Then, suddenly, he put his fingers under her chin and lifted her face to his. She felt drowned by her tears and knew that she must look wretched.

"I'm sorry, my lord," she whispered. "I'm sorry for how I look."

"You look like a whipped child," he said ruefully. "But when you wash your face, you'll look better."

"And tonight," she said bravely, determined to say what she wanted him to know, "tonight it will be dark, my lord, and you . . . you can pretend it's Sarai with you."

His face softened with a quick compassion. "Poor little one," he said.

He bent his head to hers and kissed her. At first, her mouth was still and cool under his, but something moved in her heart. This was Abram kissing her, her benefactor, her master. Instinctively, her lips softened and moved in response to his.

He lifted his head, and his eyes were merry. "You'll do," he said. "And in the dark—or out of it—you'll be Hagar to me."

"My lord," she said. There was nothing he could have said that would have pleased her more.

"Don't cry any more," he said. "Pray if you want to, but don't cry. Pray that between us, we'll make a child for Yahweh. Will you do that?"

"Yes, my lord."

He stood to leave. "Oh, and I want you to understand how it will be. I'll share your tent—and only yours—until a child is conceived."

"But what about my lady? She. . . ," Hagar began.

"Sarai understands. There mustn't be any wasting of the seed. If Yahweh wants me to have a son, then we must think only of making a child. Do you understand?"

"Yes, my lord," she said meekly.

"Then . . . do as Sarai says. Eat in your regular place. Live as you've always lived—except that at night we'll share your tent."

"Yes, my lord."

He made a gesture of farewell with his hand and turned to leave, but suddenly stopped. "Why wouldn't you let Meryet talk to you?"

She felt her face burning. "I thought . . . thought that you would teach me, my lord."

He smiled with genuine affection. "Thank you," he said. "That's gratifying for an old man to hear."

It was on her lips to protest that he wasn't old, but she was afraid it would sound coy. So she only smiled at him and watched him stride down the path.

For a long time after Abram left, Hagar sat in complete stillness. Her mind went over and over the words that had been spoken and the things that had happened while Abram was with her. No other man, she thought solemnly, could have done so much to comfort a girl in her position. She remembered the strength of his arms and the warmth of his lips. But most of all she remembered the words, "you will be Hagar to me."

With such a man, she thought, a woman would be safe.

And then she thought, How can Sarai give him up? Hagar was not at all sure that under similar circumstances she could do what Sarai was doing.

It was late afternoon when Hagar went back to the tents. She felt weary from her weeping, dazzled and drained from the beating of the sun. But there was no longer any fear in her, and she supposed her face would reflect her calmness.

Sarai greeted her with the usual words. "You're back at last. It's a good thing there was no work to do."

"I'm sorry, my lady," Hagar said.

"It's all right this time. Tomorrow there won't be any time

for dreaming. There's new wool for spinning and grain to be ground," Sarai announced.

Hagar felt a sense of gratitude. It was Sarai's way of saying that life would go on, that their whole existence was not going to be changed.

"Yes, my lady. I'll do anything you ask me to."

"Fine. You can start by getting out bread and figs and goat's cheese for supper. My lord should be in from talking to Eliezer in a few minutes."

"Eliezer?" Hagar's voice was startled. She had assumed Abram had gone up to the hills to check on the flocks after he left her.

"Of course, Eliezer. When Abram comes to your tent tonight, it will be with the knowledge of everyone. This isn't a secretive, dishonest thing we're planning," Sarai said.

"I . . . I'm honored, my lady," Hagar murmured.

It seemed that Sarai wanted to say something, but she turned away. "Fix the food," she said. "Meryet will be over after supper to help you bathe and put on fresh clothes. You understand . . . I . . . I can't do it."

"I understand," Hagar murmured. She wanted to run to Sarai, to comfort her, to tell her that she loved her. But that would have been presumptuous. So, "I'll get the food," was all she said.

Neither Meryet nor Hagar had much to say during the time they were together. Hagar wanted to be left alone with her thoughts, and Meryet seemed to sense this.

It was only when Meryet was smoothing Hagar's hair that she spoke lightly. "This reminds me of the night I fixed you to go into Sarai's tent for the first time. Do you remember? You were such an angry little thing, jerking away from my hands, fussing about everything I did."

But Hagar didn't laugh with her. "You were planning even then," she pointed out. "You knew right from the beginning that you could use me profitably."

"Would you have preferred that I just pushed you in with

the rest of the slaves? Would you have preferred the things that happen to little slave girls who have no one to take care of them?" Meryet's voice was suddenly bitter. "You dream too much, little cousin. You want life to be good to you, but you're unwilling to pay the price. And nothing comes free. Or haven't you figured that out yet?"

"I figured it out long ago," Hagar said, the bitterness of her words matching Meryet's.

"Good." Meryet was brisk. "Then pay the price and do it willingly. Abram is a great man. You saw how great the night King Melchizedek came. And not only great in the plan of Yahweh—he was able to deal with King Bera and King Birsha as though *they* were the nomads and *he* was royalty. And you've been chosen to bear his child. What more do you want?"

"I don't know," Hagar said sullenly. "I don't want to talk about it."

So—don't talk," Meryet snapped, and her hands were far from gentle as she pulled Hagar's hair back from her face.

There was no lamp lit in Hagar's tent, and Abram stumbled over a tent rope as he approached. The quick, earthy word he uttered was oddly reassuring to Hagar. He was just as he had always been—quick tempered, good, strong, weak. Nothing was going to change that.

"Hagar," he said. "Are you there?"

"Yes, my lord." Her voice trembled in spite of herself.

"Where?" he grumbled. "Put out your hand. Why didn't you leave the lamp lit?"

"I . . . I wasn't really sure you'd come, my lord," she admitted.

"Nonsense! There. Take my hand. All right, I've found the pillow. Wait until I take off my robe."

He lay down beside her, and she lay rigid, waiting for his next move. But he only stretched and sighed with weariness.

"One of the ewes dropped a lamb," he said. "Completely

out of season. We had a hard time with her."

"Is she all right?" Hagar asked, pulled out of her apprehension by the mundane conversation. "Is the lamb healthy?"

"Both well," Abram said comfortable. "A birthing is always a good thing. First there's nothing—only pain and the animal's fear—and then, like a miracle, the lamb is there—whole and perfect and yelling for food."

They laughed together in the old familiar way.

"Your hair smells sweet," he said. "After the stink of the fold, you smell good."

"I'm glad, my lord," she said.

"If I have to lie with someone," he said as though he were just discovering the fact himself, "I'm glad it's you. Here, put your head on my shoulder. There. Are you all right?"

"Yes, my lord."

"Then . . . ," he said and put his lips on hers.

Simeon's kisses, she thought dazedly, had not been like this. Nothing in all her life had prepared her for the way she would feel when Abram held her in his arms.

17

The only sound in the still morning was the click of the clay spindles as Sarai and Hagar spun the woolen thread. Although several weeks had gone by since Abram had gone to Hagar's tent, the two women were still a little uncomfortable when they were together, so the conversation which had once rattled freely between them was now more often stilted than casual.

"My lady," Hagar said at last.

"Yes?" Sarai's face was quiet and withdrawn.

"My lady, may I tell you something?" Hagar asked.

"Haven't you always been able to tell me things?"

"Yes, my lady, but this is . . . different." Hagar hesitated and then went on. "Do you remember the day I found you crying so terribly—just after we had left Egypt—when you had just discovered that you hadn't conceived a child?"

Sarai's face warmed. "I do remember. I remember how you seemed to understand even though you were only a child."

"But I didn't truly understand, my lady. I just couldn't stand to see you cry," Hagar admitted. "Only . . . well, I wanted you to know that now I understand a little better."

Sarai looked at her inquiringly, and Hagar helped with the words that Sarai seemed unable to say. "I've just discovered that I'm not pregnant yet," she said.

Sarai drew in her breath with a long sound like a sigh. "You're young," she said at last. "Meryet hasn't conceived yet either. It may very well take a few months. I was prepared for that."

"I'm sorry, my lady," Hagar said humbly.

"I'm hardly the one to be critical if another woman doesn't conceive in a week . . . or a month. Or even two or three. I'll be patient and . . . and you must be, too."

"Yes, my lady," Hagar said but she kept her eyes on her work. She didn't dare look directly at Sarai for fear her mistress would see the relief and joy in her face. She wanted, more than anything in the world, to bear Abram's son, but selfishly she hoped that it would take several months at least for the seed to take root.

For the first time, Hagar was discovering the joy of having someone she loved entirely to herself. Abram shared his thoughts and accounts of his activities with her, and she was just beginning to dare to open her heart a little and tell him some of the things that she had never shared with anyone before. To be able to talk with Abram, held in his arms, free to touch his face with her fingers or lay her head against his chest and know that he wouldn't draw away was a happiness beyond anything she had ever known. Every day she told herself realistically that this was a temporary thing, that it was only because Abram was who he was that he treated her as though she mattered, that in a few days or a few weeks, or at most a few months, she would lose the precious hours of sharing. But her heart hoped for as many nights as possible.

Sarai gave a small sigh. "I suppose the one who has to be patient is my lord. I know how difficult this is for him. He looks older; have you noticed?"

The tone was not really malicious, but Hagar's quick anger blazed.

"If my lord is suffering and aging under his hardship, he doesn't show that side of it to me," Hagar retorted, hardening her heart against the pain she was inflicting.

Sarai stared at her. "You can't possibly believe he enjoys being with you?"

"*You* can't possibly believe he doesn't?" Hagar said, her voice as cold as Sarai's.

"You should be beaten," Sarai said furiously and it was the first time the threat had been made since Hagar had come to them.

"If you're going to have me beaten," Hagar retorted, "do it *now* when there's absolutely no danger of miscarriage."

Sarai slowly lowered her head. "Go away," she said shakily. "Leave me."

"Gladly," Hagar said and flung her thread aside. She started to run, as she always did, toward the corrie in the hills, but before she had gone many steps, she found her path blocked by Meryet. Hagar tried to push past her, but Meryet held her arm with a grip that would not loosen.

"You fool!" Meryet hissed. "I heard what you were saying—you and my lady. What's the *matter* with you?"

"There's nothing the matter with *me*," Hagar answered sullenly. "You might ask my lady the same thing."

"Hagar, stop it! Come here—back of my tent. I want to talk to you."

Hagar submitted resentfully, and when the girls were far enough away from Sarai, Meryet pushed Hagar down to sit on the ground. She squatted beside her, and her face was fierce.

"You've just admitted to her you're not pregnant," Meryet said. "Don't you know this would be the perfect time for her to change her mind about you?"

"Do you listen to everything that's said in the camp?" Hagar asked sarcastically. "Your ears must be as long as a donkey's ears."

Meryet ignored the insult. "*Does* our lord enjoy being with you?" she asked anxiously.

"*It's none of your business!*"

Meryet pulled back a little from the venom in Hagar's voice. "I'm only worried that you might harm his marriage, and that wouldn't be good for this tribe."

"Harm his marriage," Hagar repeated bitterly. "I could as easily bring Yahweh down from the heavens. But I will *not* be taunted by her!"

"How else can she endure what's happening?" Meryet asked reasonably. "I thought I'd made that clear to you before the first night."

Hagar's anger began to dissipate before Meryet's logic. It was wrong to be insolent to Sarai, and Hagar knew it. She had swallowed a million insolent words over the years; why was she suddenly bereft of ordinary caution and good sense?

"You've got to apologize to her," Meryet ordered.

"I'm sure I could have figured that out for myself," Hagar said, but her voice was still angry. Not for anything in all the world would she admit to Meryet that she was ashamed.

"If you're smart," Meryet said, "you'll try to keep your own feelings out of this. You'll destroy everything if you fall in love with him."

Hagar's heart jerked. The words that she had not even let come into her mind had come out of Meryet's mouth as cool as pebbles. Fall in love with him. . . . Because of course that was exactly what had happened.

And what good would it do her? He was a man who could care about a great many people, but who could be in love with only one. And that was Sarai.

I wish I were dead, Hagar thought wildly. I wish I could run away. I wish the Pharaoh's soldiers had killed me, too. The frantic, tormented thoughts raced through her mind and Meryet watched her shrewdly while the silence grew between them.

"Well, all right, then," Meryet said with resignation. "It's too late. You've already fallen in love with him. Doesn't that make you more than ever anxious to have his child?"

Hagar's head came up, and her eyes met her cousin's.

"What do you mean?" she asked.

"Just what I said before," Meryet said. "You've admitted

you're not pregnant—and you've shown Sarai that you want
her husband. A stupid combination of things to do if you
really want him for a little while longer, if you want the
privilege of being the mother of his firstborn son."

She paused, waiting for her words to sink in.

"It's not hard for slaves to apologize," Meryet suggested.
"They acquire the habit early in life."

Hagar could not help the small, rueful smile that tugged at
the corner of her mouth. For the first time, she felt a tiny
sense of conspiracy with Meryet.

"I'll throw myself at her feet," Hagar said.

Meryet's smile was broad. "We all get wiser as we get
older," she said with relief. "And . . . I'll tell you a secret. I'm
already pregnant. I didn't tell Sarai because it would only
make her feel bad."

"But you'll have to tell her soon," Hagar argued.

Meryet shrugged. "She'll feel better about it if the announcement takes a while. She'll just think the baby has
come early when it's born."

"I'm glad for you," Hagar made herself say. "I hope it'll be
a boy."

Meryet was cheerfully philosophical. "It probably won't
be. But Dothan says an older sister can help a boy."

Hagar smiled, but her heart twisted. Life was so certain for
Meryet.

"I'll go back to my lady now," Hagar said and felt Meryet's
hands pat her back with encouragement.

The short walk to Sarai's tent seemed shorter than usual,
and Hagar wasn't at all sure what she would say when she
stood facing her mistress.

Sarai looked up, her face hard. "I thought I sent you
away."

"My lady," Hagar began, "Oh, my lady, I'm sorry. I'm
truly, truly sorry. It's only . . . only because I know my lord
loves you so much and . . . and I guess I wish someone loved
me that way, too. But I shouldn't have said what I did. I was
wrong. . . ."

The last words were muffled against Sarai's robe as Hagar threw herself on the ground and buried her head in Sarai's lap in the old way.

Sarai sat so still for so long that Hagar began to think she would never reply. What will I do, Hagar thought wildly. If she won't forgive me, what will I do?

"Get up, girl," Sarai said at last. "I shouldn't have said what I said either. I didn't think I'd be jealous. I didn't. But...."

Hagar sat back on her heels and looked at her mistress. "You have no cause to be jealous, my lady," she said dully.

Sarai looked down and bit her lip. "I wish I could believe that," she said. "If what I said to you were really true... if my lord *were* looking older, I wouldn't. But... haven't you noticed? He looks younger every day!"

The last words were said in a voice of rising panic. Hagar's blood jerked like a giant pulse beat, but Meryet's words had been said too recently to be forgotten.

"No, you're wrong, my lady," Hagar said softly. "Haven't you ever noticed? He always looks older when he first wakes, when his hair is all rumpled so that the gray shows more plainly? And you haven't been seeing him like that the last few weeks. You only see him when he's wide awake and dressed and ready for the day. He always looks younger then."

Sarai's face crumpled. "Truly?" she whispered as though she were a child begging for reassurance.

If I could only hate her, Hagar thought fleetingly. It would be so easy if I could just hate her, but I can't. I've loved her too much too long.

"Truly, my lady," Hagar said gently. "It's you he loves. He told me from the beginning."

Sarai tried to blink away her tears, and Hagar's heart squeezed with pity.

"When he's with me," Hagar offered, "he's only gentle and kind. You know him better than anyone, my lady. He couldn't be otherwise. But...," and the next words were hard to say. "But I'm sure that he . . . he pretends you're the one he's with."

Sarai lifted her head with her old pride. "We won't talk about it anymore," she said. "Not at all. When you think a child is conceived, then you'll tell me that. But until then, we'll talk about the spinning or how to fix the food, but nothing more. Do you understand?"

"Yes, my lady."

"Now, come and get at your spinning. You tangled the thread when you threw it. See if you can straighten it."

"Yes, my lady, and thank you. I'm . . . I'm sorry."

"No more," Sarai protested sternly. "No more, I said."

Hagar bent her head submissively and began to straighten the knotted string. How much of what she had said to Sarai was true, she wondered, and how much of it was due to Meryet's warning? Well, it didn't really matter. The important thing was that Abram would continue to come to Hagar's tent and that Sarai's suffering had been lessened.

"Look, my lady," she cried suddenly, "I got it all untangled."

"Good," Sarai said and her smile matched Hagar's. "I'm sure *everything* will be straightened out in time!"

They smiled again and turned to their spinning. Neither of them saw Meryet creep away from the area behind their tent, so neither of them saw the smile of satisfaction that turned up the corners of Meryet's mouth.

18

"My lord," Hagar said in a hesitant whisper.

"Um?" Abram responded, half asleep.

"May I talk to you?"

"Can't it wait?" But he turned toward her and put his arms around her.

"I've been trying to get up the courage to talk to you for three nights. Or four. Only you always fall asleep—or I get too nervous," she said.

He had shared her bed for three months now, and it was perfectly natural for his hands to move gently on her shoulders.

"Poor child," he said as he always did when his fingers encountered the old scars from the whip.

"Are you really awake, my lord?" she asked.

"If I have to be," he grumbled. Then his voice suddenly sharpened. "What do you have to tell me? Does it have anything to do with us?"

"Yes, my lord. The moon is nearly full again, and . . . and. . . ."

"Do you think you're pregnant?" His hands tightened on her shoulders until she almost cried out with the pain.

"I . . . yes, I think so."

His voice was husky when he finally spoke. "Are you certain?"

"Not certain, my lord. No one can be certain, I've heard,

until two months have gone by. But I thought I should tell you."

"Yahweh's name be praised," Abram said, and his voice broke. "And you, little Hagar. How can I ever show my gratitude to you?"

Just love me, she wanted to cry out. Oh, please love me, share your heart with me. But she couldn't say the words. It wasn't that she was too proud to beg for his love. It was that she knew he would have to refuse.

"My lord," she said instead. "I want only to serve you."

"And Sarai, too," he said. "Your obedience to her has been wonderful. I know how happy she's going to be."

"She'll be happiest that you're coming back to her bed," Hagar said before she could stop the words.

Abram was silent. "I'd be a fool, wouldn't I," he said finally, "to pretend that she wouldn't care—or that I haven't missed her? But if I said these had been unhappy weeks, I'd be lying. Can you believe that?"

"Oh, yes, my lord," she whispered, undone by his admission. "I've been too happy to ever believe that you . . . hated me."

He cradled her against him. "Hate you?" he protested. "Nonsense! I've always been fond of you, and now you tell me you might be carrying my child."

His voice was filled with wonder and his hand rested almost reverently on her stomach.

"Will you go back to her tent tomorrow?" she asked at last.

"No, not until you're certain. It would be too hard for her—if I came back and then had to leave her again."

A few more weeks, Hagar thought gratefully, a little longer to have him here beside me.

"Are you happy, my lord?" she asked after a few minutes.

"I'm more than happy," Abram said. "I feel young and strong. I feel that nothing is too difficult for me to do. I was getting old, Hagar. Old and afraid. But you and Yahweh have changed all that. You've given me the one thing in life I've prayed for."

"I shouldn't have told you until I was sure," she said, "but I thought you'd want to go back to Sarai's tent as soon as possible."

"I've told you before," he said severely, "that you think too much. Just be still—in your mind, I mean—and let Yahweh's goodness fill you. Sleep now. Can you sleep?"

"Yes, my lord," she said and wished that this moment could last forever.

Hagar had gone to her private corrie only a few times during the months that Abram had shared her tent. No matter how troubled or angry or sad she was during the day, she knew that night would come when Abram would hold her and talk to her and listen to her.

But on the day following her admission to him that she might be pregnant, she went alone up the steep path. It was time, she decided, to begin to learn to be solitary again. Even though she and Abram had decided not to tell Sarai or Meryet what Hagar suspected until she was sure, Hagar knew that her time of happiness was ending.

The late winter rains were over, and the miraculous spring blossoming of the desert spread a carpet of color at her feet. Life wasn't really ending, she comforted herself, just because Abram would no longer share her tent.

It would have been easier, Hagar thought, if I had never had a time of joy. Better to have gone lonely all my life. But hard on the heels of that thought came another. No, she was wrong. To have had Abram even for a little while was better than not having him at all.

I'll try to be content, Hagar reflected. Maybe Yahweh will give me the grace to be content. Especially if there's going to be a baby. Surely I'll amount to something in the eyes of everyone—even Sarai—if there's going to be a baby.

She sat on the rocky ledge that she considered her own and gazed out over the wide plains. She wondered briefly about Lot and Zahavith and whether things were really as bad as Meryet had said. At least, thanks to Abram and to his

God, this was a decent place where she was. And if she were
being used to fulfill someone else's dream, at least she was
treated with gentleness and respect.

"I hoped I'd find you here."

The words came with no warning, and Hagar felt her
heart jolt with sudden fear.

"Simeon!" she gasped. "Where did you come from?"
How did you get here?"

"I came across the hill, ahead of the rest of my caravan. A
small caravan, but my own." His grin was proud.

"So soon?" she asked, holding him away with her questions.

"Money speaks loudly," he said, "and Abram was generous. Why are we wasting time talking? Come here."

He pulled her to her feet and crushed her against him.
"And what do you mean 'So soon?' " he murmured close to
her face. "It's been forever."

His mouth came down on hers, and she felt every fibre of
her body wincing away from him.

"What's the matter with you?" His voice was harsh with
anger. "Is this how you treat the man you've been promised
in marriage? You didn't act like this when I kissed you
goodbye."

"I'm not promised to you," she said breathlessly.

His hands were rough on her shoulders. "Abram promised me."

"He didn't. He said perhaps."

"Well? What's to change that? He hasn't promised you to
someone else? He isn't the kind of man who would do
something like that. What's the matter with you?"

"Simeon, listen," she begged. "Things have changed.
Something has happened."

"Something has definitely happened," he said hotly. "I go
away, leaving a girl who's warm and soft, and I come back
five months later to find someone who pulls away from me
as though I were something filthy."

"Come and sit down," she said. "Let me talk to you. Let

me try to explain."

"I don't want explanations," he muttered. "I just want *you*." And once more his mouth came down savagely on hers.

A sudden anger gave her the strength to twist away. "You've *got* to listen to me," she said in a brittle voice. "I'm not—not free to marry you."

"You've never been what *I'd* call free," Simeon snapped. "You'd have more hope of freedom with me than . . . or has Abram given you to Dothan, after all?"

"Dothan's married to Meryet."

Simeon nodded. "And as it should be. So what's different about you?"

She looked at his face and knew a tiny touch of fear. He was very angry, and he had certainly never been trained in the ways of gentleness.

"Abram's God has promised that Abram should have a son," she began, hoping to make her story convincing.

But Simeon interrupted. "What does Abram's god or child have to do with you or me? That's his concern—his and his wife's."

"But Sarai is barren," Hagar said. "You knew that."

Simeon was silent, staring at her. "Has he taken you for a second wife?"

She shook her head.

"Well then?"

"But he *has* taken me," she said. "And I think . . . I think I'm carrying his child."

He struck her before she even knew his hand was raised, and she shrank back, her hand lifted to her bruised cheek.

"Slut!" he hissed. "You tried to tell me that women were cherished here, that this tribe had a god who taught goodness. And then the girl who was promised to me is used by the chief for his pleasure."

"No, not his pleasure," she cried. "Only to carry out Yahweh's promise."

"And if there is really a god as great as you think this

Yahweh is, and if he'd made a promise, wouldn't you think
he'd be clever enough to work things out without your
help?"

Anger began to burn through Hagar's fear. "It wasn't *my*
idea," she snapped. "It was Sarai's—and Meryet's. Even my
lord's. What choice did *I* have?"

For a long time he was silent, glaring at her and breathing
hard. When he spoke, his voice was low. "No choice," he
said. "I could accept that, though it seems strange that a girl
whose virginity was protected for years should suddenly
find herself in bed with her master. But there's more. Even if
he took you to bed, even if you're carrying his child, why did
you pull from me as though you couldn't bear to touch me?"

She lowered her eyes, unable to face the fierce intentness
of his.

"I'll tell you why," Simeon said, his voice still soft but
almost venemous. "I'll tell you why. You've fallen in love
with him. You think you're going to be able to keep him."

Her chin went up. "I *don't* think I'll be able to keep him.
He loves his wife and only her."

"But you love him," Simeon accused again.

She was silent, turning away from his burning stare. She
could see his fists clenching, and she wished that they
weren't alone up here in the hills. There was suddenly no
charm in being in such a solitary spot.

"But you're not really sure you're pregnant?" His voice
was deceptively soft.

She felt a little shiver of fear touch her. "I think I am," she
said. Surely, if he thought she were pregnant, he wouldn't
touch her.

"But you're not sure."

His hands on her arms were strong, too strong for her to
dislodge.

His foot tripped her and she fell heavily to the ground.

"Oh, please," she begged, reduced to groveling by his
violence. "Please. Abram's seed mustn't be defiled—please!"

"Defiled?" His breath sobbed in his throat. "Do you think

I'm only an animal. . . ."

His hands yanked and she felt her robe tear.

Protest ripped out of her throat. "No," she screamed. "No! Oh, no!"

The sound of running feet forced itself through the frantic pounding of her blood. It gave her the strength to roll away from Simeon, and she screamed again.

"Shut up!" Simeon said through his teeth, and then he seemed to freeze.

She twisted her head and saw that Simeon was staring toward the path. He had heard the footsteps, too.

"What is it? Hagar, are you all right? I was coming down from the pasture and I heard you cry out."

It was Abram, breathless, frightened. "You!" he said, appalled. "What are you doing to her?"

Simeon struggled to his feet. "You said I could have her," he accused, and his voice shook.

Hagar's fear died abruptly and pity filled her.

Abram sighed deeply. Turning, he called to those who had followed him. "Go on back. It's all right. She isn't hurt."

Then he turned to Hagar. "You're *not* hurt, are you?"

"No, my lord," she said, pulling the torn robe around her. "He . . . Simeon . . . was terribly upset, that's all. I don't think he would have harmed me, my lord."

Simeon looked down at her, and she realized that his eyes held tears.

Abram stared from one of them to the other. "I'm the guilty one," he said. "I *told* Sarai we had promised her to you."

Simeon, still breathing heavily, dropped onto the ledge and covered his face with his hands.

"I should have killed you, old man," he said in muffled tones. "If I were not in your debt, I would have."

"You're not in my debt," Abram said. "My gift to you only balanced what was owed."

"Why did you take *her?*" Simeon cried. "Weren't there a dozen other women who would have served? Why the one *I* wanted?"

"Because she belongs to Sarai," Abram explained. "And the child will be Sarai's."

Simeon glanced at Hagar. "So you end up with a man who doesn't love you and a child that won't be yours," he said. "I could have done better by you than that."

Hagar was silent. If it weren't for Abram, she would have loved this man, and what he was saying was true.

"I'll pay you," Abram began, but Simeon flung himself around to face the older man.

"Keep your gold," he said furiously. "No, on second thought, give me all you think she's worth. Will it be one small lump, my lord, or two? You're the only one who knows how much she's really worth in a man's bed."

"Be quiet!" Abram roared. "Be quiet and leave this place. And never come back. If you had been civil, I might have said you could have her in a few years, when the child is weaned. But I won't tolerate insolence like yours. Get out and stay out!"

Simeon stared at Abram a minute and then turned to Hagar. "I only wanted to love you," he began and his voice broke.

Without another word, he turned and ran, and Hagar heard his feet sliding on the rocky path, and then gradually silence flowed in and filled the little spot.

"Are you sure you're all right?" Abram asked at last.

She got to her feet. "Yes, my lord."

"He shouldn't have talked that way, insulted me like that. What did he expect me to do?"

"It's all right, my lord," she said in a tired little voice. "Truly. It's all right."

Simeon wouldn't have waited long enough for the child to be weaned anyhow, she thought. He was young and his blood was hot. It was better this way. Better that she just stay here. After all, there were still flowers that blossomed after the rains.

19

Hagar turned sleeplessly on her pallet, feeling her loneliness as sharply and painfully as she had felt it the first night that Abram had gone back to sleep in the main tent. He had been gone for more than two months now, and still she longed for him. It wasn't the lovemaking she wanted; she hadn't had time to become skilled in pleasing a man. It was the simple touching and the warmth of his arms holding her that she wanted. It was having someone who would talk to her and who would listen. There were nights when she thought she couldn't bear it, nights when she thought she would have to throw herself at his feet and beg him to come to her tent, just to talk to her.

But of course she couldn't do that. She was a slave, after all, and he was wholly in love with Sarai. All she could do was to weep in her pillow and yearn for what she had once had.

At least, she comforted herself, I have his child in me. She laid her hands over her stomach. "I wish you'd start to grow," she whispered to her unborn child. "I want to really *know* you're there."

As if in answer to her quiet whisper, a quick pulse fluttered in her body. She lay perfectly still. Meryet had told her that a baby's fist movements were like a sudden heart beat.

Was it possible that her baby had moved?

"Child of Abram," she breathed, "move again. So I'll know."

For a while there was nothing, and then she felt the tiny thrust again—the pulse of a life that was not her own. In two months, I'll be able to detect the movement with my hand, Hagar thought. Meryet's baby kicks so sturdily that sometimes the pile of wool she's spinning moves in her lap. She says Dothan laughs when he sees it. But I . . . I have no one to laugh with me.

The baby moved again, and the flutter brought a surge of stubborn pride to the girl. I don't need anyone, she thought. I won't weep any longer for Abram. I certainly won't think of Simeon. I'll think only of this baby. And of me.

The weeks moved on, and Hagar's pride in herself grew with each movement of the child she carried. When her body began to thicken, she carried herself with an arrogance that had not been seen in her since she was a child.

Sarai saw the change in the girl, and her own irritation grew in proportion. Wasn't it enough that she had given up her husband for four months, Sarai thought—enough that she had to bear the humiliation of knowing that another woman could bear his child? Was it necessary that she had to endure the girl's insolence as well? But when she mentioned it to Abram, he told her it was only her imagination.

"I think, my lord," she said one night, "that the girl has worked her way into your heart."

It was the first she had suggested anything like this to him, and she was astonished at his reaction.

He sat up and faced her with a severity she had rarely seen in him. "Stop it!" he commanded. "Are you daring to accuse me of infidelity?"

"No, my lord," she said, shaken by the anger in his voice. "No . . . it's only . . . ."

"Listen to me. I didn't think I'd ever have to discuss this with you. I thought you would be intelligent enough to make such a discussion unnecessary."

Her breath caught in her throat.

"Who told me to lie with Hagar?" he demanded. "Who?"

"I, my lord," she admitted after a minute. "But I...."

"No. No excuses. *You* insisted that I do what I did. You gave me no peace until I consented. What did you expect me to do—lie with the girl with loathing in my heart? Did you want me to create a child with hate?"

"Then you *do* love her?" Sarai said.

"I *like* her," he corrected. "I like her very much. She's a good girl, an intelligent one. But you have no reason to be jealous."

"Jealous, my lord?"

He did not soften at the pain in her voice. "Yes, jealous. I won't stand for it. I swear to you, Sarai, if you fling her at my head, I'll . . . I'll marry her and share her tent as well as yours."

Sarai gasped as though cold water had been flung in her face. His words knifed their way into her heart.

"I mean it," he said harshly. "I still don't know if I've done what Yahweh wanted. And Simeon was wronged. I did a dreadful and shameful thing when I wronged a stranger who came to my door. But I did it. And now it's over. I don't want to listen to any talk about Hagar. She's *your* slave, and you handle your problems with her in your own way. Do you understand?"

She was silent and his voice cut like a whip.

"Do you understand me?"

"Yes, my lord," she whispered.

He lay down and turned his back to her, but it was a long time before either of them slept. When Sarai woke next morning, Abram was gone. Without a touch, she thought in pain, without a word. She knew she had made him angrier than she had ever made him before, and fear moved darkly in her heart.

"Hagar," Sarai said a few days later. "I want to talk to

you."

Hagar had been grinding grain, and her back ached cruelly. She was glad to sit back on her heels and rest. "Yes, my lady?"

"It's about this habit you have of going alone up in the hills. I don't want you to do it any more."

"But, my lady...."

"Don't argue with me," Sarai snapped. "It's not safe for you up there. Look what happened the day Simeon came."

"Simeon isn't likely to come back, my lady."

"Well, there are other men in the hills. Until the child is born, stay near the tents."

Hagar felt anger begin to burn in her. They had taken everything else away from her. They had no right to her sanctuary.

"You've never forbidden it before, my lady."

"Well, I'm forbidding it now. It's not safe, and it's not seemly," Sarai said.

"Not seemly, my lady?"

"People could gossip about you. They might say this child isn't Abram's."

All at once her fury seemed to destroy the discretion that had bridled Hagar's tongue so long. "Or is it you?" she spit out without the courtesy of a title. "You're afraid I'm meeting Abram up there, aren't you?"

"Watch your tongue, girl," Sarai warned.

"I won't," Hagar retorted. "Why did you start this thing if you were going to act this way? You *knew* how it would be. You knew you were barren. You...."

Sarai's eyes were blazing and her voice crackled with anger. "Shut your mouth! You have no *right* to speak to me that way!"

"Haven't I? Carrying my lord's child must give me *some* rights around here."

"How *dare* you?" Sarai's hand struck Hagar's face so hard that the girl staggered under the blow.

For one second, Sarai's face reflected a horror at what she

had done, and a quick apology from Hagar might have brought a healing.

But Hagar was close to hysteria. "Shall I get you a whip, my lady?" Hagar asked shrilly. "Then you can beat me with greater skill."

"I don't need a whip," Sarai said, panting with rekindled rage. "You're an ungrateful, wicked, insolent. . . ." And with each word, she struck Hagar's face.

The girl would not permit herself to duck or evade the blows, and physical pain as well as black humiliation engulfed her.

Finally Hagar cried out, "I'll go to my lord about this. I will. He'll. . . ."

"It won't do you any good," Sarai shouted. "He told me to handle you in my own way. He said you were my slave and I could do what I wanted with you."

Hagar stared at her mistress with such dreadful despair that Sarai's hands stilled themselves and fell at her sides.

"*He* said that?" Hagar whispered. "My lord said that?"

"Why should I lie to you?" Sarai said harshly.

Hagar stared without moving for a long minute, and for a while Sarai endured the burning gaze, then her eyes dropped. Without another word, Hagar turned and walked away and Sarai let her go.

The girl was heading for the hills, Sarai realized, deliberately flaunting her mistress's authority. But I'm too tired to stop her, Sarai thought.

"My lady." It was Meryet, worrying at Sarai's elbow. "My lady, should I try to go after her?"

Sarai looked at Meryet's unwieldly body. "No," she said wearily. "Let her go."

"My lady," Meryet said, choosing her words with great care. "My lady, you don't really think she's meeting our lord up there?"

Sarai looked at Meryet with sudden distaste. "Do you hear everything that's said?" she asked.

"You were . . . speaking very loudly," Meryet murmured.

Sarai's shoulders slumped. "I suppose everyone else heard me, too."

"You have a right to talk the way you want to," Meryet protested. "She's only your slave. But she's not meeting Abram up there. She's an insolent, hardheaded girl, my lady, but she's honest. She'd never do that. Even if Abram were the kind of man who would want it. And you know he isn't, my lady."

Sarai's face crumpled and the tears began to flow. "I didn't think I'd feel like this," she confessed. "I never dreamed I'd be jealous. I thought . . . I thought . . . ."

Meryet's arms about Sarai were gentle and strong. "Come into the tent, my lady. I understand. I do understand. It's just that you wanted Abram to have a child, but you would have preferred that . . . it be accomplished by miraculous means."

There was a tiny hint of teasing in her voice, and Sarai's tension began to relax slightly.

"It isn't easy to share a husband you love," Meryet went on. "For many wives, it would be nothing to give their slaves to their husband. But you're . . . you're different, my lady."

Sarai submitted herself to the ministering hands, the soothing voice.

"And Hagar's different," Meryet explained. "She's strong and intelligent, and she isn't willing to be as humble as she should. But, my lady, don't hate her for it. The baby will have some of her strength, too. You wouldn't want a mindless wench to carry Abram's child."

"I know," Sarai said. "I know."

Meryet glanced anxiously toward the hills where Hagar's figure was only a speck, toiling in the distance. I should send someone after her, Meryet thought, remembering the terrible look on Hagar's face, but maybe she'll be all right after she's been alone for a while. She always has been before.

There was no time in the late afternoon for Meryet to worry about Hagar. Dothan came in from pasturing the flocks and there was supper to prepare and the usual evening tasks to perform. Moreover, Meryet had been feeling uncomfortable all day. Her back ached, and she felt a curious sense of apprehension.

"My lord," she said abruptly after they had eaten.

Dothan looked up.

"Will you go for your mother?" Meryet said, her face drawn with the suddenness of her pain. "My time has come, I think."

"Should I ask Sarai to come, too?" he asked, putting his arms about her.

"No. She has her own troubles with Hagar," Meryet said.

Dothan looked his surprise. "Hagar?"

"It doesn't matter, my lord. Only get your mother. And then, until you are permitted to come back, you'll stay in your father's tent, my lord."

He held her closer. "I'll miss you," he said. "Will you be all right?"

"If the child and I both live," she whispered, "somehow we'll endure the time until you return."

He kissed her, and for a minute they clung together, and then he felt her body tense with pain, and he put her from him.

"I'll get my mother," he promised and ran to his father's tent.

During the long, difficult hours that followed, Meryet had no time to think of Hagar, or even to wonder if she and Sarai had had a reconciliation when the angry girl had come down from the hill.

In Abram's tent, Sarai served the evening meal, and Abram looked at her with inquiry.

"Where's Hagar?" he asked.

"She was . . . well, very insolent, and I punished her, and she ran up the hill. She hasn't come back yet," Sarai said.

"Punished her? How?"

"You told me she was my slave, my lord, and to handle any problems in my own way."

"But she's pregnant with my child," Abram reasoned. "I'd like to know how she was punished. Did you scold her, you mean?"

"I struck her, my lord. Several times." Sarai's voice was expressionless.

Abram stared in astonishment. "You, Sarai? *You* struck her?"

Sarai only nodded, but when she glanced at Abram, expecting to see anger on his face, she saw only sorrow.

"You've changed," he said. "You've become a different woman."

"She was *very* insolent," Sarai defended herself.

Abram looked tired. "I don't really want to hear about it," he said, "but it's my responsibility to keep peace in this tribe. Maybe you'd better tell me what happened."

The words came out haltingly, slowly, with many false starts. She wanted desperately to make Hagar look bad in Abram's eyes and to make herself the one with whom he would sympathize. But the honest core in her which had hated the lie they lived in Egypt would not allow her to tell anything but the truth.

"Did you really think she was meeting me on the hill?" Abram asked, his voice cold.

"No, my lord, not really," Sarai whispered.

"Then why did you accuse her?"

"I just wanted to hurt her," Sarai cried. "She walks around here as though she were a princesss and I were her servant. She . . . ," and the words trembled to a stop as Abram stared at her.

"The girl only did what you told her to do," Abram said.

"I didn't tell her to love you," Sarai protested, and then stopped, stricken. She had never intended to reveal to Abram what she suspected, what she had seen in Hagar's eyes.

"If she loves me," Abram said, "then that's something you'll have to try to overlook. The important thing is that a child is going to be born."

"My lord," Sarai whispered, seeing again the look on Hagar's face when she struck her, "I was wrong. I'm the one who was wrong."

"The sin is mine, too," Abram conceded heavily. "I didn't wait for Yahweh. I took things in my own hands."

"For me, my lord," Sarai said brokenly.

"For both of us," Abram amended. Then he got slowly to his feet. "I'll go after her. Can you trust me up on the hill?" he asked bitterly.

The question was like a whip on her flesh. "My lord, forgive me," she wept, and the words were a cry to Yahweh as well as to the man who left the tent without another word.

Abram was back sooner than she had anticipated, but the look on his face was grim.

"She's not there," he said harshly. "She's not anywhere. She's gone."

Sarai looked at him in horror. "Gone?" she repeated. "But there are wild animals and evil men. . . ."

He only nodded. "It's too dark now to start a search. We'll have to wait until morning."

"But morning might be too late, my lord," Sarai protested.

"I know. But there's nothing we can do. And I saw Dothan. He says that Meryet is in labor. Maybe you'd better go over there."

"But what will *you* do, my lord?" Sarai asked.

"I? I'll pray that Yahweh will protect Hagar and my child. I can only hope that Yahweh will listen."

They were silent, and at that moment a scream sliced through the night.

"It's only Meryet, my lord," Sarai said and knew her own relief to be as great as that she saw in Abram's eyes. If Hagar were hurt—or killed—because of her jealousy, Sarai knew that her burden of guilt would be too heavy to be borne.

20

The path had never seemed so steep, and Hagar's breath rasped in her throat as she climbed away from the tents. At first, she was aware only of the pain in her face, and her finger tips touched the swollen place over her cheekbones and then winced away while sobs wrenched themselves out of her throat.

But gradually, as she struggled up the path, a greater pain filled her heart. Sarai had struck her—not only once but repeatedly. Sarai. Sarai who had been her mother, mistress, comforter and model since Hagar had been a child. For ten years now, Sarai had been the center of Hagar's life, the star in her skies. The new, unexpected, unwanted love she felt for Abram had nothing whatever to do with the way she felt about Sarai.

And now Sarai hated her. She must hate her or she wouldn't have struck her so savagely or have been so consumed with jealousy.

It's not my fault, Hagar thought. I didn't do anything. Her foot slipped on a loose pebble, and she fell jarringly to her knees. Instinctively, her arms cradled the child in her body. If anything happens to the baby, she thought, it will be Sarai's fault.

She struggled to her feet, still holding her arms protectively across her body. No, she wasn't being wholly honest with herself. It wasn't all Sarai's fault. She, too, had been insolent and cruel. She had flaunted her pregnancy. She had been arrogant.

"Can you possibly think of it as an honor?" Abram had said. But she had looked on it as an accomplishment for which she deserved all the credit.

Still—Sarai had struck her. I was to be treated as a second wife, Hagar thought, not as a common slave.

She reached her place of sanctuary, and dropped, breathless, onto the stone ledge. She stared almost blindly around the little corrie, hardly able to see through her tears the rock on which she had sacrificed the statue of Sobek, the place where Abram had held her and said, "You will be Hagar to me," the slope down which Simeon had slid when he came to tell of Abram's victory, the level place where Simeon had tripped her in his rage and pain.

How much has happened to me here, she thought. It's more like home to me than my own tent. Oh, I wish I didn't have to go back. I wish I never had to see Abram and Sarai again as long as I live.

Her gaze moved slowly out to the horizon. I could go to Sodom, she mused, and then rebuked herself. Her mind must be addled by Sarai's blows to think so stupid a thing.

Simeon. The name flashed into her mind with the clarity of light. Would Simeon take her in? Would his desire for her be greater than his anger? Would he accept her, carrying Abram's child as she was?

In the distance, along what she knew was the caravan route, a tiny puff of dust boiled. Was it possible that it would be Simeon's caravan? Did she dare risk trying to reach him?

But if it weren't Simeon, she might be killed; she would certainly be taken as a slave. But I'm used to that, she thought bitterly. If Sarai is going to beat me, if she's going to hate me, I might as well belong to someone else. Or even be dead.

But what about the child, something in her said.

I'll be careful, she promised herself. I'll go only close

enough to see if it's Simeon's caravan. I won't get hurt.

She knew, in a muddled way, that she wasn't thinking clearly, that she was acting like a child. But she felt driven by her grief and her despair. Maybe I can even find my way to Egypt, she thought wildly, and saw in her mind the broad, gleaming river and the fertile fields of her youth.

"I can't go back to Abram's camp," she cried aloud. "I can't." And she started down the path that led to the watered plains.

Darkness began to overtake her before she had gone half way. It was then that some degree of calmness and sanity came back to her. What was she doing out here, unprotected, a possible prey of lions or savage men? She had been foolish, foolish to try to come down this steep path. And now it was too dark to find her way back up to her little spot in the hills or to Abram's camp.

Where can I hide, she wondered with a shiver of apprehension. Where will I be safe? She strained her eyes, trying to see in the dimness, but the shadows hid the contours of the land.

There was a drop-off somewhere along here, she remembered. Every time they had climbed up from the plains to their permanent camp, they had been careful to skirt the place that dropped so steeply beside the path. She crouched on the ground, suddenly afraid of move another step. In her imagination, she could feel the land dropping away beneath her feet, could feel her body plunging to the rocks below. She moved her foot and felt something hard and round. Cautiously, she touched it with her hand. It was a stick. Someone had probably used it as a staff to help climb past the dangerous place and then had dropped it when the path leveled out a little. She took it gratefully and got carefully to her feet. She could push the stick before her and be safe.

Moving as slowly as though she were old, she crept down the path, hoping that she might find a more sheltered place to spend the night. It never occurred to her to ask Yahweh for help. She had left Yahweh back at Abram's tents.

Her stick hit against something large and solid. She moved up and ran her hands over it and recognized it with a little cry of gratitude. It was the altar Abram had built to Yahweh the first time they had climbed this path. The pile of flat stones had served as a place to sacrifice a lamb in praise that the journey was nearly ended. And the stones had been left standing, as all of the altars he had built to his God, to remind any who came this way that a man had worshiped here.

Beyond the altar, she remembered, was a small spring, and a semicircle of rocks that had sheltered the worshippers from the wind. She would be as safe here as she would be anywhere. She groped her way past the altar and found the rocky shelter she was looking for. The spring ran down the lip of the first rock, just as she remembered, and she drank thirstily. Then, gently, she bathed the hurt places on her face. She was intent on trying to pat the cool water on her cheeks without hurting herself too much when she was suddenly aware of a sound.

She crouched in startled stillness, straining her ears to hear, but silence filled the night.

She tried to recall what the sound had been, whether it had been the rattle of stones under someone's foot or the rustle of an animal moving on the rocks. But she couldn't remember. She bent to the water, and the sound came again. It was a rushing whisper that swept over her with insistence. At first, her fear was greater than her ability to listen. But gradually, she grew very still. There was something familiar about the sound. She had heard something like it once before, but she couldn't remember when.

Her eyes had begun to grow accustomed to the darkness, and the first stars gave a faint glimmer of light. Hagar turned slowly, certain that she would see something or someone. But there was nothing for her to see except the darker shape of the altar against the night sky.

The altar to Yahweh. Hagar's breath came out with a great

sigh of relief. Perhaps Yahweh came back to the altars Abram had built. Perhaps Yahweh would protect her.

Then the sound came again, growing until her head was filled with it. And in that instant she knew what it was. Abram had explained it years ago when she had asked him what it was like to have Yahweh speak to him.

Abram had said, "The Voice fills me until I can't hear anything else."

Now she knew. Although she was only a woman, only a slave, the Voice filled her until she could hear nothing else.

Hagar, maid of Sarai, the Voice said, *where have you come from and where are you going?*

"I'm running away from Sarai," Hagar said. "She struck me, and she hates me, and...."

But the Voice cut across her explanations. *Return to your mistress and submit yourself to her.*

"But how can I?" Hagar wept. "She hated me when I left; she'll hate me all the more because I dared to run away. She'll never forgive me, never, and I'm afraid...."

The Voice was silent, but Hagar could hear the command as though it shouted and echoed from the sky above her. *Return to your mistress and submit yourself to her!*

Submit, the Voice said. There was no room for insolence or arrogance in submission, Hagar realized. If this was Yahweh speaking, then he was telling her not only to go back to Abram's tents but to be as loving and obedient as she had been before Sarai had chosen her to bear Abram's child. Yahweh was placing the responsibility on her shoulders, not on Sarai's.

"But what about *me*, Lord?" Hagar whispered, panic churning in her. "Maybe they won't have me back. Maybe Abram won't claim the child as his."

But the Voice rang with promise. *I will multiply your descendants so greatly that they cannot be numbered for multitude.*

Hagar sat opened mouthed. *Her* descendants? Too numerous to be counted and worthy to be noticed by Abram's God? It was unthinkable, or would have been if it were not for the certainty of this sound in her head.

She felt again that she had heard the sound before, some-where, briefly. She searched her memories, and abruptly, she remembered. The day that Lot had been sent away, she had wakened to a sound. She had thought at first that it was Abram praying, but she had realized even then that it was more than Abram's voice. And now, years later, huddled alone in the dark wilderness, she was hearing the Voice again, hearing with the clarity with which Abram must have heard.

"What about this child, Lord?" she begged.

The Voice answered, *Behold, you are with child, and you will bear a son.*

Hagar's heart leaped. A son. Not a daughter who would be only a disappointment, but a son.

You shall call his name Ishmael, the Voice went on, *because the Lord has given heed to your affliction.*

The affliction seemed all at once to be nothing because she was no longer required to bear it alone.

He will be a wild ass of a man, the Voice proclaimed, *his hand against every man and every man's hand against him.*

I've been too angry while I carried him, Hagar thought humbly. I've been haughty and unkind. The poison of my anger has gone into him. I'm to blame.

The Voice did not contradict her, and she began to weep again, sobbing out all of her fear and shame.

When she finally opened her eyes to look around, she saw to her astonishment that day was breaking in the east. She must have slept, slept safely, and the night was over.

I've had a dream, she thought dazedly, and knew at once that it had not been a dream. Each word that the Voice had uttered was burned clearly in her heart. For some incom-prehensible reason, the Lord God Yahweh had spoken to *her*, a slave girl who had broken all the rules.

Yahweh actually looked down and saw me, she thought in awe, and a great trembling seized her as she prostrated herself on the ground in front of the altar.

"You are a God who sees," she whispered and thought of the carved, blind eyes of Sobek and Hathor. "And I am alive after you have seen me and spoken to me. There is no other god as great as you, O Lord. Yahweh, Abram's God, you are mightier than any other."

If the Voice were to speak in the morning light, Hagar thought soberly, it would say, "Go now and do what you've been told to do."

She smoothed her hair with wet hands and beat the dust out of her robe. Then, taking the staff which had been her eyes in the night, she turned and started up the hill.

Sarai had slept very little. She had gone to Meryet's tent late, as Abram had suggested, but she wasn't needed there. The labor was over and the baby, a pretty little girl, was safely beside the sleeping mother. After a few words to Dothan's mother, Soshannah, Sarai, relieved that no one had asked about Hagar, went silently back to her tent.

If you let Hagar come back safely, Sarai bargained with Yahweh, I'll never strike her again. I'll be as gentle as I used to be. I won't think about the fact that Abram shared her tent. I'll... I'll think only of the baby.

I've hardly thought about the baby, Sarai realized with shame. And the baby will be mine, delivered into my arms. Hagar has only been a way of getting the baby born. She thought of the fresh perfection of Meryet's child, and then visualized Hagar and the child she carried lying dead somewhere, torn by animals or attacked by men.

Sarai shuddered away from the thought. Please, Yahweh, she begged. I'll be kind to her. I swear.

She slept at last and did not wake until the sun shone through the flap of the tent.

Abram knelt outside the tent, cramped and cold and wretched. He had lain down on the bare ground during the night and had slept, worn out with watching and praying.

But at dawn, he had wakened and struggled again to his knees, aware, as he had never been before, of his age.

He heard Sarai stirring in the tent and tried to harden his heart against her, but he could not. He got clumsily to his feet. If Yahweh had not heard him now, then he would never hear him. The girl was either safe or she was not. And if she were safe, Abram would find her; if she were not, then Yahweh would have to forgive them all. It was as simple as that.

But the baby, Abram's heart cried, the child I've hungered for all these years. What will I do if the child is never born?

Sarai turned as Abram entered the tent, and neither of them said anything. Abram opened his arms and Sarai ran into them. They clung to each other, seeking the comfort of human warmth.

A sound at the tent door startled them apart.

"Hagar!" Abram cried, his voice vibrant with relief.

"Hagar!" Sarai echoed and with no hesitation ran to the girl.

Before Sarai could reach her, Hagar had dropped to her knees. "Forgive me," she cried. "Oh, my lady, my lady, forgive me. I've been so wicked, so arrogant. . . ."

But Sarai's hands were pulling her gently erect. The sight of Hagar's face, bruised and swollen, brought a cry of sorrow from Sarai and a sharp indrawn breath from Abram.

"No," Sarai said, "it's you who must forgive me."

The two women held each other, and their tears seemed to flow in a single flood of remorse.

"No more weeping," Abram said gruffly. "We've all wept enough."

Hagar, startled, looked at him and saw that his eyes were rimmed with red.

"It's a new day," Abram announced. "From this time on, there will be no more anger or jealousy or insolence. There will only be three people waiting to have a child."

Before she went to her tent to rest, Hagar went to the

hiding place where she kept the small bundle containing the
tiny statue of Hathor. She had kept the goddess for senti-
mental reasons, but she knew now that none of the reasons
justified the presence of a foreign goddess in the tents of
Yahweh. Certainly she who had spoken to Abram's God,
who had been seen by him and had been given words of
promise, had no right to the small replica of an Egyptian
deity.

I have Yahweh now, Hagar mused, tossing the statue onto
the refuse heap. She felt no sense of regret, seeing the little
idol tumble in among the mutton bones and broken bits of
clay. She felt, instead, a sense of lightness that was as near a
feeling of freedom as she had known since the day the
Pharaoh's soldiers had burst into her father's house.

21

"She's a beautiful baby," Hagar said to Meryet. It was easy, she thought with some shame, to be enthusiastic about Meryet's child, knowing so certainly that her own baby would be a boy.

Meryet glanced proudly at the child at her breast. "She's healthy and good. It's always a miracle when the first one lives. Or the second or third, for that matter. She looks like my mother, doesn't she?"

"Yes, she really does. I wonder what my baby will be like?"

"Like Abram, I hope," Meryet said soberly. "It will be so much easier for Sarai if he . . . or she . . . is nothing like you."

Hagar looked up to interrupt, but Meryet waved her to silence. "Oh, I know things are going well now, but when the baby's born, it's going to be Sarai's and if it looks like Abram it will seem more her own. Of course, if it's a girl, I don't know what she'll do. They still won't have an heir."

"It's not going to be a girl," Hagar said.

"I talked like that, too," Meryet agreed cheerfully. "I'm lucky because it really doesn't matter. Eventually, I'll bear Dothan a son."

"I already know," Hagar insisted. "Yahweh told me."

Meryet only laughed at her. "Yahweh wouldn't speak to a slave, and a woman slave at that. If you think he did, you

193

had a dream."

There was no use arguing, Hagar thought. It was enough that she and Abram and Sarai knew what had happened that night on the mountain path.

Meryet's baby finished nursing and began to look around. Although she was less than two months old, her eyes were as bright and curious as her mother's.

"Let me hold her," Hagar begged and Meryet laid the baby in her arms.

A wavering smile turned up the corners of the baby's mouth, and Hagar laughed with delight. "Look," she cried. "She's smiling. She must know I'm a relative."

For once, Meryet seemed indifferent to her child's actions. "Hagar," she said, "I want to talk to you."

"You're always wanting to talk to me," Hagar said carelessly. "You're either making suggestions or plotting my future. I don't know why I even listen to you."

"You don't most of the time," Meryet said ruefully. "But I hope you'll listen this time. It's important."

The baby clutched at Hagar's finger, and the feel of the tiny satin fist was enchanting. "Well?" Hagar asked absently, not even looking up from the child in her arms.

"You love Yafah, don't you?" Meryet asked. "You haven't always loved me—maybe you never have—but you love my baby."

"What's wrong with that?" Hagar asked. "She's a lovely baby."

"You didn't know you'd feel this way about her, did you?" Meryet asked. "I mean, you never paid much attention to other babies in the tribe."

Hagar finally looked up and met the anxious look in Meryet's eyes. "What are you trying to tell me, Meryet?"

"Have you really accepted the fact that your baby will be Sarai's child?" Meryet asked bluntly.

"Well, of course," Hagar began and then her voice slowed. "But I'll nurse him and care for him and...."

"You'll nurse him—or her," Meryet interrupted sharply,

"but that's all. The baby will be Sarai's and Abram's. They'll keep it in their tent, and my guess is that Sarai will never share their tent with you again. The baby will grow up thinking Sarai's its mother and you're only a slave. Have you really thought of that?"

Hagar stared at her cousin. She had Yahweh's promise, hadn't she, that her descendants would be too numerous to count. So why did Meryet's words move so coldly in her heart?

"I knew the child was conceived so that Sarai and Abram would have an heir," Hagar said at last.

"Your mind knows that," Meryet agreed. "But your heart thinks of it as *your* child—your child to cuddle and love. But it won't be. Do you remember one time saying to me that Sarai was different from most women, that she wouldn't give her child to a slave to raise? It's true, Hagar. You knew Sarai very well, even then, when you were only a little girl."

Hagar was silent, staring down into Yafah's small face. She saw the baby's mouth fold into petulance and the eyes pinch shut with distress and then a shrill wail sounded. Hagar lifted Yafah to her shoulder and patted her with gentle hands, feeling the small knees draw up in pain and then relax again.

"I don't think I can bear it," Hagar said suddenly. "He's not going to be a placid, good baby like this one. He'll need me."

"Oh, Hagar, how do you know what he'll be like? Or even if it'll be a boy?"

"I just know," Hagar said stubbornly. "Sarai will spoil him and then . . . ."

"Sarai most certainly will spoil him," Meryet predicted. "And if you can't accept that, you're going to be as unhappy as you were several months ago. Start making up your mind now to accept it graciously. It it's a girl, maybe they'll let you keep her."

"It won't be a girl," Hagar said dully.

"I'll share Yafah with you," Meryet offered with unexpected generosity. "Yafah can think of you as a second mother. It might help."

Hagar pressed her cheek against the small head that nestled in her neck. "Thank you," she said. But what solace would Meryet's baby be if her heart yearned for Ishmael, the child Yahweh had promised?

The pain started in the middle of the night, and for some time, Hagar lay alone, waiting to see if the child were really going to be born. Meryet had told her how it would be, and when the pain came at short intervals, she went to the door of Abram's tent.

"My lady," she called. "My lady, can you come?"

"Is it the child?" Sarai asked, her voice rough with sleep.

"Yes, my lady."

"Then go into your tent and wait for me. I'll come in a minute."

Sarai shook Abram's shoulder. "My lord. My lord, wake up. I'm going to Hagar's tent. The child is coming."

Abram's hand caught her arm. "Shall I call Soshannah? She's skilled in these things."

"Yes. If the child is to be delivered onto my lap, there must be another pair of hands. But wait until I see whether or not we need her yet."

"And when he's born—my son—you'll be the one to bring him to me, won't you?"

"Yes, my lord. Now let me go."

In a few minutes Sarai was back at their tent. "Go for Soshannah now, my lord. The girl has waited until it's nearly time."

Waited alone, Abram thought with pity. When the boy is born and when he's weaned, I'll find a husband for her. I'll make it up to her for what she's done for us. Then drawing his robe around him, he went quickly to Eliezer's tent.

The labor was longer that Sarai had anticipated and more difficult than Hagar had ever imagined. The hours crept by, and daylight came and still the baby would not come.

"My lady," Hagar gasped. "I'll die before he's born. I'm never going to be able to give my lord his son."

"Yes, of course you are," Sarai said strongly. "Don't give up now. Be brave just a little longer."

Her hands were gentle, wiping the sweat from Hagar's face with a moist, cool cloth. "Come now," Sarai urged, "try again."

"Do you hate me, my lady?" Hagar cried wildly.

Sarai bent over the frightened girl. "Of course I don't hate you," she said. "Don't be silly. This isn't the time to think about that."

"Hold my hands," Hagar begged, and Sarai lent her strength to the girl.

"Now," Hagar gasped. "He's coming now, my lady."

Soshannah laughed briefly. "Now we'll see whether or not it's a boy. There's the head, my lady," she said to Sarai. "Sit here and the child will be born to *you*."

It was a custom blurred by antiquity, but all three of the women knew what to do, and when the child, red and squalling, drew his first breath, he was on Sarai's knees, and it was her hands which kept him from falling when the cord was cut.

He's beautiful, Sarai marveled, and her body ached as though the pain had been hers. He looks exactly like my lord. She wrapped him in the clean cloth that she had ready and held him against her breast. She was hardly aware of the ministrations being done to Hagar. She and the child in her arms might have been alone in the tent.

"May I see him?" Hagar whispered.

"Look!" Sarai's face was as proud as though the girl on her pallet had had nothing to do with this thing. "He looks like my lord. Exactly."

Hagar gazed at the tiny red face. He had Abram's broad forehead, strong chin, and wide mouth. Even the ears were set on the little head as Abram's were. But as she gazed, the eyes opened, and she saw the long, dark, narrow eyes that had been her father's.

"His eyes are not as round as Abram's," Sarai discovered, but her pride did not waver. Then she seemed to suddenly realize what Hagar had gone through. "Are you all right?" she asked kindly.

"I think so," Hagar said. "May I hold him, my lady?"

"Not now. Abram wants to see him. I'll bring him back later for you to nurse him. Try to sleep."

Hagar watched the women with a sense of desolation. She had never wanted anything as much as she wanted her own child. Even her longing for Abram had been smaller than this terrible need for the boy who had been carried in her body. But Meryet was right. The baby would be Sarai's and Abram's son. Even Yahweh, she remembered, had promised no more than that the child would be born and that it would be a boy.

Sarai came into Abram's tent, and he saw the look on her face with a feeling of great relief. This was what he had hoped for, prayed for—that Sarai would accept the child as her own.

"It's a boy, my lord," Sarai said. "Look, your son."

Abram's knees shook in a shameful manner. He was undone by the miracle of this child in Sarai's arms.

"Let me sit down," he said humbly.

When he was seated, Sarai leaned down and put the baby in his arms. "See, my lord," she said. "He's very much like you. It's as though he were made in your image."

"Not the eyes," Abram said. He almost said, "He has Hagar's eyes," but he stopped the words in time. Hagar must be forgotten as soon as possible.

"Well, he can't be exactly like you in every detail, I suppose," Sarai said, but her voice was content. "But he's beautiful, isn't he?"

Abram looked down at the child, and he felt love wash through his body like a flood. He had waited a long time for this moment, but Yahweh had been merciful and had allowed him to hold his own son in his arms before he died.

"We'll call him Ishmael," he said.

"The name the girl suggested?" Sarai asked.

"The name Yahweh gave him," Abram corrected. "I believe Yahweh really spoke to her. I don't understand but I believe."

"She's only a woman, my lord, only a slave."

"But she gave us a son," he said gently. "The Lord made a covenant with me, and now I have a son to inherit the land that was promised to me. It's not so strange that Yahweh would come to the girl who made this possible."

Sarai was too intent on the baby to even listen to what Abram was saying. Her arms had been empty for years and now she had a child to hold. Not just any child—not an awkward, half grown slave as Hagar had been when Sarai had taken her for her own comfort—but Abram's own son. Stroking her finger along the top of the little head, Sarai discovered that it didn't matter that Hagar had borne him. He had been delivered to *her*. She had a son at last.

The baby turned his face from one side to the other with a blind, seeking motion, and his lips moved. "He's hungry," Sarai said. "I'll take him back for feeding. Shall we leave him in her tent, my lord?"

Abram looked at Sarai and his heart melted with its new burden of love. "Leave him long enough to feed," he said. "Then if you don't mind carrying him back and forth when he cries, we can keep him in here with us."

"Thank you, my lord," Sarai said and they smiled at each other with love.

"Hagar," Abram said several months later when Hagar had begun serving in their tent again. "Before you take Ishmael to feed him, I want to say something."

Hagar waited impatiently. She hated to be cheated out of even one minute of the private times she had with Ishmael. Only in her own tent, when he nursed, could she say her foolish little love words to him, sing the old lullaby songs her mother had sung to her.

"When the boy is weaned," Abram said, "In three or four years, when he's weaned, we'll find a husband for you. We'll try to give you a life of your own."

"I'll be too old, my lord," Hagar said steadily.

"Nonsense!"

"No, my lord, truly. I'll be past twenty five—and not a virgin. There's no one who would want me, no one I'd want to go with. I want to serve you and my lady, that's all. I've . . . well, I've had a child, so it's all right, my lord."

He looked at her in distress. "It's not fair, though."

"It's fair enough, my lord." Hagar said. "If you and my lady will let me stay, I'll be content."

"Are you sure?"

"Yes, my lord. Very sure."

She bobbed her head courteously and almost ran toward her own tent. There, behind the wall which shaded her from the sun, she put the baby to her breast. He ate with the concentration with which he did everything. When he cried, he screamed louder than any other baby in the camp. When he smiled, there was sunshine all around. His tiny hands clung with a strength seldom seen in infants, and young as he was, his feathery eyebrows could bend down in a scowl that was almost fierce.

He will be a wild ass of a man, the Voice had said, every man's hand against him and his hand against every man. Hagar had tried to tell that part of the prophecy to Sarai, but she had only laughed. He was just an unusual baby, Sarai had pointed out, because he was the child of Abram.

But it was more than that, Hagar knew, and it was her responsibility to stay near him. As long as Abram and Sarai claimed him for their own, she had to continue to serve them. She had no other choice.

And besides, she thought, looking down into the dark eyes so much like her own, he holds my heart in his tiny hands. He may never know how much I love him, because I'll never dare show it when he's old enough to understand, but I would die for him.

She smiled at him, but he was indifferent to her. It was only in Sarai's or Abram's arms that Ishmael smiled his sunshine smile. I wonder, Hagar thought with a grief that none of Meryet's words had prepared her for, if he'll ever even know that I'm his mother.

PART FOUR

PART FOUR

God said...No longer shall
your name be Abram but
...Abraham...
As for Sarai your wife
...Sarah shall be her
name...

And Sarah saw the son of
Hagar...wherefore
she said unto Abraham,
Cast out this bondwoman
and her son...

GENESIS 17:5a, 15; 21:9a, 10a

22

Hagar walked from the cooking area toward her own tent for a brief midday rest. The sun had beaten down on her all morning, and she was weary. But she stopped when she saw the two children playing in the dirt.

"Does your father know you're out here?" she said sternly to the small boy who glared up at her out of eyes that were amazingly like her own.

"He knows," Ishmael said. "He's there—see?—under the oak trees. He told Emah he'd watch me."

Emah, the childish word for mother, and Abba, the diminutive form for father, were the only names Ishmael had ever known for the two people he thought were his parents.

"How can he watch you," Hagar asked reasonably, "if you both creep around behind my tent where he can't see you?"

"He'll only sleep anyway," Ishmael said.

"I'll watch him," the little girl offered.

Hagar looked at Yafah with real affection. The little girl looked more Egyptian every day, Hagar thought. Dothan's mother's mother had also been Egyptian, and, as a result, Yafah looked as though she might have been born along the Nile.

"How can you watch me?" Ishmael demanded of Yafah. "I'm bigger than you."

"Suppose I watch both of you," Hagar suggested.

Ishmael sent her a dark look. He was familiar with her watching. Where Emah would only smile or Abba caution mildly, Hagar would use a switch that stung his legs like fire. As a result, he avoided her whenever possible.

"We'll go back where Abba's sitting," Ishmael said sulkily. "Come on, Yafah."

Hagar stood without moving until she was sure that the children were absorbed in what they were doing and were so close to Abraham that he had to be aware of them.

Abraham! After nearly a year, the new name still felt strange in her thoughts or on her tongue. And Sarah. But Yahweh had given the new name when he had demanded the new covenant. A strange covenant, requiring a strange sacrifice—the circumcision of all males in Abraham's tribe. But when it was over, the men walked prouder, confident that they bore in their flesh the mark of their God.

And Ishmael, Hagar's thoughts went on—there may not have been a new name for him, but he, too, bore the covenant seal on his body. She had thought at first that Yahweh was asking too much, but she had seen, even in this short time, that the tribe was more closely knit to each other and to Abraham's God because of the new ritual.

And Ishmael is the child of the covenant, Hagar mused. Surely *that* could never be taken away from him. She turned and went into her tent. If she were not able to openly claim her child, she found great comfort in the fact that Yahweh had marked him for his own.

The afternoon peace was shattered by a howl, and Abraham's head jerked up.

"It's mine!" Ishmael yelled in a piercing voice.

"It's not. It's mine and if you don't let me keep it, I'll tell my mother." Yafah spoke as hotly as he.

"Tell her," Ishmael howled. "You're a donkey, Yafah! Your mother is only a slave and my mother will just tell her to go back to her own tent and take care of her children. Give me that!"

The last words were emphatic, but the little girl put her hands behind her and stood her ground defiantly.

The slap was so loud that Abraham found himself wincing. "Ishmael," he shouted. "Come here."

Yafah's sobs were lusty enough, but she did not give up what she held in her hands.

She's as much a match for him as anyone, Abraham thought almost with admiration. She's got her mother's spunk.

With a glowering look at Yafah, Ishmael turned and trudged over to his father. "What?" he said, looking up through the tangle of his dark hair.

As always, Abraham felt himself rendered helpless by the mere fact that this child was here in front of him, a breathing, living proof of Yahweh's goodness.

"You oughtn't to hit Yafah," Abraham said mildly. "You're bigger than she is, and you ought to be kind to her."

"She took my best stone," Ishmael protested, his lip protruding.

"There are thousands of stones," Abraham pointed out. "Everywhere you look on the ground, there are stones."

"But that was *my* stone!" The child darted a black look at his playmate and then put on a winning smile. "Please, Abba, make her give it back."

He crawled up onto Abraham's lap and put his head against his father's chest. A child of the covenant, Abraham thought, remembering the solemn hours that had followed Yahweh's instructions. Surely this boy is blessed and will inherit not only the land which Yahweh has promised, but the knowledge of Yahweh as well. Why is he so defiant at times? Why isn't he like other children?

"Please, Abba," Ishmael said in the softest of voices.

But for once Abraham was able to resist the cajoling plea. "Don't be greedy. Go and find another stone, and if I see you hit Yafah again, I'll... I'll turn you over to Hagar."

There was mingled disappointment and anger in the child's eyes, but there was respect, too.

"Hagar's only a slave," he said with an attempt at indifference. "Emah won't let her scold me."

"Hagar is not 'only a slave,'" Abraham retorted sharply. "You're not to think of her that way."

"What way *am* I to think of her?" Ishmael asked, his eyes shrewd.

They had agreed, Abraham and Sarah, that Ishmael was not to know that Hagar had borne him. And Hagar, Abraham was certain, had never indicated to the child that he was hers. Some day, Abraham thought heavily, he'll probably have to know, but not until he's grown, not until he's a leader of my people.

"Well, you're to think of her as someone who's to be respected and obeyed," Abraham said. "Emah and I took care of her for many years, so she's almost . . . almost like an older sister to you. When she says you must do something, you must do it!"

Ishmael looked down at his dirty bare feet. "She looks out of the back of her head," he confided to his father. "She can see what I'm doing even when she isn't looking."

Abraham shouted with sudden and unexpected laughter and after a minute, Ishmael laughed with him, giggling and burying his head in his father's lap.

"Then she's a good person to have around," Abraham said.

"And must I really find another stone?" Ishmael asked, peeking up.

"Yes, you really must."

Ishmael accepted the decision with a sudden capitulation to his father's wishes. "All right," he said. "Let her have the old stone. She's only a girl."

"Exactly," Abraham agreed. "Why don't you sit here in the shade with me and rest a little while? Your face is as red as a pomegranate."

"A little while," Ishmael conceded. "Abba, tell me a story."

"Well," Abraham began, gratified that, in this one thing, he was superior to all others in holding the boy spellbound, "I'll tell you about the great flood."

Ishmael settled down with a look of expectancy.

Suddenly Yafah, who had scuttled toward her own tent with her stone, came racing toward them.

"Go away," Ishmael shouted. "This is *my* story!"

Yafah ignored the little boy. "My mother told me to tell you, my lord, that there are strangers coming up the path. Three men, she said, and dressed in fine clothes."

It was for this, Abraham thought in amazement, that I had refrained from going into my tent to sleep. Somehow I knew they were coming.

"But my story, Abba," Ishmael whined.

"Later," Abraham promised. "Run and find Emah. Tell her I need her. And Hagar, too. We're going to have guests, and we must greet them properly."

The event was unusual enough to erase Ishmael's disappointment, and he ran obediently to do his father's bidding. Abraham stood quietly, watching his guests approach across the camp compound. There was a sense of warmth in him, similar to the feeling that was his when the Voice roared through his head.

Sarah and Hagar were harvesting grain, and Ishmael's cries were the first indication they had had of the approaching guests.

"Emah!" Ishmael called, and Sarah thought his childish word for mother the loveliest name in the world—dearer than either the familiar Sarai or the still strange Sarah. "Emah, you're to come at once. Abba wants you!"

"Is he sick?" Sarah asked anxiously.

"No. We're going to have guests. You're to come, too," he added, glancing up at Hagar.

"Your face is dirty," Hagar said, hardening her heart against him as she had to do each time she saw him.

"I'll wash it tonight," Ishmael said, but he did not waste his smiles on the young woman whom his father had said was to be treated as an older sister.

"I'll wash it for you," Hagar promised.

"I want Emah to do it," Ishmael cried, remembering Hagar's brisk ministrations from the past.

"We'll wait and see who the guests are," Sarah said quickly. The child's preference for her was heartwarming, but she always found it just a little embarrassing when he was so candid about it in front of Hagar.

But Hagar seemed impervious to it. "No matter who the guests are," she said firmly, "it's time for an all over bath for you . . . now that the spring rains are bringing us water. Your mother is too gentle. You need to be scrubbed."

Ishmael darted one of his black looks at Hagar and took Sarah's hand. "You'd better hurry," he said, pulling on her. "The men are here by now."

Sarah glanced at Hagar. "I wonder who?" she murmured over the little boy's head.

They hurried toward Abraham's tent, Ishmael clinging to Sarah's hand and Hagar behind them. There was no real pain in Hagar at the sight of Sarah and Ishmael together. She had forced herself to live with the idea that the little boy had no feeling for her at all. She knew he was not to be blamed for this. Both Sarah and Abraham had taught the boy to be as he was.

But the four years that had passed since Ishmael's birth had not altered Hagar's conviction that he was *her* responsibility, although there had been a time when she might have left Abraham's tribe. Just after Ishmael was weaned, a messenger had come from Simeon's caravan and had been alone with Abraham in his tent for several hours. Later Abraham had told Hagar that if she would like to go with Simeon, he was still willing to have her. Simeon was already married, Abraham had said; in fact, there were two wives. But Simeon had never been able to forget Hagar and if she wanted to go. . . .

But Hagar had begged to stay and Abraham had seemed only too glad to send the messenger away, laden with rich gifts for Simeon but without the girl for whom the servant had been sent.

"There!" Ishmael cried when they got within sight of the tent. "There! They're sitting under the trees with my father. Abba, Abba, we're here."

He darted away from Sarah, casting himself into Abraham's lap. But for once, Abraham didn't respond. He looked up and spoke quietly.

"Hagar," he said, "take the child. Keep him in your tent until I call for him. Sarah, prepare food for our guests. Take three measures of meal to make cakes. And if you will excuse me, my lords," he added, turning to the guests who sat in the shade of the great oak trees, "I'll get a calf and prepare meat for you."

Ishmael turned to dart away, but Hagar caught his arm. "You'll do as your father says," she hissed, too softly for anyone but the child to hear.

Her fingers were so relentless on his arm that Ishmael turned suddenly docile and stood waiting quietly.

Sarah gestured to Hagar to come where they could talk.

"Take the boy to Meryet," Sarah said. "He can play with Yafah, and Meryet can watch him. I'll need you to help prepare the food and serve it. Hurry now."

Hagar saw the relief on Ishmael's face. "Listen to me," she said. "If Meryet tells me that you're unkind to Yafah or that you tease the baby and make him cry, you'll be punished. I mean, whipped with a switch that will make your legs sting for hours. Do you understand me?"

Ishmael looked up into her face. He looked as though he would like to make a bold retort but he swallowed his words.

"All right," he said, his voice sulky.

"If you'd be good," Hagar urged, her voice strangely serious, "then people would love you and life would be sweet as honey for you. Why can't you understand that?"

He wriggled impatiently under the intensity of her gaze. "I don't need to be good to be loved. Emah and Abba love me anyhow."

"Maybe," Hagar conceded, "but there's still the switch to be remembered. And your father will let me use it."

"May I go to Meryet's now?" Ishmael asked, ignoring her last words.

"Yes, I'll go with you."

"I don't need you," he said. "I can tell Meryet what Emah said. And besides, Meryet knows the guests are here. She's the one who told Abba."

I might have known, Hagar thought wryly. "All right, then, go!" she said and watched the little boy dash thankfully away from her.

It would be easy to cuddle and spoil him, she thought, just as I was cuddled and spoiled when I was small. But I don't want him to suffer the anguish I went through when I was first taken to the Pharaoh's court. I want to make him strong.

"Here," Sarah said when Hagar joined her, "take these little cakes I've mixed and put them on the hot rocks to bake. Are they still warm from the last meal?"

"I think so. I'll stir the fire a little. Shall I look for some fruit, my lady? There are pomegranates and figs, I think."

"Yes, whatever you can find. Our lord seems anxious that the men be fed well."

Abraham himself served the meal to his guests—succulent, tender roast calf, hot, crisp bread and both pomegranates and dried figs.

The men ate hungrily and then smiled at Abraham.

"Thank you," said one of them. "Yahweh will bless you for your hospitality."

Abraham stiffened. "Do you know my Lord Yahweh?" he whispered.

The men nodded affirmatively.

"Are you from King Melchizedek?" Abraham asked.

The spokesman made a sketchy gesture. "We come from the east," he said vaguely.

"Will you stay with us for the night?" Abraham inquired. "We would be honored if you chose to stay with us awhile."

"No, thank you. We've got a long way to travel. We're heading for Sodom."

"I have a nephew there," Abraham said eagerly. "His name is Lot. If you should see him, would you take him our love and our blessing?"

"Of course. But, before we leave, we'd like to see your wife, Sarah. Is she here?"

Abraham felt a quick sense of surprise that they should know her name, and then he rebuked himself. If these men came from Yahweh, they could know anything.

"She's inside the tent, my lords," Abraham said. "Shall I call her?"

"I suppose it's not really necessary," the man conceded. "I just want you to know—you and Sarah both—that I will surely come back in a year, and in that season Sarah will bear a child."

"A child, my lord?" Abraham gasped. "But Sarah is too old. I'm too old."

The man's voice was emphatic. "In a year, Abraham, your wife, Sarah, will bear a son."

23

Hagar and Sarah stood inside the tent, hidden from the men but able to hear the words clearly.

The stranger's announcement held such solemn conviction that Hagar caught her breath, but Sarah dissolved in laughter. There was a time, Hagar knew, when Sarah would not have laughed, when tears would have been her only reaction to the old promise. But now, with the security of Ishmael, Sarah's tensions had slowly disappeared. She looked at Hagar with her face crumpled into lines of disbelief and delight.

"Shall my lord and I know that kind of joy," she whispered, "now that we're really old?"

"You shouldn't laugh, my lady," Hagar breathed. "Those men are from Yahweh; I heard them say so to our lord."

But Sarah only shook her head helplessly from side to side and hid her face in her hands while her soundless laughter shook her shoulders.

"Did Sarah laugh?" the spokesman said sternly to Abraham.

"I didn't hear her, my lord," Abraham protested.

"No, but she did laugh."

Hagar looked anxiously at her mistress. The laughter had been silent, but the men had heard.

Sarah's eyes were suddenly frightened. She pushed aside

the curtain and went out into the presence of the guests.

"I didn't laugh," she declared earnestly.

The man's face was kind but his voice was solemn as he contradicted her. "Yes, you did. You laughed because you think such a thing is altogether impossible."

"But it *is* impossible, my lord," Sarah said breathlessly. "It has been years since. . . ."

"Is anything too hard for the Lord?"

Hagar felt the hair on the back of her neck rise as though a cold draft had blown across her. If Sarah had her own son, what would happen to Ishmael?

"Is anything too hard for the Lord?" the man repeated, this time in a voice so soft that it was a whisper. "I tell you truly, I'll return next spring, and a son will be born to you, Sarah."

He stood up then, and the other two men stood with him. "We must start on our journey," he said to Abraham.

"I'll walk a way with you, my lord," Abraham said, casting an anxious glance at Sarah who stood as though she were turned to stone.

"We'll welcome your company," the guest said, and he looked at Hagar. "You'll see to your mistress, won't you?"

Hagar nodded, and the four men turned and started along the path that angled downward toward the plains.

Hagar helped Sarah into the tent, helped her lie down with a pillow under her head and wiped her face with a cool cloth. Finally, certain that Sarah would sleep, Hagar slipped out of the tent and stood hesitantly, twisting her hands together in a wringing motion.

She had to talk to Abraham, to ask him about Ishmael's future, and yet she was reluctant to follow him and the other men. Finally she ran to a higher spot and looked down toward the valley. In only a few minutes, she saw three men emerge from a clump of trees and move down the path. They were too far away for her to distinguish their features, but since there were only three of them, Abraham must have started back toward the camp. Well, then, she could run and meet him and ask her question. Sarah would surely sleep for a while, and Ishmael was safe with Meryet.

She expected to find Abraham around the first bend of the path but he was not there, and she began to feel apprehensive. She ran quickly toward the next bend but stopped abruptly when she reached it. Just beyond, in the thin shade of some scrubby trees, Abraham lay prostrate.

But it was an attitude of prayer, she realized almost at once, and she crouched quietly where she was. As the silence began to flow around her, she felt a sort of ringing in her head.

She heard Abraham speak in a clear, incredulous voice. "Will you really destroy the cities, Lord? Both Sodom and Gomorrah?"

Again Hagar was aware of a silent ringing in her head, but she was not able to distinguish any words. This was only right, she realized. Yahweh was speaking to Abraham, not to her. She was blessed beyond the scope of her dreams in that she could hear even this faint echo of the Voice.

"But, Lord," Abraham argued, "if there are even fifty righteous men in the city, would you destroy it?"

Abraham seemed to listen with fierce intensity. Suddenly he sat up. "My Lord," he said in a voice as normal as the one he would use in an argument with Eliezer, "would you destroy a city because only five men of that fifty were wicked? Surely you would not destroy a place where there are forty-five good men?"

Who else, Hagar thought with a mixture of admiration and fear, would dare argue with Yahweh?

"I am only dust and ashes," Abraham conceded with an effort to be humble, "but what if there are forty good men, Lord? Would you destroy the city then?"

Hagar watched the look that spread across Abraham's face.

"Oh, Yahweh," Abraham begged, "don't be angry with me. Please. But what if there were thirty good men? Would that be enough to save the city?"

There was a short, ringing silence, and then Abraham spoke meekly. "I have taken on myself to speak to the Lord, and perhaps I have no right . . . but if there were twenty good men, Lord? Would you destroy a city that contained twenty righteous men?"

Hagar held her breath, half expecting to see Abraham struck down for his audacity.

"Just one more time, Lord," Abraham pled. "I promise I won't ask again. But if there were only ten righteous men, Lord? Would you spare an entire city for ten good men?"

Hagar heard the ringing drain out of her head and for a few minutes, she felt as spent as Abraham looked. Then strength began to come back to her, and knowing certainly that Yahweh had left this place, she dared to get to her feet and approach Abraham.

She ran fearfully toward him.

"May I help you, my lord?" she asked.

He looked up at her, and his eyes were dazed. "The guests," he said in a shallow, hurried voice. "They were angels. We entertained angels and were unaware of it."

"But, my lord, what would you have done differently if you had known? You gave them food and water and made them welcome. You even believed their prophecy, didn't you?"

He nodded. "But Sarah laughed," he murmured in distress.

"It didn't make them angry, my lord. I don't think it did. And she . . . she was struck silent when they asked if anything was too hard for the Lord. I don't think you need to worry, my lord."

"Well, time will tell," he said and then added heavily, "I've been talking with the Lord God Yahweh."

"Yes, I know. I heard you."

"Did you hear Yahweh, too?" Abraham asked in astonishment.

"No, my lord. He was speaking to you. I had a . . . a sort of ringing in my head."

Abraham seemed hardly to hear her. "Yahweh is going to destroy the cities of Sodom and Gomorrah. I've tried to talk him out of it. He said if there were ten good men—surely there are ten?—he won't do it. Maybe I've saved the city."

"My lord," Hagar said humbly, "Lot doesn't even deserve that kind of love—that you would dare to argue with your God for him."

"I promised him," Abraham said, taking her hand to pull himself to his feet. "I promised Lot I would pray for him. Yahweh understands."

They began to walk along the path. "From things Meryet has said," Hagar offered, "there might not even be ten righteous men. Even Lot's daughters are married to evil men. Maybe only Lot and his sons are good. That's not ten, my lord."

Abraham stopped stricken. "Perhaps I should have asked Yahweh to spare the city for *one* righteous man?"

"My lord," Hagar suggested, "would you want so much evil preserved? Maybe if you had just prayed for Lot and his family—that they could escape from the city. . . ." She didn't know where the idea came from or how she had dared to suggest it.

"I'll do it," Abraham said eagerly, starting to walk faster. "I'll fast and pray and make sacrifice. For Lot."

It was almost as though he had completely forgotten the promise of a miracle, Hagar thought.

But then Abraham turned to her and his face was like a light. "If Sarah is to have a child," he said, "then I am blessed above all men, and it's only right that I should give myself in prayer for those who are not so blessed."

"Yes, my lord," Hagar murmured. She had followed Abraham with a specific question to ask. She had wanted his assurance that Ishmael would still be the child of the covenant even if Sarah had a baby. But she found she couldn't intrude on Abraham's concern for Lot. I'll ask him later, Hagar thought. If Sarah really does have a child—no, I know better than that—*when* Sarah has her child, I'll ask Abraham about Ishmael. That will be soon enough.

For the rest of the day and all during the night, Abraham prayed and fasted and burned animals for sacrifice. He asked some of the men to pray with him, so they were kneeling together in the dawn when the dull, muted explosion erupted over the rim of the distant plain. Terrified, they stared at the horizon where a crimson glow, smeared with darkness like ashes, spread in the place where once the cities of Sodom and Gomorrah had stood.

"Lot, my son, my son," Abraham moaned. But then a note of hope crept into his voice. "Yahweh has surely heard our prayers. I believe that our God is able to save Lot and his family."

The people stared at the horizon and seemed unable to even grasp what their eyes were seeing.

"The time for prayer is past," Abraham announced in a strong voice. "Now we must work. All of you, get about your business. Lot is in Yahweh's hands."

It took three days for the terrified, ash-covered messenger to reach Abraham's tent. He was Simeon's servant, he declared in an exhausted voice, and Simeon had sent him because he knew how worried Abraham would be. Lot had escaped! Yes, he was sure. His master, Simeon, had seen the family hurrying across the plain toward the little city of Zoar.

"Yahweh's name be praised!" Abraham cried, interrupting the account. "He heard our prayers!"

"But Lot's wife, my lord," the messenger said, "she didn't escape. She lingered so long, looking at the city that she . . . she was covered with brimstone and ashes. She stands there like a pillar of salt, my lord."

The words were hushed with the horror of what he was saying, and Abraham listened in stricken silence.

It was Sarah who cried out, "Oh, poor Zahavith!"

There was terror as well as pity in her voice, and Abraham

tried to comfort her but she would not be comforted.

"Perhaps she mocked the Lord as I did," Sarah wailed.

"You didn't mock Yahweh, my love," Abraham said softly, signaling Dothan that the messenger be fed and cared for. "You only laughed. But now you believe, don't you? You believe as I do!"

Hagar watched Sarah's face as grief gave way to hope and hope gave way to certainty. Next spring, Hagar thought with mingled awe and apprehension, Yahweh's promised miracle will take place. A son will be born to Sarah in her old age.

"There's another thing that my master told me to say," the messenger announced to Dothan as they walked away together. "He said to tell your lord that Simeon's caravan still travels on the route to Egypt from Damascus—on the route that skirts the Negeb. If the girl ever changes her mind. . . ." His voice trailed off.

Dothan nodded. "Thank you. I'll tell my lord. I think my lady, Sarah, will need Hagar for the next several years. But there may come a time—yes, tell your master that I suspect there may very well come a time. . . ."

24

"Hagar!" Abraham's voice shook her awake. She had been dreaming of him, and, for a few seconds, she thought she was back in the time when he had shared her tent. She even rolled toward the sound of her name, expecting the feel of his arms.

"Hagar! Wake up! It's the child. He's coming."

"I'm awake, my lord," Hagar mumbled. "Give me only a minute."

"Hurry!" Abraham's voice was urgent. "I don't want to leave her alone, and I must take Ishmael to Meryet's tent. She needs you right away."

"Get Soshannah, too, my lord," Hagar said. "I'm not clever at this. I can only be ... a comfort to her."

"Of course. I know. Hurry."

Sarah's moans met Hagar at the door of the tent.

"Why isn't a lamp lit?" Hagar asked with irritation.

"I couldn't bear that my lord see me like this," Sarah gasped.

"How foolish you are," Hagar said, making an effort to keep her voice gentle. "He loves you enough to see you under any circumstances. Here, let me go out and get a live coal. In a minute we'll have light and, if you like, a bit of food to nourish you."

"No, wait until Soshannah comes and let her get the light.

Don't leave me, Hagar. I'm afraid."

Hagar reached out and caught the hand that was groping for hers. "There's nothing to be afraid of, my lady. Yahweh has promised you a son. What's there to worry about?"

"I might die," Sarah wailed.

"Oh, nonsense! If Yahweh didn't want you to be the child's mother, he would never have made you pregnant in your old age. Have you thought of that?"

"He might punish me because I laughed," Sarah said fearfully.

"Is he such a God, my lady?"

"I don't know." Sarah's voice stopped short with pain and then struggled on. "I don't seem to know him as well as you do. You're the one he spoke to."

"Do you still worry about that, my lady? But that's foolish. What else would have brought me back to Abraham's tents? Perhaps you've never needed to be spoken to like that," Hagar said, her voice as soothing as though she were comforting a sick child.

Soshannah came to the door of the tent. "Is there no light?" she asked.

"Will you get a live coal?" Hagar said. "My lady didn't want me to leave her."

"But I did more than laugh," Sarah persisted when Soshannah had left. "I didn't have enough faith. I should never have told Abraham to lie with you. I should have had enough faith to wait for this child."

"But, my lady, if you had waited—then Ishmael wouldn't have been born," Hagar protested. "Think of the joy he's brought you."

"Oh, Ishmael . . . ," Sarah said, and her voice dismissed him as though he were of no consequence. Then she cried out suddenly, and Hagar reached for her hand.

This wasn't the time to be worried about Ishmael and his inheritance, Hagar rebuked herself. This was the time for all three women to concentrate on the task of bringing a child to birth.

The pain was gone, and Sarah felt drowned in peace. She looked again at the baby on her arm, and she thought she couldn't bear the amount of joy that filled her. She had thought, holding Ishmael the night he was born, that she was happy, but she hadn't known what happiness was.

This, *this* was happiness—the miracle of the baby that Yahweh had sent her—not through the body of her slave but out of her own body. She and Abraham and Yahweh had created a child.

"May I see my son?"

Sarah looked up to see Abraham at the door of the tent. It wasn't proper for him to come inside, but at least his eyes could touch her with love and pride.

"Here, Hagar," Sarah said. "Let my lord see the child."

Hagar hurried to obey, but her heart was breaking. Everything she cared about had changed during this night, she realized. Nothing would ever be the same again.

Hagar placed the baby in Abraham's arms and tried not to look at his face. But she couldn't help seeing the joy that blazed from his eyes and curved his mouth into an elated smile.

"Yahweh's name be praised!" Abraham exulted, and there was nothing solemn in his voice. Laughter seemed to bubble in the words. "What shall we call him, my love?" he asked, looking over at Sarah.

And she laughed with him, feeling as though she would never have to weep again. "Shall we call him Isaac, my lord? I laughed when I heard the prophecy of his coming, and you laughed now, seeing him. Shouldn't we give him a name that means laughter?"

"Isaac," Abraham murmured. "Child of laughter. Child of promise. In eight days we'll include him in Yahweh's circumcision covenant."

"My lady should rest," Hagar murmured, but she knew it wasn't really Sarah she was thinking of. She didn't think she could bear to see Abraham's joy any longer. "Let me take the baby back to my lady, my lord, and we'll let her rest."

"Of course," Abraham answered. "But it's morning, and I want to bring Ishmael to see the baby. Will that be all right?"

"My lord," Sarah began, but Hagar's voice was stronger.

"Oh, yes, my lord," Hagar said, forcing herself to sound casual. "Ishmael will surely want to see his brother for a minute."

"Then sleep, my love," Abraham said to Sarah. "When Ishmael and I come back, you won't even hear us."

"Ishmael is always noisy," Sarah said fretfully when Abraham was gone. "He'll disturb the baby... and me."

"Oh, no, my lady," Hagar said. "You know I can always make him mind. You won't have to worry."

A touch of shame darkened Sarah's face. "You know I love Ishmael," she said defensively. "It's just...."

"You're just tired, my lady," Hagar injected smoothly. "Any woman who has just delivered a child is reluctant to have the older children around at first. It's perfectly natural."

"Is it?" Sarah asked, her voice fading with drowsiness. "Then, when I'm better, I'll feel differently?"

"Yes, my lady," Hagar said firmly. "You'll feel differently."

While Sarah slept, Hagar sat beside her and looked first at the baby and then at the sleeping mother. Oh, please, she found herself crying silently to Yahweh, oh, please, don't let this baby come between Ishmael and the two people he loves so much. There needn't be a problem, Lord. There can be two sons, equally loved, equally cherished. Please, I'll do anything... anything if you'll only keep Ishmael in their hearts.

Abraham came cautiously, quietly through the early morning, holding Ishmael by the hand. "You have a brother," he said to the sleepy child. "You have a little brother."

"Will he take my stones?" Ishmael asked.

"He's much too young to bother you at all," Abraham promised. "He'll only eat and sleep for a very long time yet. You'll have lots of time to get used to him before he's big enough to play with you."

"Will Hagar take care of him?" Ishmael asked.

"Perhaps. And Emah, too. Emah will take care of him most of all."

Ishmael stopped still and stared up at his father. "I don't want Emah to take care of him," he said. "Emah has to take care of me."

Abraham looked helplessly at the little boy.

Hagar, who had come to the tent door to look for them, heard Ishmael's remark, and she spoke clearly, "That's silly, Ishmael. Doesn't Yafah's mother take care of all her children? Certainly Emah can take care of two little boys."

"I want her for myself," Ishmael muttered.

"Well, come and see your brother," Hagar suggested. "Perhaps you'll like him so well that you'll want to share Emah with him."

"I don't think I'll like him at all," Ishmael said.

Hagar's heart plunged with despair. What could she do or say that would make this stubborn child behave as he should? She couldn't resort to the switch here, and even if she could, she doubted that it would do any good.

"Wait here," she said softly. "I'll bring the baby for you to see."

Ishmael stared past the door to where Sarah lay sleeping, worn out from her labor. "There's Emah," he said to Abraham. "Why is she sleeping in the day?"

"She's tired. Having the baby made her tired. In a few days she'll be up and around as usual. Look, here's Hagar with Isaac."

Ishmael looked down sullenly and then found his eyes pulled up by the intensity of Hagar's gaze. It was almost as though she were commanding him to behave.

"Here, sit here on the pillow," Abraham urged. "Could he hold the baby, Hagar? Would it be safe?"

"Yes," Hagar said decisively. "Here, Ishmael. Bend your arm. Here's your little brother."

Ishmael sat obediently, bent his arm as directed and

looked into the tiny face of Isaac. The dark look on Ishmael's face smoothed itself out into something like relief.

"He's only little," he announced.

"Shh!" Abraham said. "You'll wake Emah. I told you he was only little."

"He'll have to mind *me*," Ishmael confided in a loud whisper. "I'm the firstborn, so he'll have to mind *me*."

"Who told you that?" Hagar asked sharply.

"Meryet," Ishmael said, absorbed in the baby on his lap. "Isn't he red? Was I red like that when I was born?"

"Yes. And perhaps Isaac will grow up to be as handsome as you," Abraham said, his proud, happy gaze going from one boy to the other. "Now give him back to Hagar. Come on, we'll go to breakfast. Meryet has said she'll feed us," he added for Hagar's benefit.

Hagar bent to get the baby, and her eyes met Ishmael's.

"Don't drop him," he said.

"I won't," she replied seriously.

The baby wailed with a thin, high sound, and Sarah woke with a start. "No," she cried out, "no, Ishmael, stop!"

"What's the matter, my lady?" Hagar asked. "Ishmael's nowhere around. Meryet's keeping him."

"It must have been a dream," Sarah said with a long sigh. "I dreamed that Ishmael was hitting Isaac . . . hitting him over and over."

"Oh, no, my lady," Hagar protested. "Ishmael was here while you were sleeping. He *liked* the baby. Truly he did. I've never seen him so gentle."

"But the dream was so real," Sarah fretted.

"Don't think about dreams, my lady. Think about your baby and his hunger. That's why he's crying. Will you nurse him or should we find a wet nurse among the women in the tribe?"

"Of course not. He's *my* child, and I'll nurse him."

They worked together until Sarah felt comfortable and Isaac was nursing with small, contented sounds.

"Hagar," Sarah said, looking intently at Isaac's head, "I think maybe Ishmael ought to start sleeping in your tent."

"In *my* tent, my lady?"

"Yes. Isaac will cry at night to be fed and it will wake Ishmael. He's not a heavy sleeper like some children are. He'll do better with you."

Hagar's voice was very low. "Are you sending him away so soon, my lady?"

Sarah's eyes were angry. "I'm not sending him away. Meryet's children sleep in a tent with a young slave. You know that. So do many of the children in the tribe. What I'm suggesting isn't unusual at all."

"But will Ishmael understand that, my lady?"

"Why wouldn't he understand it?"

"Because he loves you, my lady. Because he's too young to see it as anything but punishment. He doesn't love me, you know."

"Well, that's your own fault," Sarah retorted. "Why have you always been so harsh with him?"

"Because," Hagar said. "Because I've been afraid for him, and I wanted to strengthen him for the hurts that life would hand him."

Sarah was silent for a long time. When she finally spoke, her voice was determined. "Listen, Hagar, listen to me. I still love Ishmael . . . of course I do. You can't love a child since birth and get over it in a day."

"It isn't a day, my lady," Hagar argued. "You've had a year."

Sarah stared at the younger woman and then her eyes slid away. "This child at my breast was given to us by a miracle. Ishmael was given to us by our own selfish scheming. Can I help it if I feel differently about them?"

"No, my lady." Hagar sounded as defeated as she felt.

"I'm sure Abraham will always claim Ishmael as his son, and I know I'll always care for him. But our first responsibility is to Isaac. *Your* first responsibility is to Ishmael."

Hagar moved toward the tent door, and then she stopped.

She spoke quietly, but for this moment she was not a slave. "Don't you think I know that?" she asked. "Why do you think I stayed here when Abraham would have found a husband for me, when Simeon offered me a place with him? I stayed because Ishmael needed me, because I *knew* someday you would stop loving him. . . ."

Her voice trailed off, and she stood in miserable silence, shocked at her own daring.

Sarah stared at the girl and slowly turned her head away so that her voice was muffled and indistinct. "Then you won't mind taking him into your tent, will you?"

"No, my lady," Hagar said. "I won't mind at all."

To everyone's astonishment, Ishmael went quietly and unprotestingly to Hagar's tent that night. Abraham assured him it was only a step in becoming a man and Sarah was kind to the little boy and promised that when she was feeling better, she would play any game with him he wanted to play. Only Hagar seemed to see the pain and desolation in the child's eyes.

But she promised him nothing and offered no solace. She made a bed for him and saw to it that his feet were clean. She pretended that she didn't hear his weeping because she knew that he would struggle away if she tried to hold him. Only after Ishmael slept, his breath catching in his throat in ragged sobs, did she allow herself to touch him, to wipe the tears from his face, to press her cheek against his. Maybe, she thought drearily, he'll be aware of my nearness and think it's Sarah and be comforted.

25

When Isaac was three years old, the tribe was forced to journey a long distance for summer pasture. For the first time in several years, the spring rains had been late and sparse, and the pasturing areas in Hebron were drying up. For safety's sake Abraham had insisted that the entire camp travel along with the shepherds since they were to be gone a number of months. Sarah grumbled and complained as she always did when they moved, but Hagar worked silently.

Her silence was no virtue, and no one realized it more than Hagar herself. Since the night of Isaac's birth, she had pulled herself into herself as a small land turtle might pull itself into its shell. She had been bruised enough, she felt, and the less she shared herself with others, the better off she would be.

The day before they left, she ran up to her private sanctuary in the hills to impress the familiar stillness and peace into her mind for remembering while they were gone. To her astonishment, Ishmael followed her.

"What do you do up here?" he said. "Emah says you're silly to sit alone in this place."

"Your Emah just likes different things than I do," Hagar said carefully. "I like to be quiet and I like to be alone."

Ishmael climbed up onto the rock ledge, and drew his knees up so that his chin rested on them as his arms wrapped around his legs. He was silent for a while, and then he said, "I like it, too. I like it even better than the camp."

"I'm glad." Hagar smiled.

"Why couldn't we sleep up here?" Ishmael suggested.

"It's dangerous. There are wild boars, and besides there's no water. We couldn't wash or have water to drink."

Ishmael shrugged as though water weren't important. "I could take care of you," he said generously. "I could fight off wild boars."

Her look was solemn. "I'm sure I'd be safe with you here," she answered, "but it's better for us to stay at the camp."

The silence stretched between them, but it was not awkward. They were comfortable together, Hagar realized.

Ishmael looked at her slantwise. "Isaac would be afraid up here."

"I'm sure he would be. Of course, he's very small."

"He's three years old, nearly old enough to be weaned," Ishmael announced. "Yafah told me."

Hagar only gave an assenting murmur.

"Will he sleep in our tent with us?" Ishmael asked. "After he's weaned, I mean?"

"I don't imagine so," Hagar said, selecting her words with care. "You didn't come into my tent until two years after you were weaned."

Again the silence and then Ishmael spoke in a carefully careless voice. "And besides, you're not really Isaac's mother."

She almost answered with a casual agreement, then the words he had said stung her to awareness. "Well, of course I'm not," she said. "Why would you say that?"

He glanced at her and then shifted so that his eyes were staring out over the plain.

"Yafah says you're *my* mother," he said in an expressionless voice.

Her heart jerked, and she felt breathless and frightened. She hadn't prepared herself for this. It should be Abraham whom the child talked to, not her.

"Yafah talks too much," she muttered at last. "She's always chattering."

"Is it true?" Ishmael asked bluntly.

"You should talk to your father about things like this."

"I did. He just said to wait until I'm older. I don't want to wait until I'm older. And besides," he went on, "if it hadn't been true, he'd have just said I was being silly."

"When you're older, you'll understand better," she said faintly.

"I'm old enough," he said, and his eyes looked straight at her.

"Well, for years and years," Hagar began almost as though she were telling a story, "your Emah wanted a baby. She prayed and prayed to Yahweh, and every year she wept because she still didn't have a little boy. Your Abba loved her very much, and he felt as lonely as she did. He prayed to Yahweh, too, and always Yahweh said that someday there would be a son."

His eyes were intent on her face.

"But they got too lonely to wait, and so . . . your Emah asked if I would have a baby for her. You were . . . you were carried in my body, but when you were born, you were born onto Emah's lap. So, in a way, we are both your mother."

He sat thinking, and then he sighed deeply.

"Then why has she stopped loving me?"

Why indeed, Hagar wanted to say bitterly, but bitterness would not help this child. So she spoke as gently as she could. "I don't think she has stopped loving you. I only think she loves Isaac because he's still a baby . . . and. . . ."

"And because she's his real mother," Ishmael finished bleakly.

He put his head down on his arms, and for a minute she was afraid that he was crying, but when he lifted his face, she saw no sign of tears.

"She's afraid," he said in an oddly adult voice. "She's afraid because I'm the firstborn, and because my father loves me."

It was the first time Hagar had heard him use the mature

word for "father."

"It doesn't matter," Ishmael said after a few minutes. "My father loves me . . . he'll always love me."

"I'm sure he will," Hagar agreed. "He's a great man, your father, and he doesn't take away—or give—love lightly."

I'm the one who should know, she thought. How terribly I loved him, but he never even pretended to give me anything but a kind of affection. How I could love him still if it would do me any good. But I've learned to live without his love or even to think about it very often.

They sat a little longer in silence and then Hagar stood up.

"I must go down," she said. "There's a lot to do."

Ishmael slid down from the ledge. They turned to walk out of the sheltered corrie, and her worn sandal slipped on one of the stones.

"I'll help you," Ishmael said and reaching up, he took her hand.

"Thank you," she said steadily, but her heart was singing.

They walked down the rough path without speaking, but just before they reached the camp, the child looked up at Hagar.

"I don't mind," he said. "That you're my mother, I mean." He pulled his hand from hers and raced away toward Meryet's tent and the comfort of Yafah's constant companionship.

Hagar stood watching him, feeling the foolish tears prick her eyes. This was her moment of happiness, she knew, and it could never be taken away from her. Ishmael might be angry and insolent many times, but she would always have the memory of this moment for her solace.

When the tribe was traveling, there was little time for conversation, but one night Hagar met Abraham outside her tent. He looked tired and worried, and she hated to add to his burden of concern, but she felt it was important that he should know what had happened.

"My lord," she said quickly and quietly, knowing Ishmael

was asleep not too far away. "I must tell you something about the boy."

"Ishmael?"

"Shh! my lord. He's sleeping there in the tent."

"Has he misbehaved again?"

"My lord, he's a strong-willed boy and sometimes an insolent one. But he's not really bad. Why does everyone suspect the worst about him?"

Abraham grinned. "He makes a lot of noise. People notice that."

"My lady notices it particularly." It was a statement rather than a question.

"Sarah is nervous since Isaac was born," Abraham said with some apology. "She worries about him and gets upset if *any* of the children tease him or take his playthings."

"Yes, my lord. I want to tell you something. Have you a minute?"

"Of course."

She told him everything that had been said up on the hill, saving only the last statement for her own heart, and Abraham listened with distress.

"Is he terribly unhappy, do you think?" Abraham asked.

"No, my lord, not terribly. He missed my lady very much at first and cried night after night." She saw Abraham wince with pain, but she saw no reason for making this particularly easy for him. "He doesn't cry any more, my lord."

"We never know," Abraham said slowly, "what we do to other people. I wish that Yahweh would give us specific laws to follow so that we might do better. It seems to me that all I do is make mistakes."

"Oh, no, my lord, not you."

"You should know better than anyone," he said gravely. "I can only ask you again to be patient with your mistress and with me. I may not always approve of what she does, but I love her and I think Yahweh must love her."

"Yes, my lord, I know."

"Well, thank you for telling me. And you say the boy is

reasonably content with you?"

"Yes, my lord. I think so."

Oh, more than reasonably, her heart rejoiced, thinking of the sturdy feel of the little hand helping her down the steep path, the apparently casual words, "I don't mind—your being my mother, I mean." How right she had been to stay! What if Sarah had pushed him away and there hadn't been anyone to take him in?

"Good!" Abraham said. "He's still my son, Hagar, and will always be—no matter what."

For some reason the last three words sent a chill through Hagar. She tried to shrug it away, but it persisted long after she lay beside the sleeping Ishmael. There's trouble in store for me, she thought, worse trouble than any I've ever known before.

The tribe skirted the Negeb on their way south, and Hagar felt her skin crawl with a crinkle of horror as she looked down on the desolate wastes from the path that curved along the flanks of the hills.

And, as before, when they were safely past the desert area and back in a land where there were springs and wells, there was a desire to celebrate their newly established security.

"We'll have a feast," Abraham announced to the gathered tribesmen. "It will be a celebration of our safe journey past the Negeb, combined with the celebration of Isaac's weaning. We'll roast a calf and we're sure to find greens growing—maybe even some leeks. We'll sing and dance and praise our God with happy hearts. Do you agree, my people?"

They shouted their approval of his suggestion. The past weeks had been difficult ones—filled with hard work, dangerous traveling, meager food. It was a welcome idea to make merry and to eat with abandon. This valley where they were had wild grain growing in it and there were date palms and gnarled gray-green olive trees.

For several days the women worked and planned, and the

men laughed and told jokes as they herded the animals out
to pasture. Abraham was everywhere, usually with Ishmael,
and sometimes accompained by both of his sons. He had
never been so happy, Abraham thought. Here in this strange
land he couldn't see out over the plains that had held the
cities of Sodom and Gomorrah, so for a little while he could
even stop worrying about where Lot had gone and what he
was doing. He could concentrate on Yahweh's goodness and
on the richness of his life.

"If we didn't have Isaac with us," Ishmael declared as they
went from place to place, checking on arrangements, "we
could walk much faster, Abba. Isaac's too little to come with
us all the time."

Abraham looked down at Ishmael. "I always took you
with me when you were that little," he said.

"Really, Abba?"

"Of course."

"I'm big," Isaac said.

"Not as big as I am," Ishmael bragged.

Isaac looked at his older brother under lowered brows and
kicked Ishmael in the shins.

Ishmael howled and reached over to punch the smaller
boy in his little fat stomach.

Isaac's breath puffed out and he sat on the ground to raise
his voice in pain and indignation.

From nowhere, it seemed to Abraham, Sarah came flying.
She lifted Isaac into her arms, soothing him with crooning
words.

"He hit me," Isaac wailed, pointing a chubby finger at
Ishmael.

Sarah's anger blazed. "How dare you?" she cried. "My
lord, why can't you watch them? Why can't you control
Ishmael?"

"But, my dear," Abraham said mildly, "Isaac kicked
Ishmael first."

"How could his soft little baby feet hurt?" Sarah demanded.

Abraham looked at Ishmael's face and saw the anger that darkened it.

"Take Isaac with you, my love," Abraham said hurriedly. "I'll take Ishmael with me."

Sarah looked at her husband over the head of the weeping child. "This can't go on forever," she said. "You know that. Either Ishmael has got to change, or something must be done. I can't stand to see him treat Isaac this way."

"Come, Ishmael," Abraham said. He tried to give Sarah a warning look, but she was too busy mopping Isaac's tears to notice it.

"I didn't do anything so terrible," Ishmael muttered as he and his father walked away.

"You shouldn't punch him. He's too little."

"He kicked me."

"Can't you overlook a baby's kick?"

"Then he'll go on kicking me all my life. And someday he'll be bigger. Must I overlook it then?"

The child's logic was almost frightening, Abraham thought. "I don't know," he admitted to his older son. "I only know it's important for you to be good."

"So I won't upset Sarah?" Ishmael asked.

Abraham stopped in astonishment. "*Who?*"

"Why should I call her Emah any longer?" Ishmael reasoned. "She's not my mother."

Abraham shook his head. "Oh, Ishmael, Ishmael, don't talk like that. You'll only cause trouble for yourself."

Ishmael took his father's hand again. "As long as you love me, Abba, nothing can hurt me."

The celebration turned out to be all that anyone had hoped for. Laughter and song and fellowship filled the air, as Abraham's tribe ate and drank and sang and danced. Even the children were allowed to stay up late and eat foods not normally permitted.

Isaac, as the honored guest of the banquet, was passed from one person to another, given the sweetest morsels of food, hugged and kissed until he was quite indignant.

"Kissing for babies," he sputtered, scrubbing at his face.

"Then come with me," Ishmael said, "if you want to be with boys."

"Boys!" Isaac agreed with emphasis, and took his brother's hand.

In only a few minutes, they were part of the squealing, noisy crowd of boys who were taking advantage of the late hour and the lenient attitude of the parents.

"Isaac's too little to play with us," one of the boys said. "Take him back to his mother."

"Not too little," Isaac said stoutly, clinging to Ishmael's hand.

"Let him stay," Ishmael said carelessly.

"Stay!" Isaac agreed with delight as he watched several wrestling boys roll toward them.

Ishmael had only looked away for a second, it seemed, when the struggling boys on the ground rolled into their legs and sent them both tumbling. Isaac's voice lifted in its usual wail of protest.

"Oh, hush up," Ishmael said. "Don't be such a cowardly baby. If you want to play with boys, you're going to have to act like one."

Isaac stared at his brother and then shut his mouth. But Ishmael felt his shoulder taken in a rough grasp.

"Don't talk to him like that. Did you knock him down?"

Ishmael looked up into Sarah's face. There was only anger in the eyes that had once brimmed with love.

"Ask Isaac," Ishmael said.

"You're insolent," Sarah flared. "Isaac, did he knock you down?"

Isaac shook his head, but Sarah didn't even look at him. Her hand tightened on Ishmael's shoulder, and she shook him harshly. "You leave him alone, do you hear?" she said. "He could be hurt playing with these roughnecks—these friends of yours. Come on, Isaac, come with Emah."

"No," Isaac shouted, but she lifted him and carried him

away, while Ishmael stared after them with burning eyes.

The celebration was finished, and Sarah finally got Isaac to sleep. Abraham watched her warily, knowing that she was disturbed about something.

"It's got to stop, my lord," she said abruptly. "I won't let Isaac grow up with Ishmael—playing his rough games, listening to his insolence, being pushed around. Isaac is *our* child and he shouldn't have to share his inheritance with . . . with a slave's child."

"A slave's child, Sarah? But mine, too."

"Not the legitimate son, my lord. Not the heir Yahweh promised."

"Be reasonable. I can't just send them away as you've asked me before. What do you think I am?"

"Listen, my lord," she said, her words intense, "I've had an idea. We can send them out toward the caravan route. Someone will take them in and deliver them to Simeon. He's always wanted to marry her. Wouldn't it solve all of our problems? You'd finally keep your old promise to Simeon—and Isaac would be the only true heir, without . . . without any interference."

He spoke quietly. "You've figured it all out, haven't you?"

"Yes, my lord. I'm right. I know Yahweh would tell you I'm right.

"But, Sarah, Ishmael is my son!"

"True, my lord. But Yahweh didn't tell you to lie with Hagar. Isaac is the child Yahweh promised. O, please, my lord, think about it. I'll never—I swear to you—I'll never be happy until Hagar and Ishmael are gone."

As faint as an echo, Sarah heard the venomous words of the angry woman in the Pharaoh's court. "Someday you'll ask your god to take this worthless wretch out of your house." Well—the prophecy had come true. It wasn't that she hated either Hagar or Ishmael. She wasn't heartless, was she? Oh, surely not. She only wanted Isaac's inheritance to be secure.

26

Abraham sat dazed and incredulous, staring at the morning sky. Surely he had misunderstood God. Surely Yahweh had not really said that Sarah should be obeyed in this shocking thing. But the echo of the Voice sounded louder in his head than his own feeling of anguish and remorse.

Send your handmaiden out, the Voice had said.

There was little comfort in the promise that Ishmael would grow and marry and have children. Ishmael is my firstborn, Abraham thought bleakly, and can I let him go into this strange wilderness?

He didn't know he was murmuring the words aloud until he glanced up and saw Sarah watching him with elation shining in her eyes.

"My lord, Yahweh has told you I'm right," she cried softly. "How could you even doubt it? Isaac's inheritance must be kept safe. You should know that."

I loved her when she doubted Yahweh's promise, Abraham thought sadly, but I'm not sure if my love can survive this new fanaticism. Perhaps with Hagar and Ishmael gone, her zeal will gentle itself and she'll once more become the Sarah I loved.

"I'll tell Hagar today," he said wearily and could not meet Sarah's eyes.

Abraham looked for Hagar after the morning meal. His

heart lurched in his breast with queer, plunging strokes, and he tasted bitterness in his mouth. He saw her at last at the far edge of the camp, with only Ishmael and Yafah to keep her company. She was playing some little game with them, and she was laughing. She doesn't laugh often, Abraham thought. Poor child! And it was almost as though his fingers had encountered the remembered scars on her shoulders.

"Hagar," he said. "I have to talk to you. Send the children someplace else to play."

Hagar saw his face, and the dread which had been walking close to her for several days came close enough to touch her with coldness. "Go and play," she said tensely. "Don't bother my lord and me."

The children looked at her and saw something which made them go, without protest, to the other side of the camp.

"Yes, my lord?" Hagar said.

"Hagar, I don't know how to say this to you. Yahweh told me what to do but he didn't tell me how to do it."

"Yahweh, my lord? Are you sure it wasn't my lady?"

He looked at her uneasily. "What do you mean?"

"You're going to send me away, aren't you?" The words were said with no expression, but he could see how her hands twisted together.

"Yes," he said. He sought desperately for words to soften the blow, to make this easier for her, but he could find none.

"I can't leave Ishmael, my lord," she breathed. "I can't."

"You won't have to leave him."

"You mean, my lord," she said carefully, "you are sending us both away? But he's your firstborn son."

Abraham swallowed. "I know. But Yahweh. . . ."

Her calm began to shatter. "Don't keep blaming it on Yahweh, my lord. Not when it was Sarah who put the idea in your head."

"But Yahweh spoke to me," Abraham insisted. "Do you think I could do such a thing without his approval?"

She stood stricken. "You mean Yahweh has rejected me?"

she whispered.

"He said that Ishmael would be the head of a mighty nation, that his descendents would be numerous."

"But what about *me*?" Hagar cried, and he shifted uneasily under the anguish of her voice.

"We're near the caravan route here," he said. "And this is the time of year Simeon travels this way. I thought. . . ."

"Do you plan to send a group of men to protect the child and me? Do you plan to send a dowry?"

He felt no anger at her bitterness. It was no more than he deserved, even with Yahweh's decree to back him.

"Our plans weren't clear," he mumbled, "but I'm sure. . . ."

Her grief and despair spilled over and became a hot, blazing anger. "We don't need anyone," she said in a strident voice. "Besides, if someone goes with us, Ishmael will know he's being sent away. I won't let you do that to him. I won't let you be so cruel. I'll leave with him, now, this hour. He'll think we're only going for a walk to find a new shelter in the hills."

He started to interrupt, but she spoke even more shrilly. "I don't want your protection *or* a dowry. I don't want you and *I don't want your god!*"

The last words were wrenched out of a throat aching and tight with tears she was too proud to shed.

"Wait," he begged, reaching for her.

"No, don't touch me. Don't pity me. I've served you well, my lord. As payment, at least let me keep some dignity."

She whirled away from him and raced to her own tent where she stood trying desperately to calm herself. She could accept Sarah's willingness to send her away; she could almost accept Abraham's compliance with his wife's wishes. But she thought she couldn't bear it that Yahweh had rejected her.

I had begun to really believe that he was a God to worship forever, she thought, but he doesn't care for me any more than Sarah does.

The flap of the tent opened, and Meryet came in. "I heard

you shouting at Abraham," she said softly.

"When have you ever *not* heard me?" Hagar retorted.

"You *can't* go away alone," Meryet gasped. "You could get lost out there. You know how the paths twist and change, how the hills all look the same. We're not that far from the Negeb. Hagar, be sensible."

"If anyone goes with us, Ishmael will know his father is sending him away," Hagar insisted. "I won't permit it."

"But, Hagar. . . ," Meryet began.

"No, I'm making the plans now," Hagar said. "But I'll promise you this. If Ishmael lives to be a man, I'll send for Yafah to be his bride. If he's rich enough to suit you, that is."

"Oh, Hagar!" Meryet's grief was genuine. "Don't mock me."

"I wasn't mocking. I mean it—every word."

"Then—if you want him to live—let me find someone to go with you. We'll think of something to tell Ishmael. Please, Hagar, let me talk to Dothan before you go. Or, better yet, to Abraham."

Hagar pretended to consider Meryet's suggestion, but she looked at the ground so that her eyes would not meet her cousin's. "I think you'll find Abraham up at the higher pasture," she said at last.

"Oh, Hagar, you're finally being sensible." Meryet flung her arms around Hagar and hugged her breathlessly.

Hagar had all she could do to keep from throwing herself on Meryet's breast and weeping out her agony and despair. It would be the last time she would ever see Meryet, she knew, and although there had been hard words between them, there had also been a tough cord of blood and memory.

"Wait here," Meryet said, and hurried toward the high pasture.

Hagar watched her until she was out of the camp and then she hurried over to where Ishmael was playing with Yafah. To her dismay, she saw Abraham standing close by, watching his son with eyes that were filled with sorrow.

Without glancing at Abraham, Hagar called out. "Ishmael, do you want to come and help me find another corrie here—another secret place?"

"Can I go?" Yafah begged.

"Not this time," Hagar said. "Maybe sometime again."

"If *I* say so," Ishmael added. "Maybe I'll tell you about it," he added generously to the little girl.

"Come," Hagar said impatiently, knowing that unless she left very soon, her courage would fail her.

"Wait!" Abraham hurried toward them.

"My lord!" Hagar warned.

He pulled back the hands he had stretched out to his son. "I . . . I just wanted to give you my water skin," he said humbly. "I've just filled it. In case you should get thirsty," he added to Ishmael.

Ishmael slung the bag around his neck as though he had carried it many times.

"Thanks, Abba," he said. "Come on, let's go."

Hagar took the offered hand and turned her back to the man who had been the center of her world for more than half of her life. They were both silent, and she would not even allow herself to turn and look at him. She knew that his longing eyes would not be on her but on the little boy who trudged along beside her.

"My lord!" Meryet was breathless. "I've been looking all over for you. I thought you were up in the high pasture."

Abraham looked up, slowly focusing his sight and thoughts on the young woman who stood in front of him. "No . . . no," he said vacantly. "I've been right here."

"My lord, you can't allow Hagar to go out alone. She's hardheaded and stubborn, but she'll die out there. She doesn't know this country at all."

"She didn't want the boy to know they were being sent away," Abraham tried to explain.

"You can't let Ishmael's feelings matter more than his life, my lord. Please. Get some strong men to go with her."

"It's too late," he said. "They're gone."

"Gone, my lord?" For once Meryet had no plan of action. She simply stood and stared at the man who looked so suddenly old.

"Yes, they've been gone ... for ... I don't know ... an hour, maybe two."

Meryet thought of the long climb to the high pasture, of the time wasted while she drank from the spring there and talked to Dothan, of the long walk back. Two hours at least. Why hadn't she guessed that Hagar would deceive her?

"Oh, my lord," Meryet cried, and she was suddenly weeping, pulling at Abraham's sleeve, "you can't let them go out like that. You've got to try to find them."

"But Yahweh told me to let her go."

"But did he tell you to let her go *alone*?"

Abraham shook his head from side to side in a helpless, almost palsied gesture. "I didn't mean to let her go alone," he mumbled. "Yes, go find someone. Tell Eliezer to send a few men to find her and the lad, to lead them safely to the caravan route. Yes, do it at once."

Meryet ran, grateful for instruction, relieved to have something concrete to do.

It was full dark when the men came wearily back to the camp.

"We couldn't find her, my lord," they reported to Abraham. "She wasn't on any of the regular paths. We walked great distances, but we didn't even see any footprints, and there's no wind to blow the dust away. They're just... gone."

Abraham heard them in silence and turned away in despair. Alone, outside his tent, he began to pray. "Oh, my God, my God," he wept, "what have I done?"

Through his pain and shame, something cool and sweet moved. It was not so much the sound of the Voice as the memory of words once said. Is anything too hard for the Lord?

Abraham lay very still, letting the question fill his empty, bruised spirit. It wasn't really a question because the answer was implied in it. *Is anything too hard for the Lord?*

"Forgive me, Lord," Abraham whispered in a voice that was tired but peaceful. "Forgive me for doubting you and your plan. I'll put my son and my handmaiden in your hands, Lord. I don't see how, but I know you can save them. I believe. I believe."

Sarah's hands were very gentle, lifting him from the ground. "Come, my lord," she urged. "You must rest."

Already, Abraham realized, she was different. Perhaps it was for this that Yahweh had agreed to send Hagar and Ishmael away. And if life would be sweeter for Sarah now, then surely Yahweh had some good thing in store for Hagar and for her son.

27

It was Ishmael who found the little spot, high above the path, amazingly like the rocky sanctuary above the campsite in Hebron.

"Here," he called in delight, climbing up over the rocks. "Come on up here. You can see all over."

Hagar followed him, although something seemed to warn her not to leave the path. Still, the rocky corrie seemed familiar and comforting, and she was glad to sit down. The summer heat was almost overwhelming, and her throat felt dry and scratchy.

"We'll have a drink of water," Ishmael said, "and then we'll go back to camp. Here, you drink first."

He handed the skin to her, and she took it carefully.

"I'm not really thirsty," she lied. "Are you?"

Evidently his pride would not let him admit to a thirst that a woman didn't share. "We'll save it for later," he said airily. "Shall we start back?"

She couldn't tell him. At least not now. She would have to find the courage before nightfall, of course, but for now, she couldn't tell him that his father had sent him away.

"In a minute," she said quietly. "Just let me look for a while."

Her eyes were anxious, scanning the landscape in front of her. Meryet was right, the hills did all look alike, and the scarred earth seemed to bear the remnants of a hundred trails. But along the horizon there was something that might be a sort of road. If they went down the opposite side from the one which they had climbed, and if she were careful to keep the sun to her left, then surely she would be able to find the place she was seeking.

"Here," she said finally, "we'll go down here."

"We didn't come up that way," Ishmael protested.

"But it goes in the same general direction. We'll find the path all right."

He came with her, and to her relief, he spent so much time hunting for odd stones and chasing the tiny lizards that scuttled, rustling, in front of them, that she knew he had lost all sense of direction.

"I'm thirsty," Ishmael said at last. "Here, take a drink."

She let the water touch her lips but kept herself from swallowing. She watched his greedy gulping with mingled satisfaction and apprehension. It was good to be able to ease his thirst, but every drop that was swallowed meant there would be less for later on, when it really mattered.

She had been unable to keep the sun over her left shoulder. The paths twisted and turned, heading this way and that, branching off in places where it was impossible to determine whether they were really going east or west.

"I want to go home," Ishmael announced suddenly. "I want to go back to my father."

Hagar felt anguish slice through her. She wanted to go back too, but Abraham had sent them away. Yahweh had rejected them.

But Yahweh spoke to me once, Hagar reminded herself. Then her new bitterness pushed the memory away. He had spoken to her only because she was carrying Abraham's child, only because she had stumbled onto one of Abraham's altars. She was foolish to even think Yahweh could care for her out here in this lonely place.

But he could have cared for us in Abraham's camp, her painful thoughts went on. He didn't have to tell Abraham to send us away. Why—oh, why?

They trudged in silence for a while longer, and then Ishmael interrupted her thoughts. "I'm hot," he complained. "I'm hot and thirsty. I want another drink."

"No," she said harshly. "Save it for later."

He stared at her. "No, now. I want it now."

She snatched the skin from his hands and held it beyond his reach.

"You're only wasting it," she shrilled.

For a few more seconds, he stared into her face. "You're mean," he screeched. "You've always been mean. I'll go to my father. He'll give me all the water I want."

He whirled around on the path and started running headlong across the plateau on which they stood. She was astonished at the speed with which he ran. Surely he was too tired to run like that.

She pulled her robe above her knees and began running after him. For one terrible minute, she was afraid that she wouldn't be able to catch him, that he would just disappear from her sight. But she moved as swiftly as a young deer, panic and love giving her strength. She caught up to him just as he fell into a depresssion in the sand. She saw, with pain, the bloody marks on his legs where the spiney bushes had scratched him.

She lifted the weeping child, wiping the sand from his face with her hands. "It's all right. Look, here's the water. Go ahead and drink."

He drank greedily, and she saw some precious drops spilled down his chin.

"More," he demanded when she tried to take the skin from his fingers.

"Yes," she said dully. "Why not? Here—drink all you want."

He looked at her shrewdly and then tied the skin shut without drinking. "Later," he said, turning his face away. "I'll drink it later."

Hagar looked at his averted face. He grew more like Abra-

ham every day. Even the narrow Egyptian eyes were
shadowed by brows that were dark and heavy like his
father's.

No wonder Sarah was jealous, Hagar reflected. He's a
beautiful and a bright child, and Abraham loved him. Maybe
he would have even loved him more than Isaac if we had
stayed.

But . . . to just send us out into this desert, she thought,
and for a minute she was afraid she would be smothered by
the pain that filled her.

"We're lost," Ishmael announced. "You know that, don't
you?"

"I'm . . . I'm afraid so."

"If we just wait," Ishmael said, "my father will send men
to find us. There are always searching parties sent out for
people who get lost."

"We've been gone a long time." Hagar murmured.

"Then they'll look for a long time. After all, my father
loves me."

But no one has ever loved *me*, Hagar thought bleakly.
There was no self-pity in her; it was too late for self-pity.
There was only a final and terrible honesty. Sarah used me
for her own comfort, Abraham held me in his arms, Simeon
wanted me once, and Meryet . . . Meryet shaped my life . . .
for her own good more than mine. But no one has ever really
loved me.

Not even Ishmael, she knew. Oh, he had accepted her, but
a few minutes ago, he would have left her willingly for
Abraham and the coolness of Abraham's wells.

Ishmael sat down wearily, and then curled up on the sand.
Perhaps he'll sleep, she thought. Lifting the skirt of her robe,
she made a sort of shade and when his breathing indicated
he was asleep, she smoothed his hair with her other hand.
Her arm ached, holding up the cloth, but she knew it
wouldn't be for long. How long could they endure the heat
and the thirst?

Her thoughts whirled in an unending circle, but slowly

she reached back into her memory to that other time she had
huddled, shaking and afraid, on the dark mountain path. As
clearly as though it had been yesterday, she heard the words
of prophecy that had sent her, humbled and subservient,
back to Sarah's tent before Ishmael was born.

Behold, you are with child, the Voice had said. *You shall bear a
son, and shall call his name Ishmael because the Lord has heard
your affliction. . . .*

He saw me then, Hagar thought. The God of Abraham
saw me then and pitied me, frightened and angry and insolent as I was.

"Then why not now, Lord of my lord?" she beseeched,
but softly so that she would not wake Ishmael. "Hear me
now. See me again."

There was no sound except the small moan of the wind
and the hissing of the blown sand. She hadn't really expected anything.

"I'll make me a god of my own," Hagar said in a clogged
whisper. "I won't even think of the god of Abraham. I'll
make a small god like Sobek or Hathor."

There were several pebbles there, and she gathered them
into a pile. She broke off tiny twigs from the scrawny bush
that struggled to push above the sand, and she made arms
on the stone figure. With trembling hands, she wiped kohl
from the lids of her eyes and dabbed rude features on the
stone face.

"I'll call the god Little Re," she went on in her rough, dry
whisper, "and I'll worship it and. . . ."

But the little god was ugly, she thought as though scales
had suddenly fallen from her eyes. It was grotesque and
bloated, and it did nothing for her. She felt none of the
certainty and serenity that had bathed her tired spirit when
Yahweh had spoken to her.

"This pile of stones can't help me," she whimpered in total
despair. With a quick, convulsive movement, she broke the
small statue apart and brushed it into nothingness.

Then the tears came, all the tears that she had held back

with such stubborn pride when Abraham had talked to her, when Meryet had come into her tent. She abandoned herself to weeping and tasted the bitter salt on her cracked lips.

"Why are you crying?" Ishmael pushed aside the robe and looked at her with questioning eyes. "Are you angry because I ran?"

"Oh, no," she said, trying to stop the sobs that wrenched out of her. "No, not angry."

"Then why?" he demanded.

"Because we can't go home," she said before she could stop the words.

A look of terror crossed his face. "Not go home?" he cried, struggling to his feet. "But I told you. My father will look for me."

Hagar hid her face against her hands, but she felt the urgency of his fingers against hers.

"Look at me," he begged. "It's true, isn't it? My father *will* look for us."

"No," she said in an expressionless voice, "No, he told us to go. We aren't supposed to go back."

She expected him to wilt in fear and grief against her, but to her amazement, she saw his face harden with anger.

"But *I* am the firstborn!" Ishmael shouted, and there was only fury in his voice.

. . . *His hand shall be against every man*, the Voice had said, *and every man's hand shall be against him*. . . .

The rest of the prophecy might be doomed by the death that lurked in this desert, but this much of it was true. Even against his father, Ishmael dared to stand erect.

"Yes," Hagar said clearly, "you *are* the firstborn!"

The child can't live until evening, Hagar thought on the morning of the third day. The water was gone, and there was no sign of an oasis or well anywhere. Weakness seemed to drag at both of them, and the torture of thirst clawed at their throats.

By noon, Ishmael had fallen, unable to move his feet any

longer. Once more, Hagar knelt and held up her robe for shade. But her arm was too weak, so she sank to the ground and pulled the little boy under the shelter of her skirt.

"Oh, Yahweh, my Lord," she cried in her despair, "I cannot bear to see this child die. Oh, Yahweh, my Lord, my God. . . ."

Not the God of Abraham, she thought dazedly. *Her* God!

And quite suddenly her fear was gone. She felt a curious, cool stillness fill her and surround her. Nothing had actually changed, she realized. She was probably going to die and her child would die. But even here in the desert, *they were not alone*!

With trembling hands, she unwound the covering from her head and laid it over Ishmael's face, propping it up as a shade. For a long minute she sat staring down at him.

"I love you," she said clearly in spite of her cracked lips and dry throat.

It was the first time in her life she had ever said those words. She had longed to say them to Abraham, had dreamed of saying them and hearing a kind reply. But she had never had the courage. Now she said the words to his son.

"I love you, and I'd gladly die if you could live."

Then, knowing she could not endure the agony of seeing his final breaths, she laid him under a thin bush and adjusted the scarf over his face. Her fingers lingered and she bent to touch his cheek with her lips.

"My son," she said and felt her heart break.

She was too weak to walk, and so she crawled to the next group of bushes, and there she lay on the ground, feeling the cruel sun on her uncovered head. Her heart thudded painfully, and her breath labored in her throat.

The Voice came with clarity and purity. *Hagar,* the Voice said. *What's the matter?*

It's the Voice of Yahweh, Hagar thought with trembling humility, and he's speaking to *me*!

I have heard the child, the Voice went on. *Don't be afraid, for I have heard him. And I will make of him a great nation....*

The Voice rang with the same calm authority she had heard before. There was no mistaking it. Here was a miraculous thing. Yahweh was not confined to the tents of Abraham. He could come to the desert to speak to his handmaiden.

She sat immobile, hardly breathing. Was it possible that there was, after all, only one God and that he could see *all* people?

Her eyes opened slowly. At first, she saw only the flat, harsh dazzle of the sun on sand, and then as she moved her head, seeking Ishmael, she saw the cool, green shape against the sky.

I'm dreaming, she thought, or I'm seeing a vision. But the reality of the palm fronds moving in the hot wind brought her to her knees. The sand was rough and real against her legs, and she began painfully to crawl to the small oasis that had miraculously appeared. Had she been so blinded by her grief that she had failed to see it before Ishmael fell?

The water was real. It bubbled up from the sand, and the cool, sweet smell of it washed across her face. She drank deeply, and then started out for Ishmael.

She lifted him, marveling at the strength which surged through her tired arms and legs. As though he were a baby, she carried him to the well and laid him in the shade. With reverent hands, she bathed his face and wet his hair. His eyes opened and she helped him drink.

"Did my father find us?" Ishmael asked.

"Yahweh found us," Hagar said, and knew that she would never be lost again.

They found dates to eat, and Hagar washed her face and smoothed her hair. She took her shawl and covered her head, making herself ready for whatever Yahweh would send.

They didn't have to wait long. The camels showed suddenly against the horizon, and grew larger and larger as the small caravan approached the watering place.

"They'll kill us," Ishmael cried, shrinking against his mother.

"No, they won't kill us," Hagar said. "Yahweh wouldn't have led us to this place only to have us killed. I think they'll take us with them."

"I won't be a slave," Ishmael said, his defiance suddenly returning. "I won't be a slave to any man. I'm the son of Abraham."

"You'll see," Hagar said. "They'll be kind. You'll be a son, not a slave."

"How do you know?" he asked.

"I just know."

She was so certain that when she saw Simeon on the first camel, there was not even any surprise in her. She saw his eyes widen in amazement, but then a quick joy filled his face. Even though he has other wives, Hagar thought with certainty, he'll take us in. He may be the one who will finally love me, and I think I will love him. We'll have children, and I'll tell him of Abraham's God—of *my* God—and we'll raise Ishmael to be a great man.

She stood modestly, her face covered, her eyes lowered. She heard angry and curious voices exclaiming over her presence, over the appearance of the child, and then she heard Simeon's voice.

"The maid and the child are mine," he said. "I've arranged to meet them here. They're no one else's concern."

Hagar raised her eyes then and looked fleetingly at the man who was dismounting from his camel. The years had softened him, and there was kindness in his eyes. No longer was there a blaze of undisciplined passion about him. With him, she and Ishmael would be safe. More than safe. Happy.

"How did you find me?" Simeon asked, coming close to her and Ishmael so the others would not hear.

"Yahweh brought me here," she said. "Abraham and Sarah sent me away. . . they have a child of their own now. We're not needed anymore."

He came even closer, and she felt her heart beating in her

throat.

"They sent you away? Into the desert?" Simeon's voice was very soft, the words expressionless, but she saw anger flicker in his eyes.

"To you," she said. "They hoped we would find you."

"But they sent no one to protect you?"

"And no dowry, my lord." Her courage was beginning to fray, and she was suddenly aware of fatigue.

Simeon laughed. "What do I need of a dowry? You bring me a son."

She heard Ishmael's breath go out in a long sigh of relief.

"My lord," she began, seeking words to convey her gratitude.

But Simeon only grinned at her and touched her face gently with his finger tips. "Come," he said, "give me water to drink and draw some for my camel. We have a long way to go before night."

And Hagar turned to do his bidding, as she would do it, she knew, for the rest of her life.